THE EXPANSION BOOK 4

WAR

DEVON C. FORD

PRESS

First published by DHP Publishing in 2019
Published by Vulpine Press in the United Kingdom in 2020

Cover image by Jamie Glover at eruleanfuture.com
Cover by Claire Wood

ISBN: 978-1-83919-335-4

www.vulpine-press.com

"A soldier will fight long and hard for a colored bit of ribbon."
Napoleon Bonaparte

PROLOGUE

French Alps Region, Earth

Commander Leslie Brandt tried to blink. She managed to open one eye, reaching up numbly with her fingers to clear the sticky blood away from her left eye and unglue it. Her finger traced upward, a sharp hiss emanating from her cut lips as her fingernail found the open gash in her eyebrow and the source of the hot blood.

She tried to speak, only managing a croak. She spat the dust from her dry mouth and tried again.

"Sound off," she said. Her voice didn't sound like her, either because of her swollen lips or her ringing ears. She couldn't be sure which. Nobody responded to her order anyway.

"Sound off," she demanded loudly, as though force of will could make the people in the downed dropship respond. She stood, staggering on the uneven deck. The craft had landed belly-down, at an angle. The cockpit and entire nose section to her right was gone, sheared off on impact. She opened her mouth to yell, to call for the pilots. The sight of a spray of bright blood over the inside of the distant cockpit glass stopped her. She remained clinging on to the twisted bulkhead.

Turning back to make her way down to the rear of the ship, her boot found one of her squad. The prone soldier's foot was bent opposite to the leg. Her eyes followed the limb up to the face, which was locked in a rictus of pain and gasping breath.

"Medic," Brandt called out weakly, almost falling on the injured man as she tried to step closer to him. "Medic!"

"It's me, C… Commander," the injured man said through his terrible pain. "It's Turner. Pass me… pass me my…"

His hand fluttered feebly at the tactical webbing pouches hanging down above him. The kit storage rack was so far above his head that it couldn't be reached without putting pressure on his mangled leg. Brandt snatched it down for him and watched. Her senses returned; she watched the man expertly locate and prime a dermal injector spray with painkillers one-handed before pressing it to his neck and breathing out a deep sigh of relief.

"Don't worry," he said between gulps of air. "I won't have too much; just get me to a safe triage spot and I can direct people to help the injured." He seemed to regain some sense as the pain medication began to work, looking around to try and survey the wreckage.

"Sit tight, Turner," she said, struggling down the slope of the dropship's deck.

Brandt had twenty personnel on that ship, all assigned to her command and all hoping to get through the training in one piece. Then they could get shipped to sea when the famous recon troop commander went to the Centauri system. All of their hopes, dreams of adventure, and excitement—not to mention their career aspirations—went up in smoke the minute their transport went down, painted by surface-to-air weapons.

She shook that away. She couldn't think about that. She had to deal with the immediate problems that were within her control and not the peripheral worries of those under her command. Brandt was already stressed out and pissed that she had been held back from the Ninth Fleet's deployment. She had been assigned to run training operations in the new anti-Va'alen program she had helped develop.

Noises from farther down the dropship reached her ears. She bypassed the groaning, writhing troops who were slowly regaining consciousness.

"Here's my authority, you dumbass piece of dog shi—"

"Zero," she gasped. "That you?"

"It's me, Commander," he replied groggily. Blood ran from a cut somewhere on his head, but it was already drying on his face, cracking where his skin tightened around the crow's feet by his eyes. His habit of using her callsign to address her had faded unless they were in familiar company. The trainees here just got confused.

"This damn weapons locker won't accept my authority, and I'd sure as hell like to have something that goes bang right now." He held his empty hands open to her. "A sniper without a gun is as much good as tits on a boar hog."

"Let me try," she said. Brandt guessed that the two weapons lockers onboard the dropship would open for her biometric authorization. She waved her left forearm over the lock; the dull red light flickered to a dull green light, and the door popped open slightly.

She stepped back, letting Zero wrench the bent metal open further before reaching inside. He passed the first pistol out to Brandt, following it up with two spare magazines. She took the gun, staring at it like she'd just been handed a sharpened stick in place of the advanced weaponry they had been equipped with until recently.

The pistol was the universal service design; it was the USP she had used before the singularity acceleration charges had been harnessed into the newest generation of firearms.

Worse still, since she had come back from the unnamed moon under the twin suns in the nearest solar system, she had used a captured alien rifle. The commander had been hoping to be involved in the development of even better personal weapons. Now, though, she felt as though she may as well have just picked up a rock.

Snapping herself out of the irrelevant daydream, she loaded and primed the pistol before shoving it into the elasticated pocket on the right thigh of her coveralls. Brandt organized the stunned and the walking wounded into order one by one. They began unloading the dropship to set up a triage and treatment post.

Pushing her way through the snapped branches and fallen foliage she reached the cockpit where the sickly sweet, metallic smell of blood filled her nostrils. Climbing up, slipping twice on the gore under her fingers and boot soles, she saw what had killed the pilots. The center console, somehow overloaded by the unexpected attack, had exploded and peppered their unprotected faces with superheated shrapnel. The pilots were in simple fatigues, which had no chance of saving their life. They had not been scheduled to fly anywhere near the upper atmosphere, or a training mission using powered armor. There was no cause for them to be wearing the pilot's operational flight suit that would have protected them. Brandt scanned the chip in her arm over the small gun locker and removed the two pistols, hoping that they wouldn't be needed, before reaching for the still sparking comm set beside the pilot's seat.

"Mayday, mayday, mayday," she croaked into the mic with the transmit button pressed firmly. "Training flight Epsilon Four-Four out of Virginia, following easterly flight pattern to training ground Delta Six. We have been shot down, repeat, shot down. Unknown coordinates. Unknown hostiles. Over."

She paused, resting and taking a few deep breaths before she tried again.

She had a feeling that something would happen to one of their transports sooner or later. They had few options of flight paths now that they were effectively banned from any African or Middle Eastern airspace.

"Mayday, mayday, mayday," she tried again. "This is Commander Brandt of the training flight Epsilon Four-Four en route to Delta Six training grounds, is anyone receiving, over?"

Static crackled over the damaged speakers but the noise was definitely a response. Whatever they said was drowned out by the sounds of mechanized armor crashing through the dense undergrowth rapidly approaching from her front.

CHAPTER 1

American Territory UN HQ, NYC

Two Months Earlier

"Commander," the admiral with budgetary oversight said in a tone he probably thought was fatherly, though it came out patronizing. "You see, the things is… we don't need a reconnaissance ship with that—" he chuckled in a falsely self-effacing manner "—how can I put it? That much of a substantial *credit* label attached running around in uncharted space doing god only knows what."

"Surely, Admiral," he said smoothly, "that's the very point of an advanced prototype reconnaissance ship? Isn't that the sole purpose of its design and build?"

The admiral dropped his pretense of breaking the news gently and gave him a cold look that said there was more going on that Torres didn't know.

"Now you listen to me, son," he said quietly, as though he was worried about someone overhearing him in his own office. "I couldn't give a fart of moon dust who your mommy is, so if you think your last name is going to do you any favors here then you're waiting for the wrong train, you got that?"

"Absolutely, sir," Torres said loudly, unfazed by the threatened family connection. This man, who likely hadn't a received single positive accolade ever, had probably fallen foul of Torres's mother's ambition and ability at some point in his career. She was in charge of training for the entire southern half of the continent, whereas this guy was, what? Accounting? Budget control?

The admiral seemed wary of his easy victory and stood rigidly with a degree of uncertainty.

"Now, your flight officer here will remain stationed with the *Bowkun Shar Itchy*," he said, intentionally mispronouncing the name to annoy them. "You, however, are temporarily returned to your previous posting until reassigned." He eyeballed Torres for a moment longer. "Your record doesn't hold that information, only your promotion from Lieutenant Commander. Where were you posted?"

"UNID, sir," Torres answered without emotion. Even admirals of the bookkeeping fleet should know not to mess with the intelligence directorate too much.

The senior officer looked flustered for a moment but recovered quickly and cleared his throat to end the meeting. "Dismissed," he snapped.

Torres stamped his heels together and held a textbook salute for the precise three second count that regulations dictated. Beside him Sarvanto, the tall Finn, did the same with a more relaxed approach and both men turned smartly to march out of the admiral's office.

Both maintained a military bearing and discipline until safely out of sight when Torres dropped the march and lined up a punch against the nearest hard surface. He stopped, pulling back the blow before he could break every bone in his hand. He didn't want to spend a couple of weeks in a healing glove. Instead he satisfied himself with a gesture of impotent rage, snatching off his dress uniform cap, screwing the pristine flat top up in his hand and throwing it on the polished deck to stamp on it.

"Feel better, sir?" Sarvanto asked, deadpan.

"Yes, actually," Torres said as he caught his breath. He looked up as Brandt walked hurriedly over with as much decorum as she could manage without running.

"What the hell?" she muttered, glancing around at the looks his outburst had drawn.

"I'm off the *Ichi*," he said. "Apparently she's too expensive to be flown around out in space where people haven't gone before. Does that... that *clown* even know what reconnaissance means?"

"Do you know what that means for the rest of us?" she asked.

They had known something was up when UN command had denied the crew access to their ship. Standing in their way had been a mixture of confused and embarrassed UN troops and a suspicious bunch of Hyper private contractors, the company largely responsible for developing the ship.

The summons to attend the admiral's office at oh-nine-thirty the following morning was extended to Torres with as little warmth as possible. The summons for Brandt to attend at oh-nine-thirty-five gave Torres's meeting context. He didn't expect to stay for coffee.

"I guess you're about to find out," Torres muttered as he tried and failed to return his uniform cap to a wearable format. He finally gave up, pulling the crested badge off the front and forcing the battered thing into a trash chute.

A young adjutant's voice sounded behind him. "Commander Brandt? The admiral will see you now."

~

Brandt's meeting took a whole minute more than the allotted five; at least she inconvenienced the senior officer in that one small way.

She walked out with the same stone-faced military precision that Torres had, marching straight past him muttering, *"not here,"* through gritted teeth before stomping straight into the nearest elevator. Sarvanto and Torres piled in with her in silence and all three stayed straight-faced until the doors closed.

"Son of a *bitch*!" she cursed, lining up a violent kick and putting a big dent in the shiny metal surface a little too close to Torres's groin for comfort. He stayed silent, hoping that the particular S.O.B. in question was the admiral and not him.

"Reassigned?" Torres asked gently.

"Yeah," she said, deflating slightly though ready to kill with her bare hands.

"Got command of a unit? I mean, you're going back out, right?"

"Training," she said, barely above a whisper.

"Training what?" Sarvanto asked.

"Training. And developing a threat package for the Va'alen." Sarvanto and Torres looked at one another, their eyes widening as though each were trying to get the other to speak first.

"Errr..." Torres said, trying to think of what to say. "You *kinda* are the best person in the UN for that..."

"So I get benched, my career gets tanked, and the people on my team get sidelined on the biggest missions the UN has ever conducted?" She turned on him.

"Well, when you put it like tha—" Torres began.

"We're going to Dassiova," she said firmly.

"He's at the orbital dockyards at best. At worst he's already at Mars doing build-up training with the new fleet additions." Brandt thought about it. If their fleet, or what *had* been their fleet, was still at the huge orbital stations where they had docked on their return, then they would soon be heading out to their jumping-off point at Mars.

"Try him on comm first?" Torres suggested.

"Well, duh," Brandt snapped. Sarvanto felt a little uncomfortable in the presence of two senior and decorated UN officers fighting like young siblings. "I wasn't planning on hijacking the *Ichi* and going pirate!"

They were spared any further conversation when the elevator announced their arrival at the ground floor. The voice sounded so annoyingly smug and satisfied that Brandt almost kicked it again just for good measure. And fun.

Stepping out into the atrium and passing the extortionately expensive drinks machine that actually served decent coffee, Brandt remembered the last time she had been there. It had been for her court martial. She had gone in and taken full responsibility for the lives lost during a terrorist attack that had been, in fact, engineered by her own side. She had suspected they might not have always been the good guys. That made her think of Zero, her staunch second-in-command and senior NCO who had saved her life at least twice with his unnervingly unnatural ability to put a bullet in the right place at any distance.

Zero would suffer from whatever political agenda was being played out, too. His career would be affected, and he would miss out on going to the new planets they had discovered.

More than that, she felt, other lives would be in danger because he and his rifle wouldn't be there to protect them. Training was no place for a soldier of his skill.

They exited the security gate without being checked. None of the low-level soldiers on duty wanted to stop two well-known commanders in obviously foul moods. Reaching the street they paused, when a transport pulled up beside them.

It was sleek and jet-black—too nice of a finish to be UN— and hovered at the roadside on silent repulser engines. The rear door opened, revealing a quilted cream-colored leather interior. The inside looked like an expensive limousine; it didn't match the semi-military outside.

An annoyingly familiar voice emanated greeted then from inside.

"Commanders," Levenstein said, trying to sound important. He was a company man, a Hudson-Yu Progression and Research moneyman much as the admiral inside was for the UN. Being responsible for the flow of credits gave him a power far beyond his natural station. "I'm here to extend you both an invitation."

They turned to look at Sarvanto by way of apology that he wasn't included. Seeing as he was staying with their ship whereas they were reassigned, both Torres and Brandt guessed he would be okay. Stepping inside and taking a seat, Brandt paid close attention to the only other person present. He touched a delicate fingertip to his ear and spoke softly.

"Two onboard, proceeding to rendezvous point." He saw Brandt paying close attention and treated her to a white-toothed smile that tipped the scale into unnatural.

She had to admit, the rest of him was put together pretty well. She noticed that he had a strong physique even when he was sitting. He possessed the kind of shoulders one couldn't get in a gym, but came from hours—years even—of hard training for a real fight and not just for enhancing his reflection.

"Where are we going, Levenstein?" Torres said tiredly, as though the small man didn't amuse him. He lifted the soft leather of the armrests of his seat and pulled out a glass bottle of expensive water, eying it with something nearing contempt before he opened it.

"Like I said," Ryan Levenstein answered in his whiny voice that made Brandt think of some asshole lawyer, "I'm just extending an invitation."

"From who?" Torres asked.

Long Island, NY

The small compound had a sliding gate that opened for the transport to glide through without slowing after a fifteen-minute ride from Brooklyn. A glance in the monitor showed that gate sliding closed before they'd even come to a stop. The door opened upward and the Levenstein smiled smugly at Torres and Brandt.

"Follow me, please," he said.

Brandt wanted to punch him in the throat. Or the dick. But she knew she'd have to be kneeling to guarantee the blow would land. Levenstein was head and shoulders shorter than her.

They climbed out, trying not to seem impressed with the setup, which was evidently Hyper without a single sign to show their mark.

Eyebrows were raised, expressions traded subtly between the two white-uniformed commanders of the American territory's United Nations forces, but otherwise their cards were kept close to their chests.

"Ready transport for immediate dust-off," the smooth man said softly. Brandt turned around to see him taking his fingertip away from his ear once more and giving her a winning smile.

"Dust-off to where?" she asked him.

"And who the hell are you, while we're at it?" Torres added.

"I'm afraid I can't disclose the location of the rendezvous at this time, for security reasons," he said firmly but softly, as though he was a soldier first but a politician on the weekends. "As for who I am, please call me Johns."

"John's what?" Brandt asked. She was unable to help herself from mocking the ridiculously fake name, wondering why he didn't just call himself Agent Smith.

"Just Johns," he said, turning away and leading them toward what looked like a standard dropship but finished in the same plain gloss-black as the ground transport had been

"You're going to bring us back, right?" Torres asked with mock concern. "It's just that my mom doesn't like it when I stay out after dark. She gets all cranky and grounds me."

Johns smiled as though he found the jest hilarious but was too polite to laugh out loud. Brandt and Torres saw through his fake bullshit and both marked him down as a probable sociopath.

Exactly the kind of people Hyper recruits, Brandt told herself as they walked up the rear ramp of the dropship.

Unlike the ones they were accustomed to, with their rows of hard and uncomfortable collapsible seating, this dropship had room for the same amount of cargo but seating for only half the number of troops. For the first time in their lives, they were treated to a dropship ride in the comfort of a padded seat with noise-cancelling earphones and touchscreen interfaces built into the armrests. Each seat had a numerical designation, and as Brandt settled herself in opposite Torres her screen blinked up with the text box showing 'They showing us how the other half live?'

She sat, crossing one leg over the other like she had never had room to do in such a transport before. "I think so. Is this our recruitment ploy?"

"That's my guess."

A throat-cutting gesture followed Torres's texted response. The two commanders simultaneously realized that the text comm links were likely monitored. Tapping instead at the secure comm screen on her left forearm, Brandt sent her fellow commander and now former ship's captain a message on their UN devices.

"Let's just enjoy the ride, see where it takes us."

Torres didn't respond, just caught her eye and nodded as Johns took a seat one away from Torres and in Brandt's eyeline. Torres, as though to show his contempt for the display of opulence, put on the headphones and selected an in-flight movie before the flight had begun.

Brandt selected Johns's chair and tapped out a short message.

'The midget not joining us?'

Johns looked at the display and smiled—genuinely smiled for the first time since she had seen him.

A mutual dislike of the short man could unite entire territories.

Johns put on his headphones and tapped at the screen, opening a channel to Brandt's set.

"No," he said smoothly. "Mister Levenstein is staying here. He was only authorized to do the meet and greet since you knew his face. I'll be looking after you now."

"Cool," she said dismissively. "Next time you want someone to do a meet and greet, don't send a face everyone wants to punch, okay?"

"Duly noted, Commander Brandt," Johns answered.

~

The dropship ride was short, staying in the lower atmosphere and moving fast. Brandt was originally concerned about their destination, but seeing that their position, altitude and speed were displayed on the screen beside her she doubted anything sinister was going on. She was fairly sure this was the company's ploy to recruit them; to get Torres and her to resign their commissions, take fat paychecks and be counted among the ranks of former UN private contractors on the company books.

If that contract was just guarding Hyper locations around the globe, then they could ram their offer up their rich asses, no matter how big the buyout.

As a commander in the UN she technically made eighty-two thousand credits a year, but as over a third of that was deducted for necessities as directed by the UN, she made as much as a mid-level corporate lawyer did. She knew that, because a very good friend of hers spent his days with mid-level lawyers and she paid attention.

She paid attention to everything, so much so that she was pre-scribed a small dermal injector to allow her to sleep when she wasn't on operations.

Brandt tuned into the ship channel as she liked to do, eavesdropping on the pilots while hey followed their flight protocols.

"Roger, changing vector to zero-four-niner," the pilot said. She'd heard similar words so many times in the exact same tone from so many different pilots that she was certain such a way of speaking was a fundamental part of flight training.

"Confirm, zero-four-niner," the co-pilot answered in a slightly varied tone. "ETA two-five minutes."

She looked up, catching Torres's eye and flashing two and the five to him with a gesture. He nodded, turning to the smoothly un-memorable man in the seat beside him.

"Going to tell us how high up the food chain we're going to get here, Johns?" he asked casually.

"All in good time, Commander," the man replied, more politician than soldier.

~

Twenty-three minutes later their momentum was cut and the dropship began descending in a swooping arc. Brandt scanned through the active frequencies but found herself shut out of the cockpit commlink to the ground. It was no doubt some kind of anti-terror security procedure that the UN would still follow for a year after it became out of date.

The imagery of their route and telemetry details had gone, leaving only limited functions on the console. Before now, Brandt had seen them approaching an unmarked spit of land in the Labrador Sea north of the demarcation between the sub-territories of Canada and North America. She passed a few seconds recalling how there used to be a heavily policed border between the two neighboring countries. After the discovery of clean energy sources, the open continental borders she had known her entire life had leveled the inequalities between almost every place on Earth.

Thought of energy sources pushed her mind further down the rabbit hole as she conjured the image of the Va'alen perpetual magnetic energy device, or P-MED as the UN had codenamed it. Brandt's team had found and secured it, and she thought about whether that new technology would replace their singularity drives in the future.

The soft bump of landing struts on the deck snapped her back to the present as she unbuckled and stood.

"Ready?" Johns asked, as though saying no could delay what they had been so gracefully and politely kidnapped for.

"Lead on," Torres told him. He fell in step beside Brandt and whispered, "Don't even crack unless they give us a ship and triple our salaries."

CHAPTER 2

Hypr Island, off the Coast of Newfoundland

The private island was as much of a hive of professional activity as the small compound in New York had been. To both UN Commanders, sharing almost three decades of first-hand experience between them, that activity seemed false.

If the compound were a real military base, the whole place would have looked different. Instead, it was packed with former military who had found the soldier's life too hard or too disciplined or too boring, as well as with civilians who simply pretended to be real soldiers.

The men and women there, sporting their fancy black uniforms in contrast to the two white-uniformed UN commanders, seemed to be just trying too hard. Real troops would be out of sight, hurrying up and waiting somewhere more comfortable or scouring the base for food, somewhere to sleep, or entertainment. These contractors all seemed too comfortable, drunk on company bullshit, like girl scouts vying for the top spot in that year's cookie sales ranking.

What she did notice, however, was the quality of the weapons and equipment on display. Torres noticed too as he walked beside her, following Johns's circuitous route through the display they both suspected was for their benefit.

"New armor and weapons," he muttered to her. "State-of-the-art dropships," she muttered back.

"It's like a god dammed recruitment video," Torres scoffed. "Join Hyper," Brandt murmured mockingly. "Explore the galaxy, learn new skills and meet new people, be a pretentious ass, qualify for greater privileges back on Earth…"

"Practice looking serious even if you don't know which end of the rifle is the dangerous one; when you're wearing black and looking mean, nobody will care!" Torres added in a surprisingly good movie voiceover impression.

"This way, Commanders," Johns said as he stopped. He indicated for the two senior officers caught giggling to one another to step inside a single story building. "For what it's worth I spent four years in CP after reaching lieutenant commander. I'm sure we've worked with some of the same people over the years, and personally I can say that I don't regret stepping aside to Hyper any day of my life." With that he nodded, embarrassing them a little as their nervous mockery had been overheard, and walked through the open door.

They were met by what looked like a field command center, with a simple desk for the overall commander and a buzz of people coming and going with their eyes glued to datapads.

"Ah, Commander Torres, Commander Brandt, please come in," a man said. His above-average height was accentuated by his formal, upright manner, signaling him as a senior officer.

They stepped in beside one another as though summoned to an admiral's office, just as they had been less than an hour before. Despite being two capable, headstrong and independent officers, both fought against the ingrained urge to stand to attention until ordered to stand easy.

"Relax, both of you," the man said, his easy authority speaking volumes through his lined face and kind but shrewd eyes. "My name is Robertson. Charles A. Robertson. Formerly Admiral in the United Nations Territory of the Americas, and now enjoying life for a change. You want coffee?"

That was a lot of information for them to take in. They both knew people who had left the UN for private security jobs, thinking that the more attractive pay and easier lifestyle would make them better off in the long run. The ones who had thought they could do without the state-sponsored pension and enhanced citizenship that the UN could offer. They had even dealt with more than a few of the troops under their command wanting to sign their way out. The troops had refused the dangling carrot of signing on again for an even better exit deal further down the line. But neither Brandt nor Torres had heard of high-ranking officers leaving the UN to take up jobs with the private companies, even if it was the biggest player on the planet.

"Coffee sounds good, sir," Brandt said, more interested in the coffee than the impressive man before them.

Robertson snapped his fingers and called out for Summers, bringing forward a young woman wearing a black uniform and a rank insignia that meant nothing to either of the commanders.

"Cream and sugar?" she asked them.

"Just cream for me," Brandt said.

"Nothing for me," Torres added. "I like it hot and black." Brandt sucked in a quick breath through her nose and bit her lip as she fought down the unprofessional urge to make an inappropriate joke at her friend's expense.

The former admiral smirked, and Miss Summers pulled a face that said she was trying to suppress the urge to laugh at the unspoken joke. She stepped away and Robertson invited them to sit. They did, staying uncomfortably upright in their white dress uniforms—not cut for comfort—and waited for the pitch.

"How is *Mariana?*" he asked Torres, infusing the name with all the rich Latino culture he could muster without the natural ability to roll his r's.

Torres was caught off guard to learn that this former admiral knew his mother.

"She's good, sir, thanks." He replied hesitantly, cautiously sensing a trap or perhaps information that he didn't want to know.

"She and I came up together, going our separate ways when she got promoted to lieutenant commander ahead of me," Robertson said as his face glazed over in warm reminiscence. "No matter. Please give her my warm regards when you next speak to her?"

"I will," Torres said suspiciously.

"And your lady friend," Robertson went on, "Lieutenant Commander Eze?" He hid his smile at Torres's almost imperceptible reaction, taking care to pronounce it correctly. "I trust she is taking to her new role well?"

Amare Eze, formerly Brandt's second-in-command of the small team of recon troops onboard the *Ichi*, had been promoted on their return to Earth partly as an apology for her arrest for the crimes of treason and espionage. She had been exonerated when the real culprit cut and ran, stealing a dropship and going over to her true side of the separatist Middle Eastern Alliance.

Eze, unable to continue under Torres's command since their relationship had been outed, accepted the promotion and transferred to the *Indomitable*, Admiral Dassiova's flagship of the Ninth Fleet. She would be working under the Chief, the vaunted former senior NCO from their early careers who had elevated through experience and seniority in the special operations world to lead the fighting unit on Dassiova's vessel.

"I'm sure Lieutenant Commander Eze will conduct the role well," Torres said stiffly, firmly closing the book on that line of questioning.

Robertson smiled, taking the hint that he was heading into dangerous waters if he pursued the demonstration of intimate knowledge. He turned to Brandt instead, solidifying his superior intelligence network.

"And Commander Brandt? I hope you've been enjoying New York City? Have you tried staying on the Upper East Side for a change? We have a number of buildings there I'm sure you'd appreciate…"

"I like my digs just fine, sir," she said, anticipating his next display of knowledge. "And my liaison at the adjutant's corps is just fine, which I'm certain was your next question…"

"Ah yes, Commander Morello," he said with a smile. "A very talented lawyer with an almost robotic ability to recall procedural law, wouldn't you say?"

"I would," Brandt answered, "if I knew what you were talking about. Please, at the risk of sounding rude, we have shit to do and we'd appreciate you cutting to the chase."

Robertson smiled again, happy to end the dance. Such demonstrations weren't to his liking in the first place, but were merely the necessary display of showing your enemy how many guns you had.

"The company, that is to say the Hudson-Yu Progression and Research Company, would like to offer to employ you both, effective immediately."

Brandt sucked in air through her teeth and shifted in her chair as her coffee arrived. She took it with a nod of thanks. "Problem is," she said as she raised the cup and blew the heat off the top of the drink with her eyes fixed firmly on the mercenary commander, "we're both lifers, so we can't just up and quit."

"Again," Robertson said, "not to labor the point, but you *do* know a very talented lawyer who could undo those particular ties in a minute."

Torres sipped his own too-hot black coffee and let the richness of it fill him with satisfaction. Though he had joined as an officer and signed up for life, he would be able to organize a closed doors discussion, utilizing his mother's influence, and quietly get himself discharged from the service. Brandt, who had joined as an enlisted rank and earned fast-track promotion through blind luck, a bullet to the abdomen and keeping her mouth shut, did not have that luxury. Being a 'track,' she was in for life unless she had the money and the influence to set her on an alternative political path instead. Either that or a more lucrative position within the private sector.

"If the legal route isn't an option you like," Robertson said, "then we have some of the finest doctors on the planet who would be willing to declare you unfit for duty. You'll make a miraculous recovery, of that I have no doubt, and then you'll be free to seek employment wherever you saw fit."

"It's all a numbers game, really," Brandt said carefully.

"And numbers are things we do well here," Robertson said. "I would hazard a guess that those numbers would be at least *double* what they currently are for commanders of your experience, along with a whole host of benefits you won't get elsewhere."

"Do you want us, or just our UNID knowledge?" Brandt asked bluntly.

Robertson laughed. "Honey, who do you think designed, manufactured and distributed those chips you've both got in your arms? We did."

Brandt had heard enough even before the derogative gender remark. She sipped her coffee, as she nodded slowly and faced the former admiral.

"I'm afraid the numbers don't work for me," she said. "But even if those numbers doubled again I'd have more than a few reservations."

"As would I," Torres echoed, leaning forward to put his cup of piping-hot coffee on the man's desk. "So I think I'll pass. Leslie?"

"Oh," she said, "hard pass. *Hard!*" She too deposited her drink and stood. "Pleasure to meet you… whatever your mercenary rank is, but we need to be going now, sir."

"I'm sure you do," Robertson said with a smirk of amusement as he watched the two commanders head for the door. "One last thing," he called out, "if you stepped to this side of the fence we'd be willing to… *acquire* the *Ichi* from the UN and give it back to you. We'll put you back out there, and we won't cramp your style half as much as the UN will."

Torres and Brandt looked hard at one another for a moment. The tiny shakes of their heads communicated a dozen words each.

"We're good, thank you, sir," Torres said.

~

The dropship ride back was just as brief and uneventful, only this time instead of the large luxury ground transport there waited two simple cabs for them. Together they took one back to their assigned living quarters in the same block and dismissed the second cab, joking that the Hyper intel package missed that small fact at least.

Orbital Shipyards, Earth

The dropship sent by Admiral Dassiova arrived quickly. It landed on the blacktop of the UN compound a little over an hour after the two commanders had huddled behind Torres's forearm screen and placed the call.

"What have you two gotten up to now?" he had asked like an annoyed father being asked for bail money.

"Not over comm, sir," Brandt had said suspiciously. "Can you send us a ride up?"

Dassiova had chewed his lip for a moment, evidently considering whether he should exert his authority or not. With a shrug, he decided he should.

"UN HQ in one hour," he ordered them, cutting the link.

That gave them enough time to change, having been given officer's accommodation in the secure barracks near headquarters. That had been much to Brandt's annoyance, as she always preferred to stay in the city.

Closing their mouths against the dust and debris kicked up despite the cold and wet day, Torres and Brandt stepped toward the opening tail ramp of the dropship. It clearly wasn't staying a moment longer than it took to get them aboard. Both wearing the dark coveralls that were usually reserved for uniform onboard ships at sea, they shrugged into their jackets and grabbed seats.

Brandt caught the eye of the petty officer acting as loadmaster for the bird and indicated with both hands over her ears that she wanted a headset. He petulantly mimed back to her to put her restraints on. Commander or not, safety in the hold was his realm. She shrugged into the thick straps, annoyed at being back under the strict rules of the UN bureaucracy machine and chalking a silent, guilty point up to Hyper's offer of employment.

She hated not being plugged in, not being connected, and life without her armor was becoming psychologically difficult at times. She thought she might have to see someone about that if it got any worse. Alternatively, maybe she could get herself on a ship heading for the Centauri system and get her ass back on the front line.

Placing the headset over her braided hair she settled back to watch Torres as he leaned back and performed his most annoying trick: falling instantly asleep. She passed the time catching up on her private communications and listening to the pilots recite their universal litany until the shuddering of the atmospheric barrier assaulting the ship's shielding threatened to wake Torres. He stayed asleep until she leaned back and nudged him with her foot while listening to the pilot announce that they were slowing for the approach vector.

"O-S-Two, O-S-Two, flight Sigma Two-Five on approach. Advise heading and docking platform," the pilot said calmly.

"Roger, Sigma Two Five, Orbital Shipyard Two. Proceed eight-eight by four-seven-one. Lighting up docking platform forty-three for you now. Safe landing."

"Thanks O-S-Two," the pilot murmured back almost lazily. "Bringing her in now."

Brandt craned her neck to see out of the forward viewport in the cockpit through the open hatch. She could only glimpse a flash of the brightly lit exterior of the gigantic, skeletal space station which served as both the parking lot for vessels too large to enter atmosphere safely and those being retrofitted or built.

Sitting back with a huff, Brandt glanced up to see Torres's amused look at her annoyance. He knew she would be pissed at not getting to see the approach, and that would affect her mood for a few minutes afterwards until something else turned her attention.

They were unclipped and out of their seats before the loadmaster had stood. He twisted his face into something nearing rage as two senior officers thought themselves above the rules of his aircraft. He stood to follow them to the ramp, which they had activated themselves. He could barely believe the lack of procedural awareness of these two officers, behaving as though they were too important to follow the rules.

"Commander!" he barked, stomping toward Torres who had hit the ramp release switch. "You can't just open a hatch onboard a dropship like that! Do you know the dangers out here? We could violently decompress or have our eyeballs flash-freeze in our heads, or we—"

"Petty Officer," Brandt said, her voice full of authority, "I assure you that Commander Torres, Captain of the *Boken sha Ichi*, knows about the dangers of space."

The loadmaster's mouth hung open for a second before snapping shut with an audible clapping noise.

She watched his eyes as they switched between Torres's smiling face and her own. He had no doubt made the connection a little too late after playing taxi to one too many officers attending a meeting or wanting a tour of a ship under construction. To his credit he said nothing more. He merely shut up and stepped back as they turned to walk down the ramp where they were met by the brooding Dassiova who already seemed to have been waiting too long.

"On me," the admiral said, turning on his heel and striding away quickly.

Torres and Brandt exchanged a look and fell in behind the older man to save from being left behind. He didn't look back to see if they were keeping up, just maintained his own relentless pace through the packed walkways of the docking stations. Twice he was forced to wait as some heavy equipment was moved from a cargo area on the opposite side of the walkways and each delay seemed to start a fuse burning inside him. Luckily it never reached detonation. Their final destination was the docking platform where the fleet's flagship, the carrier *Indomitable,* was anchored.

"Sir, if we're meeting here why didn't we just fly directly to you instead?" Brandt asked.

"Because all my birds are grounded," he said stiffly. "Nothing in or out unless via the scanners of the cargo decks below."

With that he stepped up to the armored sentry on the left and scanned his forearm over the datapad on the small station. In spite of being the fleet admiral and the man in charge of that ship, and even though every one of his crew recognized him on sight, he still had to scan himself to board and wait for the screen to blink green to allow him access.

To him it felt like being patted down by security to step back inside from your own front yard.

Torres and Brandt scanned their own arms, waiting for the authority to enter. As they were no longer on the crew manifest, both times Dassiova had to scan himself again to give that authority. Once they were through, he led the way back to his quarters off the main bridge.

The doors opened, hissing aside to unveil the expansive bridge and the vast number of busy people there despite being docked.

One young voice damn near squeaked as he shouted, "Admiral on de—"

"Can it, Romano!" Dassiova barked.

"Yes, Admiral," the small voice answered. "Sorry, Admiral."

"Jesus," Dassiova grumbled. "I swear the Officer Training Academy peels these ensigns from their momma's tit and sticks them in a uniform…"

Brandt sniggered, having only borne the rank of ensign for a few months as she attended OTA Colima on fast-track promotion. Torres, on the other hand, had *been* that proverbial baby in a uniform when first posted to Dassiova's unit over a decade before so he said nothing. He didn't need to. Dassiova did it for him.

"Reminds me a lot of you when I first met you, Torres," he said. "Young, squeaky and full of ideas that life hadn't beat out of you yet."

"Well, sir," he answered, "life has taken more than a few swings now—"

"And you've done alright for yourself," the admiral finished for him as the doors to his quarters closed behind them, "even without once pulling on you mother's epaulettes from what I hear."

"You hear correctly, but the name sometimes works against me, too."

"And it also works *for* you more times than you realize. Kinda like a passive ability, if you know what I mean," Dassiova said.

Torres did, and he couldn't deny it, so he changed the subject.

"Sir, what can you tell us about our reassignments?"

"Not a great deal, kids," Dassiova said as he fumbled with one of the coffee cups bearing the UN crest. He caught it by trapping it with his body against the counter before rescuing it and pouring steaming liquid from the pot into all three he had organized in a row. Setting the mugs down at the small round table with fixed chairs, he sat and invited them to do the same. Familiar or not, neither of the commanders were so lax in Dassiova's company as to make themselves at home in his personal quarters.

"This is how it is," he said. He took a sip and recoiled slightly with a burnt lip. "We had no quarantine period on Mars like last time we returned as you know, and the Tenth Fleet under Admiral Vernay has things locked down in the CS —that's what the cool kids are calling the Centauri system now, I'm told. The Va'alen are all interned on a single planet and still not ready to negotiate, apparently, and it was touch and go whether we're heading back at all."

"You mean the whole fleet?" Torres asked him.

"Yeah. Seems that even admirals get left out of some loops, and I'm in the dark as much as most people on this," Dassiova admitted tiredly.

"So what *are* your orders?" Brandt asked.

"I'm to run system defense patrols for a month, which is what they're calling our shakeup training. I call bullshit."

"How come?" Torres asked, his coffee cup paused an inch from his mouth.

"Because training doesn't usually include inputting preset planetary bombardment co-ordinates of various strategic sites on Earth into our gun batteries," he said quietly. "And deploying our frigates in geostationary orbit over the Kuldar settlement dome on Mars with weapons locked at all times doesn't seem so friendly to our new allies."

Both Torres and Brandt set their drinks down and looked at the admiral. He stared back at them but neither faltered under his stern look. He sighed and continued.

"This is classified, so if either of you breathe a word of it I will be... *displeased*," he said, adding the heavy emphasis to imply a galaxy full of pain to anyone letting him down. "That 'roach you brought back from that moon? Well newsflash: that ain't its body. It's like a mech suit or something. There was a different thing inside driving it."

"Biomechanical exoskeleton armor?" Torres asked in shock.

"If that's what you call a little alien driving a big-ass alien armored skinsuit around and killing my troops then, yeah," Dassiova said.

Brandt shifted in her seat before speaking. "So, what was inside the Va'alen?"

"You catch the part about the Kuldar having railguns pointed at their habitation dome around the clock?" Torres asked her with a hint of sarcasm.

"No," she whispered. "No frikkin' way."

"Yep," Dassiova said. "Any of them still on our crews were shipped back to join their buddies on Mars pretty quick, and the whole thing's been discussed behind closed doors for weeks. The territory leaders, those still on our side anyway, had enough shit to deal with before they found that part out."

"Like what?" Torres asked. "The MEA?"

"More goddamned acronyms…" Dassiova grumbled. "Yes, the separatists. The Middle Eastern Whatever have caused hell. One of the UN's shipyards is lost to them, but I guess it already was when they'd built a copy of our fleet there over months without anyone knowing."

The atmosphere dropped a little as the conversation headed toward the uncomfortable subject of his former flight officer, Suranne Massey, who was now officially the American UN's most wanted for treason and espionage. If she showed her face in any territory still controlled by the majority UN factions then she would be unlikely to see the light of the sun again. She would find herself on a space station prison with an intermittent grav emitter and kid's TV playing on a short loop for the rest of her short natural life.

Dassiova doubted that in truth. He knew the shady UNID would want to take her in and make her happy to tell them everything she could recall about the newest threat to their version of democracy.

"I'm posted back to UNID," Torres said.

"And I'm creating a training package for the Va'alen threat," Brandt added, miserable at being left behind.

Just then Torres's comm device buzzed.

"Torres," he announced as he hit the icon to answer it.

"Commander," said a smooth voice on the other end, "Chase Ettington, UNID American Director. I need you in my office."

"Yes, sir," Torres answered hesitantly. "When?"

"As soon as you can get back down from the *Indomitable*," he said smoothly, bursting any bubble they may have had about their right to privacy. "Please, give my regards to Commander Brandt and Admiral Dassiova." The comm link vanished.

"Go on," Dassiova said. "I've kept your dropship standing by."

Torres nodded, disappointment evident on his face that he wouldn't get to spend even a few minutes with Eze before they were separated by billions of miles of empty space for who-knew how long.

"Mind if I grab another?" Brandt asked. "My posting isn't due until Monday and I'd like to take the weekend in New York."

Dassiova nodded his assent, and the two commanders faced each other for a silent goodbye.

"Oh, one thing before you go?" the admiral asked them. Both faces turned back to look at him. "How much did Hyper offer you?"

They both smiled. "Double salary," Torres answered. "And they said they'd get us the *Ichi* back."

"Amateurs," Dassiova scoffed. "They offered me a quarter million credits for a year to sit down and 'advise' them on everything we've done out there."

The looks on the faces of the two junior officers made him laugh before he dismissed them.

CHAPTER 3

UN Medical Suite, Los Angeles

Torres felt for his friend, but he also knew a few things that most people didn't know. He knew the reason their territory, and indeed the other territories directly and publicly allied to the Americas, were training and massing troops. Such exercises under the guise of extra-terrestrial preparation were more to do with a much closer enemy threat than the Centauri system.

He was no fool, and even with the satellite blackouts over Africa and the Middle East, the troop mobilization was obvious.

The main reason for the Ninth Fleet to be loitering in the solar system was to stall any big ideas the separatists may have about making moves on the territories that had invested the majority of their military might in their neighboring star system.

Torres knew that because he was no fool. Keeping his mouth shut and his temper in check at having lost his first ship command to politics and budget concerns had been a difficult task, but the mission he had been entrusted with transcended those feelings. He had made sure he kept promises to the people loyal to him as far as he was able. Part of that was to tell the UNID director that he needed to select certain personnel to ensure the safety and security of the mission. Those key personnel included a small team of soldiers, a pilot, and one very specific resource who had been the recent subject of legal arguments between the UN and Hyper.

Torres and his companion strode through the atrium of the UNID medical facility, staffed by a mixture of UN personnel and Hyper medical scientists whose expertise ranged from biological agents to cybernetic augmentation. The real experts in that field were at the main Hyper cyber labs in Japan. He hadn't been there, but the tall soldier flanking him had recounted his long experiences of living there on the flight from the east coast.

Walking up to the main reception desk, Torres turned his charm on the unimpressed-looking woman manning the position like it was a heavy gun trench.

"Hi there. We're here for Professor Campbell," he said.

The receptionist eyed him with evident distaste, slowly switching her gaze right and up to meet the eyes of the man at his side.

Her face dropped, almost quailing under the force of the scarred face and the unnaturally bright green eyes smiling back at her. Her mouth opened up slightly, snapping shut as she retained just enough dignity to remember this was her domain.

"I'll need you to sign in," she said, indicating a smooth screen for their handprints.

"No," Specter said gently. "You don't."

"Nobody goes in without registering," she said, pointedly. Torres sighed and stepped forward, not to the visitor's hand scanner but to the reader for staff IDs, and swept his left forearm over it without taking his eyes off the woman. The door opened, a small light blinking green. Her eyes flickered down to see the credentials of the person who had just bypassed her security protocols. Those eyes went wide as the screen showed nothing but an override authority.

"Professor Campbell's office?" Specter asked respectfully.

"Down the hall," she said flatly. "Turn left and follow the yellow line until you see it."

"Thank you," he said, the electronic twang of his repaired voice-box making her shudder.

"Gotta love the office busybody," Torres said quietly. Specter hmm'd in response. They turned left and followed the yellow line painted on the polished ground.

"Professor Campbell is expecting us, right?" Specter asked.

"She is now." They reached a door and Torres knocked, stepping back so as not to crowd the doorway. The door hissed open remotely, revealing a wide and sparsely furnished office that seemed somehow both clinical and comfortable at the same time. From behind the desk a woman stood to the sound of tiny servo motors, which only Specter's enhanced hearing picked up. His face lifted a little, sensing that perhaps someone else with elements in common with him was in his presence.

"Gentlemen," she said as stood and leaned on the desk, "Come in, please."

"Professor," Torres said as he stepped in first. "Commander Kyle Torres. My colleague is Specialist Jake Santana."

He stepped forward, extending a hand for her to shake and faltering only slightly as he took in the delicate exoskeleton showing on her arms and legs. Her handshake was soft, a hint of weakness, but her eyes were so fierce with resolve that they overcame it easily.

"Good to meet you," she said, her British accent taking him aback more than the cybernetic augmentation she wore. She turned to Specter and surveyed him with a professional eye before smiling. "Extensive work, soldier. Is that Hamada's work I detect?"

"It is, Professor," Specter said. "Let's just say the bomb I was too close to didn't leave much for him to work with."

She smiled at his jest, allowing the gravity of the whole story to be passed over with the small attempt at humor.

"I just had a call from the main desk," she said, her tone switching to one of amused admonishment. "Don't you UNID types ever just do things the easy way?"

"Sorry," Torres said. "It's ingrained in us not to leave a trail."

"Except one your own people can track," Campbell quipped back with a rebellious half smile. "Anyway, want me to take a guess at why you're here?"

"By all means," Torres answered with a genuine smile.

"You want to know if young Nathan Rogers is ready to come out and play, right?"

"Right," Specter answered. He couldn't help his nervous apprehension for the welfare of the man, his friend, who he had seen horribly injured.

"His arm is good," Campbell said as she stood again, her movements almost imperceptibly jerky. "It's better than before, in fact, if you value precision and perfection over nature. His psychological wounds are a little more... *complex*."

"I can only imagine," Torres said as he turned to glance at Specter.

"I don't have to," he muttered.

They stood, taking their cue from Campbell who had begun walking to the door. Her movements were stiff, robotic to some degree. She seemed to feel them watching her. The two men took in the subtle device affixed to her spine and running thin metal tendrils over her hips, down her legs and along her arms.

"Spinal paralysis," she said, accustomed to speaking about it. "Surgery to repair it isn't an option, so I designed this exoskeleton based on the very rudimentary design of your armor suits, but with a direct neurological control system instead of the reactive augmentation servos the suits use. It's not as efficient as a full implant yet, but it's a work in progress."

"Incredible," Specter said in genuine awe of the woman's work and her determination.

"Thanks," Campbell said, pleased with the compliment. "I'm hoping for a working template soon, but let's be honest and say that the credit tag might not make it as accessible to those who need it as I'd like."

"Ain't that always the way," Torres breathed, falling in step slowly behind her. They hit the corridor and turned right toward a set of secure doors. She waved her arm over the reader as she approached to make both doors swing open.

"Welcome to R&D," she said without grandeur. "Don't ask me where the credits come from to run this place, because I don't know and don't much care. All I know is I get the chance to help people like Nathan."

"And we're very grateful to you for that," Torres said.

"The Royal 'We' or you specifically?" Campbell asked. She swung her arms to aid her movement.

"Personally," Torres said. "He's my pilot. And... and I like him. He's what you'd call a *good egg*."

Campbell laughed gently, slightly out of breath from the effort of walking.

"He is that, Commander," she answered. "He certainly is that."

She led the way to another section of the wing, swiping them through more secure doors until she reached a physiotherapy workshop. A shirtless man in sweatpants hung by one arm from an apparatus. His upper body was bare and coated in a sheen of sweat apart from the right arm, which looked like he was wearing a long glove.

The height was right for his former pilot, but Torres didn't recognize the musculature and near-triangular back. Hearing the sound of the door open behind him, the man hanging by one arm did a single pull-up with exquisite control, lowered himself, dropped to the ground and turned to face them.

Rogers recognized them both, stood to attention and brought up his right hand in a salute.

"Commander," he said with a genuine smile. "Good to see you!"

"Likewise, Rogers," Torres said, dropping his own salute and offering a handshake. The senior officer's face twisted as he fought to control the sudden pain of the grip and Rogers stepped back hurriedly.

"Sorry, sir," he said. "Still getting used to this thing." He held up his right arm. On closer inspection, the glove appeared to be the thin rubber covering with the same geometric proportions of his other limb just like the covering of Specter's body.

"I hear that," Specter said as he stepped forward and offered his own hand to shake. "I'm not so easy to break."

The two men locked hands like rival animals, their faces showing the strain as their neurologically controlled prosthetics battled one another.

"Enough, you two," Professor Campbell said as though she admonished two schoolboys. "Don't break each other. You cost too much to fix now."

"Sorry, Mother," Rogers said with an air of cheeky humor that spoke volumes of their relationship.

She ignored his apology and picked up a datapad to swipe through screens.

"Well, the commander has work for you," she said. "Seeing as you're starting to get in the way here I'm happy to discharge you." She fixed him with a direct look. "If you think that's a good idea?"

Rogers was already throwing on a shirt and seemed incapable of hiding his excitement. "I think that's a great idea, Professor."

"You contact me directly if you have any problems with it, okay?" Campbell told him with a stern stare.

"Yes, ma'am," he answered seriously.

"Professor," Specter said respectfully, "if it helps, I have a small support staff assigned to me who are well-versed in…" He trailed off, unsure how to refer to their similarities in front of new people.

"That would be very helpful," Campbell replied with a deferent nod. "I'd rather prefer that any problems get reported to me before any intervention from the capitalists at Hudson-Yu."

Specter's eyebrows rose a little. He nodded back at her.

"You have my word," Rogers told her. "Thank you for everything you've done for me."

~

"You sure I didn't have time to shower?" Rogers asked Torres from the pilot's seat of the transport. He'd begged to fly, having been grounded for weeks after his capture and torture at the hands of their newest enemy.

"*Man* it feels good to be at the controls again," he said, interrupting the answer to his own question. He waggled the stubby delta wings of the atmospheric transport. "Me not flying is like losing an arm…"

Torres caught Specter's eye and rolled his own at the typically poor Rogers-style joke.

"You can shower at the base before we go," Torres told him.

"We meeting any others there before we head out?" Rogers enquired pointedly.

Torres sighed, explaining that his formal requests to have as many of the former crew of the *Ichi* assigned to his detail didn't get very far. In fact, Specter only came because the UN was still scared of denying his requests after the quiet legal battle for him to reassert his personal rights instead of being classed as property. Rogers had been given to him simply because they didn't know what to do with him, other than to offer him a massive pay-off and a golden retirement. Torres doubted the young lieutenant would be satisfied with a lifestyle of leisure.

"There's a few," Torres said, "only we don't have the *Ichi* any longer." He waited while Rogers cursed at length. "We have a light cruiser, and are officially classed as a diplomatic envoy."

"And *un*officially, sir?" Rogers asked conspiratorially.

Torres hesitated. He was under orders not to share the full mission brief with anyone but Captains Hayes and Halstead of the two frigates currently holding post over the alien inhabited dome on Mars.

"We're a diplomatic envoy, Lieutenant," Torres said warningly.

"Understood, sir," Rogers replied without skipping a beat. He wasn't dumb; he knew there was more to it but rank meant information, and he wasn't that high up in rank yet.

CHAPTER 4

UN Training Grounds, Virginia

The ground Brandt stood on had been in American military hands for generations. Hundreds of years of history had passed beneath the soles of her boots, and not one bit of that made her feel like she had made any progress in her career.

"Listen up," she yelled at the assembled recruits. The wind sucked the gravity from her voice, making her sound smaller than she wanted to appear before the troops stood to attention in front of her. "All of your combat training, all of your weapons drills, every last bit of hand-to-hand skills you've tried to perfect stand for the sum total of the square root of jack shit as of right now." She eyeballed the front rank, hoping for just one of them to crack a smirk or make a comment so she could establish her authority quickly and get the initial phase of being a new training CO out of the way.

"You've all had the briefings. Any one of you think you could take on a Va'alen warrior?" she asked, hoping that youthful confidence and arrogance hadn't gone out of fashion since she'd last been in the stifling confines of a unit on Earth. True to form, one great ox of a man stood higher to attention to signify his willingness to be humiliated in front of all fifty of his peers.

"Master Petty Officer Conrad," Brandt said loudly.

She called forward the man who still felt jaded at not being called Zero, like it had somehow opened the veil on his real identity and made him vulnerable. Given his new rank and position training the selected troops, he was forced to adapt to the more formal setting but talk of his reputation and abilities travelled far and wide.

"Commander?" He stepped up beside her.

"Form the unit into square," she instructed, locking eyes with the big soldier. "Not you, sugar. You stay right there."

Orders were bawled and boots stamped on concrete. One thing that hadn't changed in all the time that had passed was the need to practice drill in some form or another.

When the formation was set, Brandt began to pace around the interior of the neat box and spoke loudly for both ranks of cold troops to hear her voice. Inside the box Zero eyeballed the man a head taller and almost twice as thick as he was. No doubt the young ox with his richly tanned-looking skin and visible tattoos up his neck fancied his chances, but Brandt would wager that Zero could eat him in small portions even without a weapon.

"Now, seaman… what's your name, son?" she asked as she leaned theatrically towards him.

"Kekoa, ma'am."

"Seaman Kekoa here," she went on to the troops as she paced, "if you hadn't noticed, is one abnormally large human being. He is so large that his mother probably tried to sign him up for the UN when he was nine because it took up too many credits just to feed him!" She waited for the expected chuckles to run around the square before continuing.

"Seaman Kekoa is so big," she said loudly, "that he could probably eat most enemies he faced in one sitting." More chuckles, this time with more than a little appreciation mixed in. He was most likely popular among the others and no bully. "Hell, he's so big if we had a hull breach in space we could probably plug it with him and re-enter atmosphere!" Again she waited for the low laughter to sub-side.

"One thing he *isn't* big enough for, though, is to take on a Va'alen warrior."

Silence.

"These bastards range from seven to nine feet tall. They have four arms, two of which are tipped with spikes that are capable of puncturing armor, and the other two have claws that can take a limb off, also with their victim wearing armor." She swallowed as the vivid memory came back to her unbidden. "Believe me, I've seen that happen… I've also seen something which we now know is called *The Path of Ending*. This is where they lose a mate, who they bond with on a deeply telepathic level, and the loss of their link sends them into a berserker rage. The last one I saw do that tore through a battle mech and a CP team, unarmed, like they were training dummies."

They didn't need to know that only two of the team were CP, and that they were mostly injured after a crash. And that two of them were non-combatants, technically.

"Now the UN, in their infinite and vaunted wisdom," another chuckle, "have provided you with the latest and greatest in weaponry to combat this new enemy should the need arise for you to be shipped out to the next solar system. And when I say that the need may arise it would be because every trooper trained to a higher standard than you is already dead or in contact with the enemy. That said, you will all take three standard magazines for both pistol and rifle and you *will* re-qualify on both weapons by the end of this week or you *will* find yourselves transferred to a posting your abilities are more suited to. Where would that be, Master Petty Officer Conrad?"

"Catering Corps, Commander," Zero barked. "Also I hear sanitation is always in need of people who can lift heavy stuff. You big into your weights, Kekoa?" Zero leaned up at the huge seaman who smiled.

"I like to lift, Boss," he rumbled.

"I bet you do, sweetheart… What are these new and improved toys to be wasted on this shower of shi-it, Commander?" Zero called out in his parade ground voice, while still fixing the side of beef towering above him with the stare of a predator.

"Explosive munitions," Brandt replied. "More boom-boom for your bang-bang. And why do we need explosive munitions, Master Petty Officer?"

"Because these 'roaches wear a bio-armor like insects, Commander Brandt, and normal rounds don't do shit to them," Zero cried back. "Heavier ammo does some damage, blows a couple chunks off 'em here and there. And the accelerated rounds we use on CP—sure you pups have all heard about them—well they weren't a whole lot better."

Zero held his tongue in case he mentioned the next evolution in human small arms, the captured Va'alen energy pulse rifles which were being hastily reverse engineered by the UN and Hyper to come up with a cheap platform they could mass produce in time for the next fleet departure. They couldn't and, being unable to seek the assistance of the Kuldar, the powers that be had decided on another option.

Manufacturing of the 6mm and 12mm ammo had been started up again, those factories having been mothballed for a few years when there were more bullets being made than fired. A slight design change was made to include a tiny high-yield explosive into each projectile. It had been remarkably easy to achieve, almost as though the UN had such an illegal weapon on the shelf gathering dust just in case.

This concept of mass-producing the option made by the lowest bidder had also resulted in the refusal to upgrade their armor platforms. All of these decisions, Brandt knew in her growing cynicism, came down to the amount of credits a human life was considered to be worth by people who would never face an enemy outside of a safe, comfortable conference room.

The answer to that was an increase in UN recruitment, and for highly trained and experienced soldiers to be thrown into training roles instead of getting back to where, in the opinions of those troops at least, they were needed most.

"So you need to get close enough to them," Brandt said loudly, "and fill them with enough holes that they go down, because inside is a little soft alien who is *very* killable. Get to them and it's game over for the 'roaches. But on top of avoiding the spikes and the claws, you'll also need to avoid getting your useless hides shot by their superior weaponry, so you will all be pleased to know that there will be double the normal amount of PT over the next two weeks to keep you nice and agile."

A small groan took up in one corner of the formation, which suffered the immediate and intense gaze of a pissed-off sniper who was just getting used to his frustrated senior NCO status and enjoying wielding that particular stick.

"My first two volunteers," he crowed happily. "Consider yourselves at the top of my shit-list. Congratu-fuck'n-lations."

Silence answered that, too.

"So, Seaman Kekoa," Brandt said as she turned to face the big man again. "Still think you can take on a Va'alen warrior?"

"Only one way to know that for sure, Commander," he answered.

Brandt had to admit that he had her on that one, even if she was fairly certain of the outcome.

It wasn't just Zero Brandt had with her. She also had Payne and Turner from their mission on the forest moon in the CS. Payne was rated to instruct on fire support with the heavier guns, just as Zero took the few trained marksmen and women away for individual training. This was at the end of the two-week intense training schedule Brandt had been forced to come up with over the course of a rushed meeting. Turner, their medic, had developed a crash course in the kinds of wounds suffered when mixing with the Va'alen, which focused most heavily on catastrophic bleeds and major trauma.

The surplus of abandoned troops meant that the two surviving members of her original team would be effectively homeless and therefore reassigned. She had argued to keep them as part of her training team and have them both awarded brevet promotions to solidify their authority over the troops.

They were on their third course now. They had heard of the departure of their fleet a week prior, and hadn't heard from Torres for the same amount of time.

Brandt had managed only two nights in the city since being posted to the east coast of the American territory. Both nights had been filled with good company and less sleep than her team medic would probably advise.

More out of boredom than anything else, Brandt argued that the training she was being forced to deliver wasn't realistic enough. The troops sent to her weren't even using their armor, instead training in fatigues to officially condition their bodies before they were reliant on powered armor.

She had a worrying suspicion that the real reason was the armor manufacturing plants weren't able to cope with the requirements of so many new units being formed.

Every other week was the same; new troops arrived at oh-six-hundred on Monday morning and were thrown through intense training. They were required to use inferior, if destructively impressive, weaponry and train without the uprated protection Brandt had been the biggest petitioner of. Not only that, but the lack of situational awareness that came with the highly-connected suit software made simulated combat confusing and more difficult than it should have been.

"The answer is better," she complained to Zero on the first evening of that week's course, "not just *more*. We need experienced, trained troops in new armor with micro-shield emitters and we need the pulse rifles which I'm *sure* Hyper have already developed."

"And I need a month in Hawaii," Turner said as he walked into the office with his nose in a datapad.

His informality was ignored, as was the way in small teams who had formed close bonds. Respect was earned and freely given. His commanding officer didn't need to hear 'Ma'am' and 'Commander' every time he spoke because she knew he respected her, and that respect was mutual. Only in front of the uninitiated did they appear regimented.

"Why? So Kekoa's big sister can give you a rub down?" Brandt asked.

"I've heard she's taller," Payne added without looking up from the squad support weapon she was cleaning on the desk, "and so big that they can't find coconuts large enough to cover her…" She held up two hands, cupping them in front of herself as her eyebrows went up and down.

"Hehe, *bewbs*," Zero sniggered quietly.

"Anyway," Turner said, stopping the weak jokes. "Banging your head against the wall and saying we need quality over quantity is pointless unless you hold the keys to the treasury."

"What are you saying?" Payne asked the medic.

"I'm saying that the planet is going to go broke, resources-wise I mean, if we don't start hauling back minerals and the like from the new planets we're finding out there." He sat, dropping the datapad onto his desk and lifting a leg to rest a boot heel on it. "Look at it this way, we've built two fleets, two *entire* fleets in what? A year? Not to mention the increased production of arms and all that goes with mass mobilization, and you can bet your ass that the private companies are falling over themselves to get ships built, bought and retrofitted with Fold Drives so they can recruit five thousand miners on contract for the ass-end of god knows where. I'm telling you, this could get ugly."

"Yeah," Zero said. "But why don't you ever tell us how you feel about anything, man? Your ass is gonna be full of splinters from all that fence-sitting…"

Approach to Mars Shipyards

The modified light cruiser class ship under the command of Torres only had a crew of forty, and the bridge crew comprised of the captain, the communications officer, the tactical officer and the helmsman. Although crewed by only a few, their ship was like the frigates under the command of Captains Hayes and Halstead: a stripped-down warship, devoid of most comforts. It had been designed to operate near to resupply vessels even though it was well armed, armored, and retrofitted with faster-than-light travel and cloaking capabilities.

Beside Torres sat Lieutenant Commander Ivanov from the Russian UNID, assigned to them as part of the joint venture. To Torres, the words 'joint venture' meant joint funding, and that meant arguing over who invested more and who should be in command. Evidently the American territory had invested more than their European UN brothers and sisters.

"Dropping out of Fold Space... *now*," Rogers announced from the pilot's chair at the very front of the bridge.

Torres's stomach lurched with the slight shudder as the ship's grav emitters caught up with the transfer back to normal space. He shifted in his chair thinking that he'd never get used to that sensation.

"Mars shipyards, this is the UNS *Corvus* on approach..." the comm officer announced, hailing their destination as per protocol without being prompted.

"UNS *Corvus*," came a British woman's voice over the loudspeaker, "this is Commander Reynolds, ranking officer of the Mars orbital yards. Transmit ident codes and authority."

The comm officer turned to face Torres who nodded and tapped in the codes into his console. This new security measure had been in place since hostile human ships had begun roaming out in deep space. A brief pause ensued with the *Corvus*'s mic cut off as the codes were verified. The tactical officer turned to Torres and gave some worrying news.

"Orbital defense platforms have charged weapons, Captain."

"Hold position and do not respond," he ordered.

"What the hell...?" Ivanov muttered beside him.

"UNS *Corvus*, you are cleared to enter Mars sector. Any assistance you require from us, please let me know. Reynolds out." A collective sigh of relief passed through the small bridge crew as the weapons signatures from the multiple defensive batteries powered down.

"Standard procedure now, people," Torres said. "As sad as that sounds, we can't be too careful when it comes to security any longer."

A chorus of muttered affirmations came back to him before he gave his next orders.

"Lieutenant Rogers, lay in a rendezvous course with the *Hammer* and the *Vengeance*, in your own time."

"Aye aye, sir," Rogers replied, reacting immediately. 'In your own time' always meant that he should hurry the hell up.

"Comm, broadcast a message to the frigates informing them of our arrival. Ask where the meet is set."

Comms were relayed, and the officer turned to Torres, informing him that they were to dock to the *Hammer*. Rogers needed no further instructions. He adjusted their course accordingly. Minutes later they were slowing and rotating to match the pitch and attitude of the larger ship to attach to the dorsal airlock on the back.

"Ivanov with me," Torres said as he stood. "Mister Rogers, you have the chair."

Rogers stood, allowing the relief pilot to step into the warm seat he vacated, before walking to the big chair and sitting.

The airlock hissed open, both senior officers feeling the chill of space prickle their skin beneath their flight suits. Both men went armed; the singularity-accelerated pistols in drop-leg holsters were standard uniform at all times now. The crews of both ships were visible as the airlock opened, and were dressed similarly. Dropping down the ladder into the *Hammer*, feeling the same familiar claustrophobic sensation as being onboard their own small ship, a crewman stepped forward to direct them to the bridge.

"I'm good, Petty Officer," Torres said. "Been onboard plenty."

"Very good, sir," he answered, cracking off another salute as the men walked down the corridor.

"Impressive ship," Ivanov opined as they walked.

"Packs a hell of a punch, I can tell you," Torres answered awkwardly. He didn't know the Russian well enough to exchange idle chat with him.

They walked on in silence, passing more crew who stopped to salute as they went by, and reached the bridge. As the door hissed open, Captain Craig Hayes stood from his command chair and nodded to another officer who stepped up to join him from her spot looking over someone's shoulder at the tactical station. Both wore the rank insignia of commanders.

"Kyle," Hayes said in his gruff voice that made him sound perpetually annoyed. "Good to see you."

"Likewise," Torres said as they shook hands. The woman beside Hayes stepped up and offered her own hand.

"Nicola," Torres greeted her with a smile.

"Hey, Torres," she replied, turning a critical eye on Ivanov.

"Captain Hayes of the *Hammer*," Torres said by way of introduction, "and Captain Halstead of the *Vengeance*. This is Lieutenant Commander Anton Ivanov, Russian UNID."

Both captains shook his hand and nodded a greeting, but both were skeptical of the man. They knew Torres was UNID, but they'd fought alongside him. They had learned to trust him as a person, but the shady sub-organization he worked for remained shrouded in suspicion and mystery and thus extended to this newcomer.

"So you're a UNID mission?" Halstead asked.

"Perhaps we should...?" Torres suggested, eyeing the door to the briefing room opposite Hayes's private quarters. The captain's rooms on the smaller warships weren't as appropriate for entertaining as they were on the larger vessels.

As the door closed behind them, Torres, as polite as ever, asked if he could take a seat. Hayes and Halstead sat as well, with only the awkwardly silent Russian remaining on his feet.

"The *Corvus*?" Hayes asked with a raised eyebrow. "Pretty punchy little boat for a diplomatic mission, isn't she?"

"All they had left in the parking lot," Torres answered with evident avoidance and a small grin. "No changes here?"

"None," Halstead answered. "We rotate troops out on the airlock down below every forty-eight hours, but so far the Kuldar haven't tried to make contact or attempt any kind of breakout."

"So we're literally keeping them prisoner down there?" Torres asked.

"Hey," Hayes said, "until we know for sure they aren't just naked Va'alen warriors, what would you do?"

Torres agreed, but told them what the plan was. "I'm going in to talk with them. That's my brief. I'm to establish the full history of the alien races, if I can, and figure out who or what is which way 'round."

"Going in under a white flag?" Halstead asked.

"Yeah, I'm making no assumption here. In fact, I believe they *are* the same race only separated generations back like the Kuldar story goes. You know what Va'alen means in their language?" he asked.

The two captains looked at him blankly.

"It means 'warrior caste,'" Ivanov said. "Just as Kuldar translates into 'sub-caste.'"

"So you're just rolling in there under the assumption that they're not going to take over your mind or something?" Halstead asked. "You're going in unarmed?"

"Not exactly," Torres answered with a grin. "I have a little insurance policy I managed to get assigned to me if you catch my drift. Now, what *I* want to know is what the hell is going on in the CS?"

Hayes and Halstead exchanged a puzzled look.

"The Centauri System," Torres explained.

"That's a better question for the admiral," Hayes replied.

"He's here? With the rest of the fleet?"

"Most of the fleet is back in *the CS*," Halstead answered, "except us and the *Indomitable*, and the *Ichi* of course, and I think we're all here as a little insurance policy."

"So you're keeping the guns on the aliens and Dassiova's keeping the guns on any humans who step out of line?"

Hayes shrugged in answer. "And you're here to check the family trees of the little green bobble-heads."

Torres, fighting back an unexpected annoyance at the vague and inaccurate description of the Kuldar, set his mouth in a grim line. "I'll bet he's as pissed as we are for being benched," he said to change the subject.

"You mean having Admiral Vernay get his job?" Hayes asked. "You could say that."

"What do you know about it? I've heard literally nothing," Torres asked as he leaned forward in his chair.

"Well," Halstead started before looking annoyed at Ivanov. "You wanna sit down? You're making me nervous."

Ivanov said nothing but sat down as instructed.

"From what I've heard, the whole Va'alen presence has been corralled onto the bigger planet next to the moon your crew took a little vay-cay on. Got the whole planet sealed up tight with the help of the separatist fleet and spent the last couple months hunting down everything else left out in the wind. Any of them who didn't come back peacefully got taken out."

"What's the plan with them?" Torres asked. "Ship them home or keep them there?"

"You tell us, spy-boy!" Hayes blurted out with a grin.

"Hey," Torres said with his hands up in defense. "I'm as much of a mushroom here as you are. Plus I guess that kind of depends on what happens down there…"

"That's true," Hayes admitted. "So you better not screw it up!"

CHAPTER 5

Orbit of Planet Designated Gaia Néos, Centauri System

"Subspace comm incoming, Admiral," Vernay's comm officer told her on the bridge of the carrier *Neptune*.

"I'll take it in my quarters," the Frenchwoman responded. She rose and walked to the doorway. Sitting down at her desk she activated the console and authorized it with her biometric implant.

"Vernay here," she said.

"Vernay, it's Dassiova," came the gruff answer from millions of kilometers away. "How goes things?"

"Fine, Admiral, just fine," she lied. She felt more than a little harassed having to provide the man with unnecessary updates. She had replaced him, after all. This was *her* assignment. "How can I help you?"

"Just checking in," Dassiova said. "Seeing if you needed any advice or assistance."

"I assure you, Admiral Dassiova, I am quite capable. Should I need your help I promise I will call you directly. Captain Novak of the *Anvil* is well versed in your previous missions here and has been of some assistance. Now if there's nothing else, I must be getting back to my duties."

"Very well, Admiral," Dassiova said. "Just… just don't take your eyes off those slippery bastards, okay? Dassiova out." He cut the comm before she could respond. She shut down the console with a noise of exasperated annoyance.

Is it because I am a woman? Is it because I am not an American that they think they can call me and offer advice? No. I will not suffer this condescension any longer.

"Admiral to the bridge," the speakers announced, prompting another noise of annoyance from her as she walked back into the next room.

"Report," she announced as she strode back onto the deck of her carrier.

"Ma'am, long-range sensor arrays have picked up enemy signatures on approach."

Vernay said nothing, but marched to the central plinth on the bridge and activated a holo-display of the information.

"Send squadron three," the admiral ordered. "Jump them to..." She manipulated the display with both hands and stabbed her finger at the chosen spot. "*There.* That should get them into a position to intercept and flank. Send them now."

The comm officer relayed the orders and jump co-ordinates to squadron three. It was a small pack of light cruisers under the leadership of a senior commander. The squadron was one of four similar units ordered to intercept any remaining Va'alen units not already interned on the planet below.

"Three Squadron reports in position, Admiral," the comm officer reported, settling in to wait.

"They're still out there," Vernay muttered half to herself as she moved to look over the shoulder of her tactical officer. "After all these weeks they're still out there."

"But they're scattered, Admiral," the man running the tac station reassured her. "All of their bases are gone and any of them still free will be running out of resources."

"And also trapped here, Lieutenant Boulet," she said with a quiet hint of admonishment in her tone. "Remember that a trapped animal is an unpredictable and dangerous one."

"Squadron reports ultimatum message broadcast," the comm officer called out. "No response."

"Tell them to send it again and add a volley in their path," Vernay ordered. Those orders were relayed, and the bridge crew sat in apprehensive silence as the tense scene would be playing out thousands of kilometers away.

"Enemy contacts still not responding to hails. Breaking up formation."

"Order the squadron to take them out," Vernay snapped. "Send additional resources to their location but hold them back for now."

Those orders were passed on and followed. The holo-display in front of her showed new signatures blink into existence in a loose defensive line between the skirmish and the planet the fleet orbited.

One of the enemy signatures blinked out, flashing red briefly to indicate its destruction. At the same time, one of her cruisers blinked a rapid orange to show it coming under fire. She said nothing, fighting down the urge to micromanage ships. She had spent years of difficult experience learning how to control herself. She had to let the men and women of the squadron do their jobs. Vernay watched in silence for another minute, interpreting the flashing icons and imagining how that translated to real-world experiences on the cramped confines of the command cruiser's bridge.

"Six contacts destroyed," Boulet reported from tactical. "Two others are surrendering. Our two cruisers report damage to shields and one has suffered minor hull breaches. No serious injuries."

"Good, order the reinforcements to spread out and sweep the sector thoroughly. Bring the squadron back to their standby position.

Inform Captain Novak of the *Anvil* that he has minor repairs inbound. Notify me of the time they anticipate to get the squadron fully operational again."

With that, Vernay stood and nodded to her flight officer, an ageing but capable man named Macon, to take over control of the bridge. She walked back to her quarters and sat at the console to send the sub-space report of yet another contact with the straggling elements of the enemy forces in the system. The contact went much the same as the forty or fifty she had overseen before, with the variation that about thirty percent of them ended up with her ships being damaged and the Va'alen being destroyed.

The majority of them went for the ultimatum; electing to power down their weapons systems and shields to be escorted back to the planet where they would be effectively imprisoned until someone made a decision about their future.

She made an entry into her personal log of the mission, which was more of video diary. She recorded her entries in short bites to reference later should she want to record her version of the momentous event in human history. She spoke about her concerns of keeping a superior enemy locked up—superior in terms of physical ability and ruthless military efficiency. She voiced the ghosts of her concerns that, given greater numbers or the ability to call in reinforcements, she feared the ability of the human fleet to repel any concerted attack by their enemy.

She had yet to see a Va'alen in the flesh, or the carapace or whatever it was called, but the recorded footage she had seen did not fill her with confidence. There was something deep inside her, something primal, that sparked a fear of them. The Va'alen looked and acted like predators, like organisms higher up the food chain than humans were. That prompted fear on an almost cellular level. She knew from the encrypted briefings from Earth that they were now believed to be the same as the aliens who had been welcomed into humanity as allies centuries ago. That knowledge didn't remove the fear.

Her concerns were many, and they were serious. Her role pushed her into a corner where she had to act as jailer, hunter, ambassador and spy; keeping the Va'alen presence locked up tight on the surface was easy enough, especially given that she had plenty of ships under her command. Every one of those ships had their fingers on the metaphorical triggers ready to annihilate the settlements on the surface with a savage bombardment should the order come. Keeping them on the planet and monitoring for any signs of a breakout, like the construction of orbital rail cannons like the crew of the Ninth's frigates had encountered before, was a simple enough task. As was hunting down any remnants of enemy in the system, a task made simple by their vastly superior faster-than-light flight capabilities. Even the unavoidable engagements were a thing of relative ease, so long as she deployed enough ships to overwhelm the Va'alen fighters.

Numbers, speed and firepower were all on her side. They were quantifiable elements she could control, just as the predictability of the hostile aliens trapped on the planet was a simple enough thing to work with.

What she didn't enjoy were the interactions with the Middle Eastern Alliance; the separatist fleet. It was what kept her awake at night—twice she had visited the ship's doctor to request something that would put her under for an hour at the most. Any longer and she risked being incapacitated during an incident that couldn't be managed by her flight officer, who acted in her stead.

The separatists for their part avoided any overt practices that would cause detriment to the UN. They had established a small presence on the captured moon while the majority of their fleet added to the ring of weaponized steel surrounding the main planet, the supposed new Earth ripe for colonization. The rest of the separatists' ships had conducted long-range patrols to assist in flushing out the troublesome pockets of enemy still lurking on uninhabited planets and in floating debris fields.

Just because they had the superior numbers and the ability to travel at faster-than-light speeds didn't mean their presence in the Centauri system went without incident.

If ever the crew or captain of a ship grew complacent then the remnants of the Va'alen swarm would usually emerge unseen from an asteroid to which they had clamped. Or sometimes the Va'alen would de-cloak in staggering numbers and damage one or two ships before the ready squadrons of frigates and cruisers jumped in to destroy or scatter them into the dark void. A captain could never believe his crew safe, not in the CS.

Living under constant threat of a dangerous and wounded enemy, on top of keeping one eye on your supposed allies, created a high-pressure environment.

And Admiral Denise Vernay didn't need Admiral Elias Dassiova checking in on her every other day to add to her stress levels.

CHAPTER 6

Kuldar Habitat Dome, Mars

Torres gave a nod to one of the armored troops guarding the airlock. The officer, bearing the insignia of a lieutenant, acknowledged the nod, turned and waved his arm in a small gesture as he nodded to the others at the post. Torres stepped up to the airlock door with Specter beside him. Neither wore any armor, although both carried sidearms. Specter had no need of armor under these circumstances—he carried a personal shield emitter inside his body, which was essentially bulletproof anyway. He carried his custom pistols, one on each leg, chambered for the high caliber ammunition usually reserved for squad support and sniper weapons. Both pistols, as well as Torres's weapon, were equipped with a singularity accelerator pod which increased the power of the projectile. Neither had yet to be issued with a directed energy weapon that had been created based on the captured Va'alen pulse rifles.

The commander swiped his arm over the reader as the lieutenant stepped forward to input the security override code. He stopped himself—the door had opened without his code, negating the need for the additional layer of manual security. If the younger officer was surprised by this he didn't let it affect him for long, stepping back with a shrug. No doubt after a couple of months rotating that particular guard duty he'd seen enough weird stuff to be immune to most of it.

The door slid shut behind them, pressurizing the airlock section before opening the far end of the metal tunnel and revealing the dull red glow of the Kuldar environment. Stepping inside, Torres sucked in a deep breath and froze until the small wave of dizziness passed when his body grew accustomed to the variation in atmosphere.

"Your heart rate just went up," Specter said quietly.

"Just the increase in nitrogen and a slight drop in oxygen," Torres assured him. It was always preferable to fall back on science to explain that it wasn't nervous apprehension causing the fluctuation in his core statistics. "Wait, I'm not in armor so how did you...?"

"I see things," Specter said ambiguously.

He had dropped the 'sir' as he always did when not within earshot anyone outside their inner circle. Referring to Jake Santana as 'Specter' had been easy; the use of callsigns had been long established. Giving him the job title of 'specialist' had also been a matter of making his presence sound acceptable to people who lived and breathed correct procedure. Specter had no official UN rank above that of seaman, which had been his rank when he had ceased to be Jake Santana the first time around. Having not officially been recognized back in any official UN capacity and acting as an external contractor to the UNID, using a job title had given him the sense of rank when it mattered to others.

Ruffled feathers were often smoothed, Torres found, by a crisp salute and the liberal application of bullshit.

"Incoming," Specter said softly.

Ahead of them, through the dense foliage, showed two pairs of large, dark eyes. They had stepped inside the habitat dome created for the Kuldar, under the specially designed lamps that emitted the low frequency red light the aliens needed to thrive.

"Hello," Torres said, raising his voice. He guessed he was dealing with some of the many Kuldar children.

Hissing, clicking noises came back to them as the eyes ducked out of sight. The sounds gave Torres the impression that the Kuldar were giggling, as though he were playing some form of game like hide and seek.

"Hello?" he tried again as he stepped forward.

The hissing sound came again, this time accompanied by the rustling of leaves as the two children ran off. Torres sighed, deflating as he faced traipsing through the jungle under the dome in search of the alien leaders.

"Stand still," Specter said gently.

Torres, as attuned to that tone of voice as he was the sensors of a shrouded ship behind enemy lines, did as he was told.

"Asha?" Torres called out loud, asking for the only one of the Kuldar he knew and hoping that his presence would mitigate any possible hostility.

"I am here, Captain Kyle Torres," Asha's voice said in English, breathy and stilted. He likely had not practiced the language in weeks.

"Can we talk?" Torres asked loudly. He slowly turned around to see three of the gangly, long-limbed aliens stepping from the dense foliage with weapons leveled at Specter.

Specter seemed unconcerned, safe and comfortable in the knowledge that he could move faster than they could and overpower all three easily. His hands stayed away from his weapons and his face showed the smallest hint of a smile. Torres also made sure to keep his hand away from the weapon on his right thigh, not wanting any misunderstanding to cause a major incident.

"Now you want to talk to me?" Asha demanded angrily. "Why did you not want to talk to me when we were dragged from your planet? Why did you not want to talk to me when I begged for word to reach you? When we were taken away from every laboratory without reason? Why did you not want to talk to me after we were locked in here like your pets?"

"I had nothing to do with any of that, Asha. I swear it," Torres said. He realized that none of the three Kuldar he could see was talking to him, so Asha must still be in the trees. "I had no control over it, and I only learned a week ago why my people did that. I'm here to talk to you."

"And you bring weapons to talk?" Asha demanded angrily.

"Asha," Torres said, stifling a laugh, "if my people wanted to kill you they wouldn't send me in with a gun; they'd vent this dome into space and save themselves the need to clean up afterward."

"This does not reassure me, Captain Kyle Torres," Asha said icily.

It occurred to Torres that his diplomatic skills weren't off to the best start. Or perhaps they were; he couldn't be certain.

"Can we talk?" Torres tried again. "If you like, we can go back out and leave our guns. Will that help?"

One of the thin aliens pointing a tentative spear at the unnervingly still Specter half turned to rattle a series of clicks and hisses towards the trees, which prompted what sounded like an argument between two of them.

"Yes," Asha said finally. "Go out and come back without guns. This will help my people believe that you are not here to harm them."

He already believes me, Torres thought to himself. *Otherwise he'd include himself in that fear.*

Torres walked carefully past the spear tip, which followed him closely, swiping his arm over the airlock controls to open them before both he and Specter backed inside. The outer door shut, masking the sight of the frightened aliens, and the small pressurization sequence began in reverse. They found themselves blasted with cold air carrying a smell neither could place, and when they stepped out to their start point the same lieutenant stepped forward.

"Short visit," he said, probably smiling behind the visor.

Torres drew the weapon from his holster. He kept it pointed at the deck as he removed the magazine and turned it sideways to show the safety mechanism to the officer, proving the weapon to be safe.

"They don't want weapons in there," he said.

"And you're going in there without a weapon just like that? Because they said so?"

Torres turned to look at Specter with a smile, seeing how he eyeballed the two troops trying not to look at the prototype weapons he placed on a desk.

"I'm hardly going in unarmed, Lieutenant, but your concern for me is touching," Torres said.

The younger officer laughed, the sound coming through his suit's speakers as though it had been translated by technology.

Stepping back into the airlock—Torres realized the smell clinging to them was disinfectant from the exit procedure—the two men went back in to try and open a dialogue with the aliens who had little reason to trust humanity any longer.

CHAPTER 7

Training Site Delta Six, European UN Territory, Formerly Bulgaria

The dropship came in low and fast as the activity in the back ramped up to full readiness. Brandt, sparing herself the burden of yelling, watched and listened from the open doorway of the cockpit. Zero bawled at the two halves of the squad lined up ready to drop to the deck and find cover as she had trained them to do.

Officially the lieutenant and their senior NCOs ran the exercise, but as none of those NCOs outranked Zero, it fell to her ever increasingly annoyed marksman to show them how it should be done.

Along with Turner and Payne, Brandt acted as safety marshal and observer, providing a very biased assessment of the performances on show. She knew that even though she and her team had trained these troops, their performance would still be wholly inadequate to take on a pack of Va'alen.

Armed with their deactivated training weapons—a stupidity Brandt argued against up to admiral level until she was firmly reminded of her place—the two sticks of unarmored troops in jumpsuits squashed up on one another ready to drop and disperse rapidly.

Zero hit the ramp release, turning his back on the opening as wind and debris whipped around the landing zone mercilessly. He bawled at them over the sound and through their comms.

"Drop, disperse, get your asses out of sight and stay there. If the safety marshals have a bead on your precious little hides I can personally guarantee the 'roaches will blow it clean off. I'm looking at you, Kekoa. Find yourself a goddamned mountain or something and hide behind it. *Mooove!*"

They went, shuffling forward to make the short drop of about six feet and roll clear in the stiff grass. Zero followed, standing tall as all around him troops hit their belt buckles and attempted to make themselves invisible. Brandt and her small team followed, all of them wearing high-visibility yellow over their jumpsuits. They would have felt less out of place being naked on a parade ground than they did standing up in simulated battle wearing no armor, carrying no weapons, and deliberately drawing attention to themselves with a scrap of bright yellow material.

"Awful," Zero roared. "Absolutely, positively, stinking godawful. Lieutenant? Lead them out, objective Alpha in your own time."

Zero caught Brandt's eye and made a face, which signaled words he wouldn't use in front of his mother. Brandt fell in step beside him as their comms chattered with the orders from the officer and the dropship's engines whining back up to lift it clear of the LZ.

"What are we doing, Grip?" Zero asked quietly off comm. "Why are we training green kids for a fight they ain't gonna get to?"

"I don't think we are," Brandt told him. "I think we're being held back and kept away from something else."

"Like what?" Payne asked them.

Zero and Brandt both turned to give the young NCO a cold look; team member or not, she was intruding.

"I don't know yet," Brandt said, shutting the conversation down. "But I'm starting to think I should've taken that job offer."

Beside her Zero scoffed. "Didn't think to ask what the going rate for a top-tier sniper was while you were there, did you?"

"No, Zero, I didn't ask what the going mercenary rate for a man of your skills was. If I speak to them again, I'll be sure to check."

"Make sure they throw in dental," he said seriously. "I still get toothache thanks to the UN hack I saw last year."

They walked in relaxed silence, following the almost comical display of troops bounding and maneuvering ahead of them like children playing, when the radio burst to life.

"Ground team Commander, attention ground team Commander, flight Epsilon One Eight en route back to Virginia," came the urgent call over their comm channel.

Brandt reached for the unfamiliar radio, again missing the HUD control of her armor, which negated the archaic need to press and hold as she spoke. Before she could answer another voice cut in.

"This is Lieutenant Price, go ahead," said the young officer ahead of them.

"Epsilon One Eight, Commander Brandt, send," she said, the annoyance in her tone communicating that young Price had just made a mistake.

The pilot of the dropship came back to her immediately.

"Commander, be advised we've just been painted by hostile ground-to-air batteries to our south."

Brandt's eyes went wide. She had been expecting something similar but was still surprised when it happened.

"One Eight, advise change course and squawk friendly on all channels," she barked into the microphone.

"Done and done, Commander," came a different voice, that of the co-pilot. "We're now showing in the clear and heading home. Just thought you should know."

"Understood," Brandt answered. Her breath came rapidly but she managed to keep her voice steady. "I'll contact HQ when we reach the training grounds. Safe flight. Out."

"The hell was that all about?" Turner asked.

"MEA is my guess," Payne answered. Brandt caught Zero's eye, and both managed to stop their eyes from rolling. Zero couldn't hold his tongue, however.

"Who the hell else is going to paint one of our birds on a training run for no good reason?"

"You meant to ask *why* the separatists would be splashing one of our dropships, right?"

Turner asked Payne, coming to her defense.

"Simple," Zero said. "Just a little political muscle flexing."

"What? We can shoot down your dropships whenever we want to?" Payne asked.

"Not that simple," Brandt explained. "They'd claim we violated their sovereign airspace with a troop transport and they fired to prevent an attack. We'll claim, genuinely, that we were a training flight with unarmed troops in transport to an exercise ground. The rest of the world will believe whatever they like but both sides will have 'proof' that the other side is the aggressor. They're testing how much the UN wants to fight them and whether we're more interested in space than home."

"Damn," Payne said after a pause. "That's complicated."

"Much more complicated down here than it is up there," Zero offered, one finger pointed to the sky and the far reaches of space beyond it.

"Yeah," Turner added. "Up there at least there's a common enemy. Kind of unites us."

"No," Brandt said in correction. "It makes something else a bigger threat than we are to each other. Don't forget that our side isn't exactly the land of the angels." She remembered her company, only able to confide the full details in Zero as he was cleared to know certain elements of what she alluded to. The others weren't, so she cut off her own conversation.

"Anyway," she said, "get this shit show to double it to the training grounds so I can make that call."

ΠЧC

The restaurant wasn't busy, but by the time Brandt had got away from the training office after completing the end of week reports it was late on Saturday. Much against her personal standards she found herself walking into a steakhouse wearing her fatigue pants and t-shirt over boots still adorned with the dried mud she failed to stamp off on her way up the block.

As she walked through the doorway she saw the eyes of a diner go wide, recalling just in time that she still wore the service pistol on her right leg. For someone so accustomed to going everywhere armed, she always forgot how shocking it was for many people to see guns carried so openly. Since the UN had globally restricted the ownership of weapons outside of military and law enforcement, the sight of such a weapon in public was enough to cause a stir.

"Ah, *crap*," she cursed.

The man she was already late to meet stood up from his table to walk toward her.

"Give me five minutes," she said. "I'll go secure this in the transport."

"Don't worry about it," Commander Anthony Morello said soothingly. "There's no issue with you carrying it."

71

"You're sure?" Brandt asked, admitting to herself that if anyone knew whether she was protected by military procedure and legislation it would be her date.

"Trust me," he said confidently. She did.

"Sorry, have you been waiting long? I got away as quickly as I could…"

"Don't worry about it," Morello said. "You forget who you're talking to? Like I leave the office dead on five?"

"True," Brandt accepted. "Monday to Friday is a joke. Either I have to give them Friday off, condense the training package to only eight days and catch up, or else stay late. It's that or work Saturdays like today, which I'll probably have to anyway after that dropship incident."

"I heard about that," Morello said, raising his eyes over the top of the menu. Brandt guessed he had already read it three times over and decided exactly what he was going to have. "That hit my office within an hour of happening, I mean; the adjutant general himself was stirred to write a strongly worded communiqué to the commanders of the Middle Eastern Alliance that very same evening."

Something in his tone made her smile. "Really?"

"Oh yeah," he said with mock seriousness. "He was so moved that he even missed his afternoon nap in his office after a morning of golf."

"Someone else wrote it then?"

"Of course, but the AG signed it, made a lot of noise about how 'those assholes' should know what's good for them and give up."

"Give up?" Brandt asked him. She was trying to get a waiter's attention. She hadn't even picked up the menu, as she first wanted a bottle of the house red.

"Well, his exact words, I'm told, were for them to 'stop their nonsense and fall in line,'" Morello told her. "He even used the word *rebellion*. I swear he's been in cryo since the second war of independence…"

"Well that kind of forward-thinking is how men like that reach the very top," Brandt said seriously as she locked eyes with Morello. Neither could hold the other's gaze for long as they both cracked up.

"Come on," he said, finally letting his grumbling belly and impatience get the better of him. "Pick your meal already."

"Okay, okay," Brandt said. He lifted a hand with style to bring a waiter scurrying over.

"Sirloin, medium rare, sweet potato fries and a salad," she said. "And a glass of house red."

She had remembered that she had the transport parked on the next block and a gun on her thigh, and dropped the idea of ordering a bottle.

"Can I get the Neapolitan calzone with fries?" Morello asked. "And a beer?"

"Draught okay?" the waiter asked, accepting his nod as an affirmative and scribbling down the order before disappearing so quickly that anything else they had forgotten to add to their order would have to wait until he rematerialized again.

Morello leaned forward, making Brandt do the same. "That caused a bit of a stir higher up, let me tell you," he said in a low voice.

"Go on…" Brandt answered, enjoying the conspiratorial feel of their conversation.

"Not here," Morello said in a whisper. He noticed her disappointed look and added, "Well there's two things I *can* tell you."

"What's that?" Brandt whispered back.

"I can tell you I'm glad you made it here, even if you are late and armed."

"And the other thing?" she asked, mirroring his happiness.

Morello looked around subtly like the most woefully obvious counter-surveillance operator in the galaxy. "The other thing is that you need a shower."

Brandt sat back, unsure whether to laugh or leave, but his barely veiled look of mischief made her stay.

"How would you like to switch jobs for a week or two, office boy?" she goaded him.

"I can use a gun," he assured her. "Besides, you can have dessert at my apartment. I'll put your uniform in the machine overnight."

As presumptuous as his comment was, he was true to his word. He had the most delicious salted caramel ice cream with big pieces of fudge, which Brandt ate wearing PT shorts and a matching UN shirt that covered her waist and hung a little loose at the shoulders.

Morello watched her without shame. She stood up on her tiptoes to rest her elbows on the counter, showing him the slender and muscular thigh where the gun had been strapped earlier.

"Come on then, smartass," she said as she abandoned her perch and sat on the couch opposite him to shake out her fluffy hair from untied braids. "Enlighten me with your super intelligence."

"You mean my natural smarts or my actual intelligence briefing from UNID?" he asked, swiping a finger over a datapad and offering it to her.

She held the spoon in her mouth; she didn't want to relinquish control of her ice cream for even a second. She took the pad and rested it on her legs as she ate and read. Her eyebrows went up and stayed up until she had finished the short daily brief and handed back the pad. It was nothing she didn't already know or suspect, but she didn't want to let him feel like she was ungrateful. The intelligence, which was graded so low and uncorroborated that it was basically a rumor, was that the MEA had attempted cyber-attacks to gain data on the aliens designated as Hive Lords.

"You supposed to show me that?" she asked.

"I'll just say you beat me up and used my chip to unlock the datapad," he told her seriously.

"You know I could."

"I know you could," he said back to her with a grin. "You know how easy you front line types have it? I'm in the gym five days a week." She shot him a questioning look which made him fold in a heartbeat. "Okay, maybe three days a week *and* I watch what I eat just so my uniform keeps on fitting me whereas you just ate half a cow with trimmings and are now trying to consume all of my ice cream, and look at you? There's not an ounce of fat on you!"

Brandt stood, lifting up the t-shirt to expose a defined set of abdominal muscles and a roguish smile.

"Yeah, well," she shot back as she sat and shoveled ice cream into her mouth again. "Us front line types also get shot at and have our limbs pulled off by angry aliens. And besides, we look like this because we're always holding up the *rears* like you..."

"Oh no..." Morello said. "Oh no you did *not* just call me a rear-echelon asshole type! I'll have you know I qualify for combat every three months, even though I don't need to, and I'm one of the very few who—"

"Relax," she said laughing. "Didn't mean to hit a raw nerve there..."

Morello's face showed the anguish of a decision, like he was fighting with himself.

"What is it?" she asked.

Morello fidgeted before sitting down quickly on the coffee table in front of her.

"You've got to keep this to yourself," he said. "This is *serious*, not just like seeing a UNID briefing which you'll probably get sent on Monday anyway, but top secret classified serious."

Brandt put her bowl down and licked the spoon, fixing him with a look she hoped was serious enough for him.

"You swear?"

"Come on," she told him. "Like you said, I'll probably hear about this anyway, I'm not exactly in the dark when it comes to security clearances…"

"No, this is different," Morello said. "The UN is planning to expand. They want to create a colony on Gaia Néos. A UN-run colony with private financial backing, only…"

"Only what?" she asked.

"Only they need to deal with the internal threat before they can expand, otherwise they'll leave the Earth undefended."

CHAPTER 8

NYC, Sunday, 03:39 Hours

Brandt's comm device blinked rapidly on the soft carpet beside the bed as the call went unanswered. On the second attempt it vibrated, an urgent message. The exhausted officer stirred in the bed but did not fully wake up. The third attempt was made directly to Morello's home system and was not subtle. The small data console beside his bed, his datapad in the lounge of his apartment and his personal comm device all began beeping and vibrating at once, which snatched both of them from sleep in a panicked instant.

For Morello this was a frightening inconvenience, but for Brandt, who still hadn't told anyone of the nightmares she suffered since crash-landing on the alien moon, it was terrifying. She flew from the bed, her hands searching desperately for the weapon that her mind hadn't yet recalled was secured in the weapons locker under the seat of her UN transport parked five floors below.

By the time her brain had caught up with current events and had cut through the fog of tiredness and the three glasses of wine, she heard Morello's voice beside her.

"Yeah?" he croaked into the comm device.

"Commander Morello, please put Commander Brandt on comm," came the strict orders. Morello passed over his device rubbing at his eyes and flopping back down to the pillow to breathe and let the panic pass.

"Brandt here; who is this?"

"Commander, you need to answer your comm," said the female voice on the other end. "You also shouldn't be off-site. I thought that was made clear to you?"

"Who the hell is this?" Brandt asked, still breathing rapidly from the sudden interruption to sleep and resulting adrenaline.

"Crawford," said the voice, as though her name was rank enough. Brandt sighed in defeat. Crawford was the short-haired, severe woman from the UNID she had dealt with more than once over the course of her career. "Commander, you need to get back to the Virginia training base immediately."

"I…" Brandt began, before stopping herself. She couldn't pull the 'I've had a drink off duty' card; they'd probably just send someone in a noisy transport to collect her. She was surprised they hadn't done that to begin with. "What's the issue?"

"No issue," Crawford responded. "You just showed up as O.O.B. and this is a routine follow-up."

"On my way," Brandt said with an exasperated huff, not bothering to hide her emotions at the intrusion into her private life. She also didn't bother to challenge the weapons-grade bullshit she had just been fed. With a groan, she stood up from the bed and padded over to where she had dumped her own comm device, slipped it back onto her forearm and tightened the strap.

"I'm sorry, Tony," she said. "Get some sleep and I'll call you when I can."

"I'm awake anyway," he said as he stood up to activate a soft bedside lamp. The sudden change made them squint. "Sorry. Let me make you a coffee before you have to fly back."

Brandt said nothing, but she was grateful for the offer. Doing anything at—she checked her comm display and groaned again—

doing anything at oh-three-forty was difficult without caffeine or adrenaline, and right then she'd take either.

She looked at the pile of PT clothes where her comm had been and remembered that her uniform was still being washed. Slipping on an oversized robe she found hanging behind the door, she padded out into the kitchen area, her bare feet slapping gently on the cool tiles, where her friendly lawyer was fumbling with the coffee machine. She watched him, smiling, until he stepped away holding both hands up like he'd managed to make it work and didn't want to risk messing it up. He turned to see her in the robe and suddenly also remembered her uniform. He snapped the fingers softly on both hands and stepped to the utility area. He returned a few seconds later, seconds Brandt spent wisely by staring at the bubbling coffee machine until the first trickles of espresso began to drip into the thick, white cup waiting below the spout.

"Here," Morello said. "All clean and still warm from the dryer."

Brandt thanked him, taking the bundle and disappearing back to the bedroom. Less than a minute later she was back, wearing the clean, warm and infinitely better-smelling uniform she had arrived in. The empty holster flapped against her right thigh, until she reached down to pull the strap around her leg and secure it.

"Want me to fix you up something to eat?" Morello asked as he handed her the tiny cup of steaming liquid that he insisted on calling rocket fuel. She thought the terminology, although appropriate, was a bit out of date.

"I'm good," she said. She sipped and let the caffeine soak into her soul. "Thanks though."

"Let me get some clothes on and I'll walk you down," he said chivalrously.

Brandt smiled. She was an experienced soldier, selected and uniquely trained for special operations and one of the few human beings on Earth or in space to have survived a fight with a vastly superior alien enemy. Still, something in his protective manner made her feel special.

"It's fine, seriously," she argued. "I'm parked less than half a block away."

"This is still New York," he insisted. "You can't be too careful."

"I'll be fine. Get back to sleep and enjoy your day off."

He stood still, staring at her for a while until he relented and walked over to her.

"Just… be careful," he said finally. "There's a lot of things going on right now and I don't want you getting hurt."

As much as she wanted to laugh it off, to tell him he was going soft, she allowed herself to be wrapped in an embrace before finishing the coffee like a shot and stepping out the front door of his apartment in the middle of the night.

Despite the warm time of year, Brandt still felt the chill of the night air hit her skin through the single layer she wore. She walked out of the elevator and hit the door release button to get to the street, wondering if her UNID implant was still programmed to act as a master key. Hitting the sidewalk and turning left to the transport, her mind wandered back to the chip and on a whim, she turned back to see if a swipe of her forearm would grant her access back into the building.

As she turned back she saw a person. In itself that wasn't a big deal; she was in a city and people moved around at all times of the day or night. It could be someone on their way home after closing up a late-night bar. It could be someone on the way to an early start for any number of jobs. It could even be an insomniac like her, out for a walk to clear their mind.

But, if it were any of those things, the person wouldn't have faltered when she turned around. Wouldn't have locked eyes with her and wouldn't have flinched, to stifle the involuntary reflex of reaching inside the unseasonably heavy coat he wore. In that instant, the stranger gave everything away.

Adrenaline surging into her body overtook the caffeine. She scanned her arm over the door reader only to find that she no longer had the UNID authority to override locks; it was either that or the building was safeguarded against the technology to some degree.

"Dammit," she cursed, contemplating kicking the glass door or yelling at the top of her voice to get someone's attention. Probably the only person awake in the apartment block was Morello, and at five floors up with triple-glazed windows she had as much chance of him hearing her as she did of getting back inside on her own in the next three seconds.

The man she had startled had gathered himself and started toward her at a lumbering run. She turned and fled in the direction of her transport, reaching into her pocket for the key. She outpaced her shadow easily, glancing back to see him running after her with his left hand held tight against his big jacket, no doubt holding a weapon in place. Torn between activating her comm, which would slow her down, and getting to the safety of the transport, she ran as she held up the key fob device and hit the remote start button. Ahead of her, about a hundred paces and on the opposite side of the street, bright LED lights illuminated the street. The high-pitched whine of singularity-powered turbine engines reached her. She slid the key back in her pocket and sped up her sprint. A shadow ahead of her emerged from the side of a building. She angled away to cut across the empty street, jumping and sliding without grace over the hood of an old model ground transport. Once on the other side, she stretched out her long legs and ran faster to her ride.

Too late. A third shadow materialized from between parked transports on the other side of the road and angled to intercept her before she could reach her vehicle.

Trapped. Cornered. Unarmed.

These three thoughts hit her simultaneously and, in that instant, she knew she wasn't going to get away without a confrontation.

She slowed, not enough for the two chasing her to catch up but enough for the intercepting shadow to get directly between her and the transport. He reached inside his own jacket as she approached, his hand holding something she didn't see. She accelerated to close the gap between them before he could fully draw what she assumed was a weapon. Jumping into the air from three paces away, she slammed her knee into his right arm, which was still across his chest and knocked him solidly back to the road. Brandt went down too, unable to regain her feet after using herself as a ballistic missile. She recovered first. She threw herself on top of him, securing the right hand, which was reaching back inside the jacket, and clamping her own hand over his to gain control of whatever he reached for.

Her fingers felt a pistol grip. This was no random mugging, not by a long shot.

A knee hit her in the side of the head as the man on his back tried to shake her off him. She recovered, head ringing and still not having let go of the weapon. Her finger felt for the trigger before he could regain enough purchase to hit her again. She squeezed his finger onto the trigger once, twice, and both times the report sounded muted and not like any gunshot she had heard.

He convulsed with both pulls of the trigger, though he didn't fall limp like a man shot with a gun would. Instead, his body went rigid and he emitted a peculiar strangled noise like he was choking. She pulled out of his grip with difficulty and stood, looking down at the weapon in the light of her transport's LED headlamps. Immediately she recognized the pistol outline. It was a Hyper design, but the ammunition was definitely not singularity charged.

A boot scuff behind her made her spin, dropping to one knee and triggering off a half dozen instinctively fired rounds. The second shape that emerged in her path dropped and the rigid body skidded over the surface of the road toward her as she turned her attention to the third. They had taken cover behind a parked transport and sent rounds in her direction. She moved, leaping over the hood of another ground transport to tuck her body behind it and make herself as small as possible. She tapped at her comm device, swiping over the little emergency icon, double tapping it and holding her finger on the flashing image to activate the emergency beacon.

Rounds pinged off the metal above her; not real ricochets and not the sound of heavy projectiles penetrating her cover, but something else. She dropped the magazine out of the weapon and saw the bright blue tip of the topmost bullet, before slapping it back in the gun. They must be using some kind of incapacitation ammo. That meant they wanted her alive. They wanted her to talk.

"Just give up, Commander," said a voice which was accented in a way she couldn't place. "We only want to talk to you."

Brandt wanted to roll out of cover and come out shooting, yelling something cool and clever like 'talk to this,' but she knew when she was pinned down. As her mind raced through her available options, the sky filled with shrieking turbines and light. Automatic gunfire had the next word, and it spoke at length until the scream of engines moved away to settle down. Brandt stayed in cover.

"Commander?" a young male voice called out. "Commander Brandt sound off."

"Here," she yelled, trusting the new people without fully understanding why.

She stood, emerging from her cover with the captured pistol still held tightly in both hands. An armored shape walked toward her, the heavy footfalls reassuring her. His helmet retracted to show an eager young face and eyes that seemed older than the rest of him.

"Commander, are you good to fly?" he asked. She didn't answer immediately so he placed a gauntlet on her shoulder for emphasis. "Commander, I need you to talk to me. Are you able to fly your transport or do I need to assign you a driver?"

Brandt's eyes snapped up to him, taking in the lieutenant's rank and the bearing of a highly trained young man pretending to be filling a mediocre role. He had CP written all over him, in every word and gesture.

"I'm alright," she told him, though she did fear getting shot down during the twenty-minute flight back to Virginia. "Am I getting an escort?"

"Armed dropship above you the whole way," the lieutenant said, holding one finger skyward. "Go straight, go fast."

"Morello," she said after starting to turn away. "They know about him. He nee—"

"The commander will be moved to a secure location. You have my word."

She nodded then frowned, realizing that the word of a stranger didn't account for much. She opened her mouth to ask over the sound of more transports flying low, but he anticipated her question.

"Beale," he said. "Lieutenant Beale."

"Thank you," she said. She holstered the stolen pistol, turned and climbed into her transport.

CHAPTER 9

UN Training Grounds, Virginia

Brandt's transport landed a little after four in the morning. Despite the time of day, there seemed to be too much activity to return to normal, not that she expected it to after the attempt made on her only minutes prior.

She ignored the officer's accommodation block, electing instead to walk straight into her team's office and see what was waiting for her.

Crawford waited, along with two other plain gray suits Brandt didn't know.

"The plot thickens," she said as she sat down opposite the senior UNID agent.

Zero, hair a mess and unshaven but with alert eyes, wordlessly deposited a cup of coffee beside her. She nodded her thanks, catching his eye to answer his unspoken question with another nod and communicating with her second-in-command intrinsically. She waited for the explanation.

"As of now," Crawford began after taking a sip of her own drink, "you and your team don't leave this base. All shore leave and freedom of movement is denied until further notice."

"Care to tell me why?" Brandt asked her. She sensed some kind of amusement from the woman with a short, masculine military haircut. Brandt's own loose hair would probably remain larger than a dropship ramp until she washed and braided it again.

"You received the call from me about thirty seconds after our operatives in the Middle East and Africa confirmed a threat against our security. It seems a report has found its way out of UN control, and that report names everyone that had contact with or immediate knowledge of the aliens designated 'Hive Lords.' For reasons we don't yet know, the separatists want firsthand intelligence on these beings and they aren't willing to land on Gaia to get it themselves."

"And how did that link to me where I was?" Brandt asked. Crawford shifted in her seat and drank more coffee.

"Part of the intercepted chatter was the activation of an

insurgency team in New York. Of the few people on your previous mission only you were in the city, plus it makes sense to start at the top and work down, assuming that you would have more information on the subject than your inferiors."

Brandt felt Zero stiffen at the archaic and offensive terminology. It offended Brandt too, just as calling her team subordinates did, but she kept her face as a straight as possible.

"So you dump us in a lame assignment, keep us from getting back out there, take our ship away and now all of a sudden we're targets?" she demanded.

"To be clear" Crawford replied unfazed, "the removal of the *Ichi* from the fleet roster was not our decision, however it made sense to reassign your crew to different places."

"Why?" Zero asked. "Why does it make sense to do that?"

"Because it does," Crawford told him flatly, ending his line of questioning with an outright refusal to answer. She looked back to Brandt. "Unofficially you have all been posted to this training facility in the hope that anyone with a level of knowledge will see this as being too busy and too well armed to be worth another attempt on you. On any of you."

"And the training?" Zero asked. "We're supposed to just carry on doing it?"

"Yes." She sounded more annoyed at his interruption than she had been the first time.

"No," Brandt said as she stood. "This isn't going to work for me."

"Which element are you referring to specifically?" Crawford asked, annoyingly calm in the face of her hostility.

"Every part of it. You need to stop playing whatever game you're playing and using us as pawns and send us back to the CS where we can be useful. Where we can do our jobs properly."

"Commander," Crawford said, "will you just trust me that everything is as it should be right now, and that I think you should just have some patience and let the world turn a little backstage?"

"No," Brandt said. "I don't like playing mushrooms. We earned our spot on the fleet with blood and now we're just pieces on your chessboard."

Crawford sighed and stood.

"You have your orders," she said simply as she walked out of the office without saying another word.

~

"Grip, what the hell?" Zero asked.

"Long story," she told him. "Hang on a second." She tapped at her comm, scrolling through her recent contacts until she found Morello and hit the icon to call him. The connection was severed so she tried again. The second time the call connected, but before she could speak it gave her a flat tone instead. She tapped to try again before Zero interrupted her.

"It's blocked," he told her. "That's the same thing you get when a device is damaged or remotely deactivated."

In frustration she went back through the call list and hit the return comm icon on the missed call from Crawford. She answered, not hiding the annoyance in her voice, from about fifty paces away. In the background Brandt could hear the whine of engines readying for takeoff.

"What is it, Commander?"

"Morello," she demanded. "Where is he?"

"He's safe, but he'll be out of touch for a while. Leave it at that. And one more thing; the next time a private corporation contacts you with a job offer remember to report it as per regulations." Crawford cut the comm link dead.

Had Brandt been using a datapad instead she would likely had launched it across the room.

"So that's it?" Zero asked. "We hurry up and wait?"

"Don't we always?" she replied before devolving into another round of curses and furniture kicking. "Speaking to those... those *spooks* is like getting a horoscope reading; you never know what it actually means. Are we supposed to be grateful and wait to get back out to the fleet? Are we getting left behind? Punished? Rewarded?"

"Who knows," Zero answered. "But it's before dawn on my only day off so, unless you need me, I'm going back to bed."

CHAPTER 10

Kuldar Habitat Dome, Mars

Torres sat on the ground, his eyes closed as he immersed himself in the rituals of the Kuldar before they spoke. It was mostly pointless for him to join in. He couldn't project his feelings and emotions the way that they did to unburden their minds. He could, however, feel their anguish over certain things which gave him a better understanding of them as a people.

They were frightened. Not of the Va'alen but of humans. They missed their home, or at least the only home they had known. They didn't know what the future held in store for them; most of them feared it would be imprisonment or death. They were confused, let down, angry and scared.

All of these things Torres knew by joining in with their ritual of honesty feelings before they spoke. While each one only came to him as a raw emotion, he could still understand enough to know that humans had let these people down.

Asha, along with three others, were the only Kuldar permitted to speak with him. Torres was not allowed to use his translation device, but he could not leave it outside the dome as he did his weapon. Instead he entrusted it to Specter who stayed still and silent as he watched, listened and learned.

Asha's grasp of English was sufficient to converse, although nuanced language and phraseology made for difficult misunderstandings if the alien didn't know what he meant. Torres's grasp of the Kuldar tongue was non-existent, so the communication was unbalanced.

"You must not say again that you cannot tell us these things," Asha told Torres. "You refuse to give us the answers that we need, yet you ask that we trust you and the other humans?"

"I get that," Torres said, then corrected himself, changing his words to be less ambiguous. "I understand, but there are things I am not at liberty to tell you."

A rustle of foliage nearby caught the commander's attention and his eyes flickered to the source of the sound—a grinning Jake Santana played peekaboo with the Kuldar children who dogged their steps whenever they entered the dome.

"And yet you expect us to tell you everything about our own people, after you have kept us prisoner here without providing reasons?" Asha snapped, bringing Torres's wandering attention back to the negotiations. Torres was overwhelmed by a wave of multiple feelings. He felt angry agreement, accusation, a need for answers.

"I can see that we aren't going to get anywhere until I can give you this information," Torres admitted. "I have to seek clearance to say more, but I hope I can. I want to trust you, but too much has happened to give that trust blindly. If you could give me at least *some* answers it would help me."

He waited, feeling hints of trepidation and suspicion. He knew that Asha was more capable than many of the Kuldar of keeping his emotions from projecting. The other two must be also similarly skilled but that didn't stop the hints reaching his mind, like scents on a breeze.

"What do you want to know?" Asha asked softly. Torres swallowed, phrasing the question in his mind so that he didn't give away the secrets he hadn't been authorized to tell.

"What is the link between the Kuldar and the Va'alen?" he asked as he kept his face a stony mask.

"We have no link," Asha said. "They appeared on our home world many generations ago, according to our ancestors, and there was a war. A war which we started and lost."

"So you don't know where they came from?" Torres asked, managing not to add the question about knowing *what* they were.

"You must understand, Captain Torres," Asha said solemnly, "that we have no official records of this time. The war happened many generations before our ancestors fled to the planet where you found us. We are..." He made a curious noise like he was clearing his throat. "Many of our people are frightened by what has happened, by the dreaded Va'alen finding us and by leaving our home, and now they are frightened that the humans are just another race of warlords come to kill us."

"I assure you we are not," Torres said, wincing internally as he feared he couldn't speak for others. "Let me talk to my superiors and, if I am permitted, we can speak again tomorrow."

Asha bowed low as his companions mirrored the movement. The bow was accompanied by a hint of acceptance, of hope even, and Torres lowered his own gaze in answer before turning to leave.

"Finished playing?" he muttered to Specter as the taller man fell in step beside him to head for the exit.

"What am I supposed to do?" Specter replied innocently. "Ignore the kids? Hearts and minds, Commander. Hearts and minds."

~

Torres's call was picked up immediately, as he expected it to be, but when he was kept waiting for almost an hour his temper started to fray. He had laid out where he was in his talks with the imprisoned Kuldar and started to say what he needed clearance for, when a UNID suit whispered in the ear of the duty officer and he was asked to hold.

Fifty-nine minutes later and his right leg jigged so impatiently that his whole body shook with the movement.

"Ah, screw this," he complained to himself.

He cut the comm link showing the annoyingly slowly rotating crest of the UN. He stood, leaving the small quarters he had been given and heading for the officer's crash deck. Seeing as most of the officers were under other domes on the surface or up on the shipyards, the space set aside for officers to relax was usually empty. When Torres entered, however, it had two lieutenants playing a quiet game of cards in once corner.

Both raised their eyes and nodded to him, knowing that they didn't have to stand or salute when he entered the room given the unwritten rules of the crash deck. Torres returned their curt greeting as he walked to the vending machine. He resisted the urge to get a beer and a chaser, not only because he knew the credits for those items would be double what they were on the Lunar base where the prices were raised, but because he couldn't afford even the slightest fogginess in his brain.

Grabbing coffee from the pot, he sat and tried to massage the tiredness and frustration from his face with both hands. Leaning back in the surprisingly comfortable chair, he reached out for the coffee when the comm device his forearm bleeped and vibrated.

With a sigh he abandoned the drink and tapped the comm to open the link. "Torres here," he said, his voice croaking a little. "Not secure."

"Well get yourself secure," said a voice he recognized but didn't expect. "I'll hold."

Torres stood, pausing only to take a hurried gulp of the coffee. He tipped the remainder of the cup in a small sink on his way out of the room and fast-walked back to his office.

"You taking the long way, Commander?" his comm device complained.

"No, sir," he replied. "Give me fifteen seconds."

He counted in his head. Seeing as he'd plucked the number out of thin air, he needed to check the guess for accuracy. It was closer to twenty when the door of his quarters slid shut behind him and he spoke to the comm device again.

"Secure now," he said. "Hold on while I transfer you to a console." He tapped at the screen, swiping the open link icon towards the console as he sat. The screen blinked on and he found himself looking directly at an annoyed and amused Admiral Dassiova.

"Sir," he said in greeting.

"Torres," Dassiova grumbled back. "You know what a shit-storm you've just served up back in the comfortable seats?"

"I didn't mean to stir anything up, Admiral," Torres told him. "I just need to be able to share information to gauge the answers I'm getting."

"Well someone back on Earth just had themselves a litter of kittens. Turns out your negotiations are little more urgent than anyone knew, because things are happening in the CS which make it time-sensitive."

"Sir," Torres said in confusion, "you've lost me. Lay it out for me like I *don't* know what's going on."

Dassiova sighed heavily before answering. "The Va'alen have recently communicated with our forces in the CS and they want to talk. UN joint command doesn't want to go in blind so that makes your mission a little more important, or at least it makes them a little more anxious for quicker results. You with me so far?"

"So far," Torres responded.

"So they need more intel before they talk to the 'roaches, and *you*, son," he stabbed a finger at the screen for emphasis, "need to get it."

Torres sat back, taking it in and filing the new information in place before lifting his gaze to meet the admiral's once more.

"So where do you fit in, Admiral?"

Dassiova smiled. "I'm heading up the negotiations, or at least I will be, so you work for me again. Dassiova out."

Mars Deep Orbit, Onboard the Carrier Indomitable

Torres climbed through the airlock from the *Corvus*, which was nestled high on the carrier's back toward the forward section. The ship seemed somehow incomplete without the full complement of eight gun barges affixed to their secure docking mounts. The deployment of four of them had allowed the two frigates to dock at the shipyards and for their crews to get a few hours shore leave and stand down time.

Torres, feeling like a yoyo as he went from being the captain of his own ship to a commander visiting another, stepped onto the massive carrier's bridge and once again marveled at how it differed from his own.

He no longer had the sleek, almost designer recon ship that he had commanded the last time, but he was beginning to grow fond of his little cruiser. It was his *Raven,* as he liked to think of it, having studied a few pointless modules of Latin. It wasn't built for comfort, nor was it the technological masterpiece the *Ichi* had been, but he appreciated the solidity and simple toughness of it. If the frigates, with their devastating array of weaponry and spartan interiors, made him mindful of the old Earth military submarines, then the *Corvus* was like a fast attack sub, packing a punch but quick and nearly impossible to detect. He guessed she could take some hits of she needed to, but he wasn't overly keen on testing that theory.

A few familiar faces nodded a greeting to him as he walked through the busy stations towards Dassiova's quarters. The two weapons stations and three comm officers were on duty, in addition to the two working at tactical and the pair of pilots. Those stations alone numbered higher than his entire bridge crew. But, the carrier was the hub, the epicenter of any operation. Ships like his were simply pieces to be moved around the board.

He pressed the call button at the door of the admiral's quarters, not even considering whether to try his biometric chip, and waited until the door hissed open.

"You got here fast, Admiral," Torres said seriously.

"No point in hanging around," Dassiova replied. He shrugged his still lean shoulders into the flight suit bearing his name, rank, and the name of his ship. "Right, let's get down to it." Torres sat on invitation as Dassiova tapped at the screen of a datapad until he found the document he wanted.

"You're authorized to tell the Kuldar this." He slid it across the table to the younger officer. Torres's eyes scanned over it. He put down the datapad and fixed the admiral with a look.

"Spit it out," Dassiova grumbled at him.

"Sir, I have to speak from my gut here," he started, getting flustered and speaking quickly to cover how his last words might have come out. "We need their co-operation. We need to know what they know, or at least to gauge if what *we* know is news to them, right? How can I get any kind of truth if I'm not allowed to be truthful with them?"

"Say what you mean."

"I need to tell them what we know and ask them for their help. It's the only way this works out long term. How slow has our weapons research been since we sidelined our allies? I'm guessing it's ground to a halt, otherwise why would we be recruiting like there's no tomorrow and producing as much explosive ordnance as we can make?"

Dassiova's brow furrowed at this intimation. Neither of the men, with their history of working in special operations and being in positions of command, liked being kept in the dark or having their hands tied. Even Torres, after working with the UNID for long enough, was shocked at how close they were playing their cards to their chest.

"Those people," he insisted with a finger pointed at the deck, "aren't the enemy. The Va'alen are. Hell, even the separatists are more dangerous to us than the Kuldar are."

Something in his words made the admiral shift uncomfortably in his seat.

"Commander Torres," Dassiova said formally, "I have informed you of everything that UN command on Earth wants you to tell the Kuldar. What you do with that mission brief is up to you and very much on your head should anything go wrong. Report to me in twelve hours or unless there's anything *I* think I'd need to know. Dismissed."

Torres stood, reading between the lines of his orders perfectly as he took a step toward the door.

"One more thing, sir," he began, looking back at his commanding officer.

Dassiova's eyebrows rose, giving him the go-ahead.

"Why is this suddenly so important? Why can't we just tell the Va'alen we'll talk when we're ready?"

"Because," Dassiova said coldly, "we aren't the only people they extended the invitation to, and we don't want to be late to the table."

~

"Back again, Commander?" The lieutenant in charge of the security detail on the Kuldar dome repeated the question, as he had done every day he was posted there and saw Torres. He had relaxed sufficiently to lose the helmet of his armor, making Torres think his team was only wearing them in case he had an opinion on the matter.

Torres ignored the weak jest, as he usually did. This time he didn't even acknowledge it with a polite smile. He handed in his weapon and comm device and waited as Specter removed the prototype sidearms from his legs and handed them over to a young seaman. He eyed the weapons like they were an abomination.

"Don't play with it," Specter said. "Not unless you want a broken arm and hole in the dome."

"It's that powerful it'll break my arm?" the young soldier said with wide eyes and a voice full of awe.

"No," Specter told him. "*I'll* break your arm for messing with my stuff, so don't do it, okay?"

The terrified boy nodded dumbly and received a smile from the green-eyed cyborg.

They went through the now familiar routine of entering the dome. Torres's body had grown used to the atmospheric conditions inside the dome and only needed a small shot of oxygen every thirty minutes to keep from being lightheaded. Specter still didn't need a thing, given that he only had about half the body mass his commander did to require the oxygen.

They went through the next familiar ritual of their working day: being shadowed by the Kuldar children who hunted them for fun through the dense foliage. Each day at this time, Specter came into his own as he turned on their playful pursuers and chased them away. Torres had opened his mouth once to ask if he—if Jake Santana—had ever had children but managed to shut it in time. He recalled Brandt telling him that he had younger siblings; his natural ability to make the children laugh must come from there.

Torres was less natural with the Kuldar young, just as he was with human children, and always feared that he came across a bit creepy with kids, like he was trying too hard to be liked.

By the time the game of chase had ended they were in the small clearing near to the makeshift settlement where the negotiations, as limited as they had been, took place.

"Asha?" Torres called out, eager to speak to his contact. There was no response. "Asha?" he tried again. Both of the humans felt a wave of awe and deep respect from all sides as the foliage ahead parted and an unfamiliar Kuldar stepped into the clearing. Beside Torres, much to his great surprise, Specter took a knee and bowed his head. Torres was confused but still sensible enough to follow suit.

"Humans," the Kuldar said in whispered English, "I am the Queen Nerisha of my people. I come to speak with you now."

"Your…" Torres began, unsure of the honorific title to give her. He stumbled over his words. "My… Queen Nerisha," he said finally, mirroring how she pronounced it as perfectly as possible. "We have news. New things we must tell Asha and yourself."

She sat, sinking to the soft ground. "My Asha can hear you, just as I heard everything you have said until now. Please, sit."

They sat. Nerisha cast her large, dark eyes at Torres as the faintest glimmer of expectation tickled his senses. Mixed in with that expectation was a hint of impatience, so he spoke.

"Our people captured a Va'alen warrior," he began, "and we did something we call an autopsy on it, where we cut open the body to examine…" He trailed off as a wave of anger and repulsion swept over him before being cut off as abruptly as if a switch had been flipped. Torres took a gamble on an assumption.

"I know this may not be what your people do, and I apologize if it offends you, but we did it to better understand our enemy and…" He hesitated but ultimately decided that the full truth was the best way to keep her attention. "And to find better ways to kill them if we are forced to fight again."

Again the wave of repulsion came, this time edged with a wary acceptance that what he said made sense. At least that what Torres hoped the echoes of emotions meant.

"It is something we have always done to learn how one of our own kind died, so we can better learn how to prevent illness and death."

"And tell me, Kyle Torres," she said as she merged his two names into one, "what did your people learn from this…" she paused, trying to conjure the word in English which meant desecration in her tongue, "this thing you did to the dead Va'alen?"

"We learned," Torres said as he straightened his back and looked directly at her, "that the Va'alen is not what it seems. It is an armor. A shell. Inside is another being."

Shock rolled over him forcefully, confusing him as fear came to him from another direction, as did anger from another again. Kuldar surrounded them in the clearing, and each of them responded to the unexpected information differently.

"What being was inside this?" she asked quietly.

"It was shorter, but it looked... it looked like you and your people. In fact, it was almost identical," Torres said.

The bombardment of mixed feelings hammered him from all sides.

CHAPTER 11

UN Training Grounds, Virginia

"This is still bullshit," Payne complained as they waited for the current training group to complete their third lap of the airfield. "They can't keep us locked in. They just can't."

"Payne," Zero said, barely controlling his anger, "you did walk into the same recruitment office as everyone else, right? You did *actually* pay attention to the part that the UN, quite literally, owns your ass until they discharge you or you earn your way out?"

"Or you die," Turner added helpfully.

"Or you die," Zero added, gesturing his thanks to the medic for his valuable input to the conversation. "If they say you don't leave the compound then you don't leave the compound. It's that simple."

"It's not me I'm pissed about," Payne said. "It's the Commander. She's sweet on that lawyer guy she thinks we can't hear her talking to through the stupidly thin walls."

"You're so dangerously close to the line there, Petty Officer Class Two Payne, that I'm not sure you're going to realize when you've gone too far," Zero said carefully.

"Probably when she's busted back down to seaman and left to finish up her service guarding the men's room on the Moon," said a strong voice. It was accompanied by the heavy footfalls of a person in armor.

Something about the tone or the confidence made all three NCOs snap up to attention.

"As you were," the man said as he walked around in front of them.

They took in the armor, the lack of rank insignia and the single shield emblem. They took in the eager young face with veins visible on the exposed skin, which put them all in mind of a very fit body encased inside the polymer alloy. They took in the service pistol, one of the newer and enhanced versions, mag locked to his right thigh and the service rifle protruding over his right shoulder. It seemed similar to the one Brandt had favored before it got blown to pieces by an alien energy weapon.

"Lieutenant Beale," he said. "You're Payne, Turner and Conrad, right?"

"I prefer Zero, sir," he said as he peeled back a Velcro patch on his right arm to display the same emblem as the one subtly adorning the officer's armor.

"Zero," Beale said with a nod of solidarity before he hesitated.

It was customary when two members of the elite met to exchange callsigns and promise to not tell the story behind it unless they were bought alcohol, but the lieutenant didn't seem to want to share. This was like a drop of blood in the water for Zero who smiled like a shark and began probing.

"Your callsign?"

"Not on a team job officially," Beale replied. "I'm just 'Lieutenant' for the time being."

Zero smiled in anticipation; the handle he had been given when he qualified for CP must be embarrassing. If he'd been dubbed 'Hunter' or 'Hawk' or any other thousand names that sounded cool he would have led with that, Zero was certain. The fact that he didn't disclose it to another member of the CP when directly asked meant that it must be terrible.

Zero couldn't wait to find out.

"How many with you, Lieutenant?" Turner asked, cottoning on to Zero's line of questioning.

"Three," Beale answered. "Half of my unit. The other half is with the team commander on... another thing..."

Zero smiled at how bad the younger man was at being cagey. People like Zero made it sound mysterious and exciting, whereas Beale just made it sound like he didn't know and was trying to hide that ignorance.

"Where are your people?" Zero asked. "Need us to show them around? You found our coffee machine yet?"

"No, not yet. They're up in our dropship keeping an eye on the training ground."

"Keeping an eye on the commander then?" Turner asked.

Beale covered the slip by ignoring the question, which made Zero doubt he'd gotten used to his status just yet.

"How long since you dropped, Lieutenant?" Zero asked. "Been on the CP long?"

"Oh, err... late in April," Beale answered casually.

Turner caught Zero's eye and stifled a smirk. He could have said it was only two months ago, but the way he tried to make it more vague just made him sound less mature. Luckily for Beale, he was saved any further embarrassment by the arrival of the training squad rounding the corner of a line of large hangars.

Brandt was at the head of that line, running hard to set the pace, which all but the fittest of the troops struggled to keep up with. As always, the last few hundred meters of the morning run were a race, and the four training staff took it in turns to lead their pupils.

Others led; Brandt schooled them. She finished ahead of the nearest competition by the length of a dropship and was already standing tall with steady breathing by the time they had all crossed the line and began forming up. Much to everyone's surprise the gigantic Hawaiian soldier finished in the lead group despite his unnatural size and accompanying weight. Towering head and shoulders above his fellow squad mates, seaman Kekoa caught the attention of Lieutenant Beale.

"Whoa," he chuckled, under his breath. "*Big* horse…"

"That's Kekoa, sir," Payne explained. "Other than being a monster he's actually pretty sharp."

"I'm amazed they let him join a fighting unit," Beale said. "If I was a recruiter, I'd have him in urban pacification or a law enforcement posting."

"Yeah," Turner laughed. "Can you imagine telling *that* guy to come back with a warrant?"

Brandt walked over to them and cut their chatter short. She mopped her sweating face with the bottom of her PT shirt.

"Dismiss them for breakfast, Petty Officer Turner," she instructed.

Turner stepped away to bawl at the troops until they dressed off correctly and stood to attention in spite of their shaking legs and burning lungs. He began loudly admonishing them for being slow and unfit before starting a tirade about their personal hygiene, at which point the others stopped listening.

"Beale," Brandt said as she acknowledged the lieutenant. "A little overdressed, aren't we?"

"Just wanted to drop in on you, Commander," he said, ignoring the jibe. "Let you know my team has eyes on you."

"And *my* team?" she asked in return. "Who has eyes on them?"

Beale looked a little flustered.

"My brief is to maintain secure overwatch on all of you," he admitted, likely saying more than he should. "But the principal tag is on your head."

Brandt stared at him for long enough that everyone else felt uncomfortable. Finally, she turned away and snatched up a canteen to unscrew the lip and pour water into her mouth.

"Well, you can either lose the armor and cannons and help train this bunch of kids, or you can keep out of our way. I'd prefer the former but that's not up to me," she told him firmly.

"Ma'am," Beale began, "I'm sure you're grateful for our assistance the other morning and I'm also sure you don't think you need us here bu—"

"You're right on both points, Lieutenant," Brandt interrupted, "but your assistance wouldn't have been necessary if they'd just had the good sense to inform me personally that I was a target. That lack of intelligence, that one-way street, put the life of a friend of mine in danger and I don't like that at all. So, Lieutenant, which will it be?"

Beale took a respectful half pace backward and clasped his hands behind his back.

"You can't escape your shadow, Commander," he said in an attempt to sound enigmatic, "but I'll do my best that you don't trip over it."

Brandt rapped her knuckles on his breastplate twice to the very unrewarding sound of a dull and heavy clunk.

"Attaboy. Run along now."

They watched as Beale most definitely did not run, but walked at a confidently sedate pace away from them.

"Wouldn't tell me his callsign," Zero said petulantly.

"Gotta be something embarrassing then," she said. "Whatever." She waved a dismissive hand towards the squad. "Get this shower showered and their officer in the briefing room with his NCOs in thirty minutes."

⁓

"Our objective is to reach the LZ, make our way to the RV on foot, defend that position for a set period of time until extracted," the lieutenant leading the squad in training said. He pointed to different point of the map projected on the holo in front of the training staff and his own subordinate troops.

"Easy as that," Brandt said. She grinned at him with a smile designed to make the officer question his plan for everything that could go wrong.

"Erm…" The lieutenant quailed in uncertainty under her confident gaze.

"Threat assessment on your enemy, Lieutenant?" Zero barked, startling the younger man who outranked him by commission alone and in no other way imaginable.

"Erm…" he said again, only half an octave higher.

"Erm?" the senior NCO asked. "That's your official designation of the enemy threat, *sir*?"

The young officer regained his composure a little and straightened himself, just like he had been taught at OTA Calgary, the officer training academy in the northern reaches of the territory.

Brandt smiled to herself. She recalled the similar briefing that he did right then, the one they had sat through on how to deal with hard-ass, leather-skinned, foul-mouthed senior NCOs who showed no respect or fear of rank. NCOs that seemed willing to stand up under fire and berate everyone taking cover like they were hiding from a mild rain shower. He fixed Zero with a look he no doubt thought was confident and spoke in a faltering voice.

"The enemy is superior in both size and strength," he began. "They hold advanced weaponry which defeats our standard armor and degrades shielding fast. Despite their size they move fast, working in linked pairs. If one is killed, the other will go into a berserker rage."

"That's about right," Zero said without expression. "So what do we have that they don't?"

The question took the lieutenant by surprise as, up until that very moment, he had been drilled into thinking the Va'alen were superior in every way to human soldiers.

"We can think with clear heads," Brandt told him quietly. "We can make logical decisions without letting instincts guide our actions like animals. We can fight smart; lure them into attacking a defended position and overwhelm them. We have the numbers, even if they fight like ten of ours then we send twenty against them. We're pretty evenly matched in space, if anything we have the advantage as they can't travel at FTL speeds, but on the deck? With just one of these things?"

She paused for effect and shook her head slowly as she stood to fix him with a look designed to instill a deep wariness of their enemy.

"Get your shit together, Lieutenant. We move out in ten."

~

One of the biggest annoyances to Commander Leslie Brandt since she had found herself swallowed up into the big, bureaucratic machine that was the UN on Earth, was the strict governance of procedure. She had been armed most of the time for the last two years, even carrying concealed weaponry on the rare occasions she was stood down from duty.

Having to secure their weapons for a short training flight over the Atlantic Ocean and across the northern edge of continental Europe made her feel like she was a low-ranking grunt of a ground-pounder once more.

A few months prior she had autonomous control of a small team on a previously undiscovered habitable moon in the nearest solar system. She had been wearing advanced prototype armor and carrying a weapon that most of the planet had yet to learn was anything but science fiction.

Now, just a matter of weeks later, she was training unbloodied troops in a vague approximation of what it was like to be in contact with the Va'alen. She was fairly sure that pitting a squad or even two against a Va'alen patrol on the surface of any planet would have a disastrously predictable outcome, especially as these would be deploying with the last generation armor if any, and weaponry that was an arguable upgrade.

As she donned her protective gear, her reflective yellow vest, for the training mission, she was almost overwhelmed with just utterly screwed over she felt.

She should be out there, carrying an alien pulse rifle and wearing armor equipped with a micro shield emitter. She should be exploring new worlds and removing the threats for those who followed to colonize them. She so desperately wanted to be that trailblazer, that torch-bearing pioneer that she dreamed of being. Instead she had been hidden away from the galaxy and put to work training troops she doubted would survive their first alien encounter for anything over a matter of seconds.

"Speaking of useless things…" Zero muttered to her, snapping her back to the present and out of her spiral of self-pity.

She looked up in time to see the armored but helmetless Lieutenant Beale approaching, flanked by three other suits of armor with their helmets activated and their visors showing only a reflection.

"Be nice," Brandt warned. Most of Zero's frustration was jealousy at not being part of a specialist team, in spite of his vast knowledge and experience.

"Commander," Beale greeted her. "We'll be following in our dropship and shadowing you on the ground." He held up a hand to staunch an expected complaint. "We'll stay out of the way of your training operation."

"Do what you need to do, Lieutenant," she told him dismissively, before turning away and walking to the dropship.

She had an empty holster and a burning desire to go back to bed and replace the sleep she had lost over the last few days. She didn't intentionally make Beale's life hard, but as he was the closest to someone she could blame for being kept in the dark, then he would have to earn her trust.

She boarded the dropship, ignoring the troops under her tutelage. They dressed off neatly, ready to board the dropship and sit in their allocated seats with their straps securely fastened to hurry up and wait. She walked up the ramp, shrugging into an insulated jacket, and took a seat behind the forward section where the two pilots flicked switches and chattered to one another during their preflight checks. Turner, stowing his heavy pack of field medical supplies above his seat, sat up front with her. Zero and Payne took seats halfway down the ship to monitor and assess the behavior of the troops in transit.

They had made this run three times now, putting each course through the final training exercise and feeling as though they had achieved little in the two weeks they had each squad. In spite of such rigorous training, the soldiers would still be wholly underequipped to deal with a Va'alen assault should they find themselves in the thick of one.

"Remind me again why we have to go all the way to Russia to do this again?" Payne asked over their secure comm via uncomfortable earpieces.

"Because," Zero said as he drew the word out extravagantly, "some political bullshit happened, and our allies didn't want our territory doing the buildup training in our own yard. It's above our lowly pay grade."

"That true, Commander?" Payne asked.

"Don't you listen to ol' grumpy here," Brandt joked. "It's an important strategic alliance between the American, and the European territories which allows for joint training and a shared playbook when combating the Va'alen threat. Furthermore," she said, raising her voice slightly as though giving a rousing speech, "it is our duty, nay our *honor*, to be part of this great collaboration and perform our role in the war effort and, *furthermore*, we should be grateful that the UN has allowed us this unprecedented opportunity to provide vital training to our brothers and sister in arms."

Silence hung for a few seconds on their channel. "Political bullshit then?" Turner asked.

"Yeah," Brandt said, "so suck it up and smile."

~

The flight was noisy and bumpy, despite the grav emitter being cranked up to keep them from bouncing around too much. The ride on the dropships at extreme altitude or in the void of space was far smoother. As they were at only five thousand feet and flying fast to simulate a tactical insertion, the air currents hammered the slab-sided vessel. It was made even worse when they reached the higher ground of the European mountain ranges.

A sudden change in pitch and thrust made Brandt's eyebrows connect in the middle—they always did whenever she thought something was wrong. By the time she had snatched the headset down and clamped the cups over her ears, she heard panicked shouts over the radio channel from the cockpit ahead of her.

"Count three, incoming fast from the south," one of the pilots shouted.

"Roger, evasive maneuvers on my mark. Breaking left in three, two, o—"

"Cancel, cancel! Second missile volley from our rear."

"Activate shields and prepare for drop," the other voice said with more calm. He must be the senior pilot, Brandt guessed. The one with his hands on the controls and, she hoped, pure ice in his veins. "Mark!"

The ship lurched sickeningly as their forward momentum dropped away, replaced with a momentary sensation of weightlessness. The grav emitter powered up automatically in response and sucked the shocked human cargo back into their seats.

"Missiles from the rear overshot, still have incoming from the south," she heard over the radio. The only answer was the sudden acceleration of the dropship and change in attitude as the nose angled upward and the power surged them ahead.

In a rare moment of clarity amidst a tense and sudden situation, Brandt found herself questioning the sense in gaining altitude when the risk of getting shot down was so high. To her, it was like speeding up in a ground transport when you knew the forward repulser brakes weren't functional. Her thoughts were interrupted by an audible *whoosh* from the atmosphere outside the unsealed dropship. A split second later she heard a huge, concussive *boom* that deafened her through the earphones and shook her brain so hard the only thing in her ears was a high-pitched squeal. She heard muffled, echoed shouts from inside the ship, like she was being yelled at underwater and in slow motion. She regained just enough sense to try and call out over the comm channel they were all linked to. Before she could, the loudspeaker came alive.

"All hands, brace for impa—" the pilot began.

A second slam rocked the ship, but different this time, and as the grav emitter failed Brandt found herself floating up to the limits of her restraints; their shields had failed.

We're going down, she told herself in disbelief. *We're actually going down.*

Before any other thoughts came to her, her head hit the side of her seat and she blacked out in an instant.

CHAPTER 12

Kuldar Habitat, Mars

Torres's revelation was met with a tidal wave of feelings and emotions. The strength of the response was so strong that his eyes fluttered involuntarily, and he was forced to one knee from his standing position. Fearing that his commanding officer and friend had been the subject of some telepathic attack, Specter rushed forward to stand over him protectively.

When Specter was hit with the bombardment of emotional reaction, he too faltered but held up a hand and called out.

"Stop!" he barked, the artificial timbre of his voice resonating almost metallically.

The assault ebbed away, allowing both men to regain their senses.

"It's true," Torres told the queen, looking directly into her implacable eyes to underline his words. He breathed heavily to get over the sudden shock.

"Show us," she ordered.

"I can't…" Torres said. "I don't have access to the footage, but I can get it."

"You must," she insisted, "for we cannot take the word of the people who imprison us without proof."

"And if I show you this proof?"

"Then we will believe you," Nerisha told him.

"I'll try to get it," he promised. "But do you know *why* the Va'alen look like you do?"

Nerisha didn't answer immediately but glanced down and to one side as though looking over her shoulder. Some unspoken communication must have occurred, because Asha walked into the clearing and bowed beside his mate. He took up the story without any sign of being told to.

"Generations before now," he said, "as I have told your people before, the Kuldar fled our old world. The legends say this was because the Overlords were controlling us, but none of our people who still live know of this. Some did know of what came after, some who are long since passed, but I recall as a child hearing the stories of when the Va'alen first came to my people's world."

Torres sat, crossing his legs as his eyes stayed on the alien who had him in rapture with the tale.

"They dropped from the skies without warning, jumping from their ships to attack my people. We were once a civilization of many people, spanning three worlds in a star system very far away, but the attack of our enemy all but wiped us out in weeks."

"But your people fled," Torres prompted. "Your ancestors escaped."

"They did," Asha said, a wave of something mixed between sadness and pride radiating from him. "With just one ship, the ancestors gathered as many Kuldar as they could find and left our old worlds behind."

"That's where the Fold Drive came from, right?" Torres interrupted, earning a flash of annoyance from Nerisha's direction.

"The device you call the Fold Drive works the same way, I believe. Our people had a network of gateways linking our worlds, which were built and sent through the long journey in space to their places. They called these the origins. Our people left that technology behind when they escaped."

"And the Va'alen took over the gateways," Torres filled in. "Like the one we destroyed?"

"Yes," Asha agreed. "That one must have been moved from another origin, or else built anew, but as you say it is gone now."

"And the ship that took your ancestors away, that went to Earth where it crashed. That's how we were able to travel beyond our solar system," Torres said.

Asha gave a small smile. "Yes. I believe you humans have a saying that 'what goes around, comes around,' yes?"

"That sounds about right." Torres wondered where Asha had picked up the saying. "But none of that really explains why the Va'alen are like you."

Asha glanced at Nerisha who turned to meet his gaze intently. Torres felt nothing from them; there was not one single leak of emotion as the two aliens communicated through their directed feelings.

"There is a story... a... a *legend*," Asha said quietly after a long pause, "of a split in our people many years before the Va'alen attacked our ancestors. It says that others of our kind favored war instead of peace. I cannot say what happened to them, but if they sided with the Overlords then there is no way to know what became of them."

Asha stood, presenting himself almost formally before Torres who rose to meet him.

"I swear this to you, Captain Kyle Torres," he intoned. "We do not know what you speak of with your... your *desecration* of the Va'alen. We have done nothing wrong and have kept no more secrets from you."

116

Torres bowed his head slightly in acknowledgement. He wanted to tell them that he believed them, that he was sorry. That he was appalled by the behavior of his own race who had scooped up every Kuldar assisting the humans and deposited them on Mars to fester as though they didn't signify the greatest scientific and humanitarian discovery of all time. He didn't like being part of an organization who treated them like that.

He said nothing, however, because his professionalism was too strong and his fear of a ruined career too heightened to betray a personal involvement. He had taken a gamble sharing information he hadn't been authorized to give, but to him the gamble paid off. There was no way so many Kuldar could have hidden their terror, their shock, their confusion when he told them the hidden truth about their enemy.

"I have to tell my superiors what we've talked about," he said. "But you have my thanks for your honesty."

Torres bowed low as he backed out of the clearing and bumped into Specter behind him. He could feel the presence of the Kuldar all around him, pressing in close as though they expected something immediate from him. He fought with every fiber in his body not to break out into a run to reach the airlock exit sooner.

Specter said nothing. He kept his mouth shut until they were out of the airlock at the other end, and even then, he knew it would be better to keep his thoughts inside until they could speak securely.

~

"Hands on your heads and step out of the airlock," came the harsh, authoritative orders the second the door rolled back.

"What the hell is this?" Torres demanded.

He refused to comply until a rifle barrel was driven into his gut hard enough to double him over. He had seen the blow coming a mile off, seen the frightened eyes behind the man wielding the weapon. In that split second, he had cushioned it with a pre-emptive clenching of his abdominal muscles and bending to take the blow. He made it seem as though he had been winded as he dropped to his knees and looked up in semi-mock pain.

Behind him Specter was frozen to the spot.

"Stay right there," a voice warned, aiming at Specter but not at Torres on the deck. The speaker mistakenly believed he had incapacitated the commander.

Torres sucked in air, fighting the urge to cough and retch from the blow as he took in the scene around him. Three soldiers down, not moving. No weapons in sight and some scent he couldn't make out hanging in the air, tickling his nose with a sour smell.

Gas? How would gas take out armored soldiers?

Then he remembered. They may have been wearing armor, but with no atmospheric threat and days, weeks, of monotony on the same detail would lead to familiarity and comfort with their surroundings. That would lead to complacency. Complacency had led to this.

Torres had been out of contact completely while inside the habitat dome, his comm device left behind. The attackers seemed to know that, as the comm devices had been stripped from the forearms of every armored guard but they hadn't searched him for one when he exited the dome. As the oxygen returned to his brain, Torres recalled another thing that they wouldn't know: the fact that his friend stood behind him was more machine than man, physically speaking. He hoped he would be transmitting some kind of mayday call from the chip in his head to the waiting ships above in orbit.

Torres looked up, faking a gasp for air as he did and taking a mental snapshot of the scene.

Four men. No. Three men and one woman. All dressed as civilian workers in gray jumpsuits and the logo of some private corporation on the chest. They carried the weapons taken from the unconscious UN troops. That must mean that while they could manufacture or smuggle some kind of nerve agent to the Mars surface, they were forced to scavenge for guns. He didn't know why that intelligence was relevant, but it was information that would form a tiny fragment of the whole story later on.

"Why are you doing this?" Torres asked, making sure to breathe heavily and sound hurt.

"Because you and your abominations shouldn't be here," the one who had hit him said, his voice tense and his aim never wavering from Specter. "Out. On your knees."

Torres bit back the retort that he was already on his knees but made a show of standing slowly and clutching his mid-section before dropping back to his knees and wincing.

"Who are you?" he asked. In his experience, those who believed themselves to be righteous warriors for freedom liked to pontificate about their dogmatic aims.

"You people didn't learn on the Moon, you didn't learn from the ships we blew up back on Earth, and you still went to other worlds and brought back abominations. God didn't create these... these... *monsters*, and we don't want them here. We don't want any of them here so we're making sure they can't come back again."

Torres heard the slightest exhalation of air behind him; Specter often sighed when rolling his eyes. Of anyone alive in the galaxy, he would have some of the strongest opinions on the misguided fools who engaged in terrorism to prevent planetary expansion.

119

"You know you're crazy, right?" Specter said matter of factly.

The leader tightened his grip on the stolen rifle, which wavered as though the weight of it was too much for the man to hold.

"We're not crazy," he insisted, mucus bubbling from his nose as the adrenaline coursing through his body brought tears. "*We're* the sane ones. *Ahaha!*" He added the involuntary nervous giggle in a higher pitch to betray his words as lies. "*You're* the crazy ones, going off to other planets and bringing back *aliens*... but you can't do that anymore, oh no..."

"Tick tock," Specter said quietly.

"Yeah," another terrorist added, stepping forward with his chest puffed out in a display of peacocking. Torres suspected he would never have had the balls to show off like that if he hadn't been pointing a gun at unarmed men. "Time's up for you. Time's up for all of you." His accent was strange; Torres was unable to trace his origin on Earth.

"Tick tock," Specter said again in a more urgent tone.

"What," the lead terrorist stammered, "what do you mean?"

Specter turned to point his glowing green eyes directly at him and smiled.

"Tick tock. Time's up, asshole."

Torres wasn't paying as much attention as he could've been, but even still, what happened next happened so fast that he had to piece it together in bits afterwards. Specter reached down and picked him up under the armpits, spun him around and hugged him to his chest like he was rescuing a much-loved teddy bear. Bullets ripped the air to ping and whine as they deflected from the shielding Specter had activated as soon as he had moved like a striking snake.

Specter took two steps back into the airlock and slammed his left hand against the door control panel. It slid shut as the fools outside still persisted in trying to shoot them. His last glance before the door shut was of two of their attackers down and bleeding from ricochet wounds and the other two still pouring rounds at them impotently. The sound changed to those rounds hitting the reinforced door. Torres noticed the air go silent; the humming stopped when Specter deactivated his shield.

"Tick tock," he said with a smirk.

The first careful shot from orbit hit the hard roof of the facility outside the safety of their position. Torres stared in shock through the thick glass viewport as the contents of the guard station were sucked violently toward the jagged rift in the bulkhead. The armored bodies of the guards—he now hoped that they were dead and not merely unconscious— bounced off the walls in their race to obey the laws of physics and rush with the air into the void and escape the pressure. The terrorists, unarmored and exposed to the great black expanse, froze to death in an instant before their bodies shattered and broke apart with every solid impact until the room outside their airlock was empty and still.

"What the hell...?" Torres breathed in disbelief.

"*Corvus*, cease fire. Cease fire. Threat neutralized, recommend you notify emergency crews and get a cleanup team in here to restore atmo, over.... Roger... we'll wait. Out."

He returned Torres's look and gave him a shrug.

Mars Orbit, The Carrier Indomitable

Torres insisted that he was fine, but the ship's doctor insisted on checking him out. A few hours of reduced oxygen combined with a blow to the abdomen and the shock of everything else gave some small cause for concern. The commander was more annoyed at the delay than concerned, however.

He still wasn't sure what had happened on the surface. Without the complete facts, he couldn't be certain how he felt about any of it. His first concern was that the single burst of cannon fire, which had ripped open the sealed facility, had killed the incapacitated guards, but Specter assured him that their vital signs had flatlined. The tactical officer of the *Indomitable* had confirmed that, showing him footage of the gas attack where the team of four just dropped almost in unison.

"Killed them in seconds, sir," the lieutenant insisted. "Even if they'd been exposed in the med bay there was little chance of saving them."

Torres had accepted that, but wanted to discuss the missed opportunities for intelligence gathering when he had killed their attackers. Specter seemed less concerned, happy to have mitigated a threat to not only themselves but to the Kuldar.

Better to vent the terrorists into space as they had intended to do to the aliens.

"We have their identities, we can tell where they had their real IDs switched out for the ones they traveled on, we know how they got to Mars and we can link all four of them through credit transfers, even though different companies used double blinds so that it wasn't obvious who had misplaced fifty thousand credits in their accounts."

"I still would've liked the chance to ask one of them a few questions," he complained, shooting a look at Specter.

"Oh, you can," the tactical officer said. "There were two more of them linked to the dead ones. Our troop commander has them on a transport on the way up from the surface now. Looks like they didn't want to come though…"

"Oh?" Torres said, raising an eyebrow inquisitively.

The lieutenant shrugged. "They tried to barricade themselves in somewhere. Our new second-in-command put a stop to that plan and hacked the device they used to gas our troops." He chuckled at a memory that wasn't his to recall. "They gave up pretty quickly when they saw their own nerve gas devices activating."

A thought prickled the back of Torres's mind. "Wait, your troop second-in-command did that?"

"Yeah, she's badass... and *super* hot!"

"She's a lieutenant commander," Torres scolded, "and directly in your chain of command."

The lieutenant straightened up, recognizing he had misread his audience.

"Sorry, sir, I didn't mean—"

"So there are two prisoners?" Torres cut him off as though he hadn't spoken.

"Yes, sir. But the admiral has ordered them sedated and re-strained."

"Fine," Torres said. "I'll speak to the admiral first."

~

"Hell of a risky move, son," Dassiova said as Torres walked into his quarters.

Torres bit back his answer; he had no idea what the move even was until the precision shooting from his ship in orbit punctured the facility's containment in precisely the right spot.

"You'll believe me when I tell you it wasn't my idea?"

Dassiova chuckled. "I guessed it wasn't. But still, that was ballsy."

Again Torres kept his mouth shut, given that Specter didn't possess the physical attributes mentioned.

"Anyway, I'd like to take a run at one of the prisoners, if that's alright with you, Admiral." He interrupted his own train of thought and brought back his focus.

"Not my call," Dassiova replied without any hint of annoyance. "UNID will be here within the hour to take them away. I imagine it'll be somewhere very cold and very remote, and I also imagine they're accustomed to getting answers." Something about the way he said his last two words made Torres a little uneasy. "And yes, I mean that they'll be torturing the living shit out of them pretty soon."

The admiral finished his summary almost disapprovingly. It was one thing to fight and kill an enemy, but another thing entirely to pull out his toenails one at a time until he gave up his secrets. Dassiova gave a brief but dismissive wave to push the conversation away.

"Don't worry about it," he told Torres. "Where are we on your mission?"

"Well, I'm sure the Kuldar didn't know they were the same as the Va'alen inside their armor. You know how they are; there was no way they could all fake shock and outrage when I told them."

If Dassiova had any opinion about Torres reading between the lines and going off-book, he kept it to himself. "So what do you need next?"

"I need some footage or images of the Va'alen autopsy to prove it to them."

Dassiova shot him a look that seemed to convey the tenuous thinness of the ice he skated on, but passed no judgment.

"Just so long as you don't officially get it from me," he said. "The *Corvus* is technically serving under the *Indomitable* now, so don't tell me things I may have to lie about at your court martial."

"Understood, sir," Torres replied, having received all the blessing he would get to bend the rules. "And after that? What's the next move?"

Dassiova shifted in his seat. "The Va'alen have allegedly sued for peace and want to talk. Apparently they want something from us. Now me? I'd be happy to pack them all into freighters and jump them into the nearest gas giant, but it gets a little... *complicated.*"

"Complicated how, Admiral?" Torres asked.

Dassiova closed his eyes for a moment and sucked in a deep breath through his nose.

"Complicated," Dassiova said with heavy emphasis, "as in the fact that the 'roaches extended the invitation to talk to both the UN *and* the separatists. My guess is they'll see whoever offers the best deal and side with them."

"The cynic in me thinks that the separatists will do some shady dealings to get their hands on advanced weaponry and some tech they've thus far been denied," Torres said bitterly.

"Which is why they've sent me to get you," the admiral told him, "with a cargo hold full of civilian advisors who all think they personally have the answer. What I really want is for you to get them," he pointed to the deck, and by extension the Kuldar on the planet below, "to trust us and help. Think you can do that?"

"Officially or not officially?"

"I got the call from that Ettington creep personally," Dassiova grumbled. "Smug bastard must enjoy circumventing military hierarchy for their own ventures."

"I doubt the Directorate is feathering its own nest here, sir. Aren't we all on the same side? Apart from the separatists, that is."

Dassiova raised an eyebrow at the younger officer, seeming as though he almost felt sorry for him in his naivety.

"We'll see, I guess," he said. "Now get down there and get us an advisor. And by an advisor I mean Asha. Dismissed."

CHAPTER 13

Gaia Néos, Va'alen Camp Headquarters

"Clear a path!" roared the Va'alen Supreme Commander, Muq Da'kath.

The gathering of warriors moved aside faster as the massive, percussive crack of a warrior's carapace being struck hard rang above the noise of their gathering.

The inner ring where the largest warriors stood split open. One of the biggest of their kind on the planet—the second largest of their entire expedition—staggered back into the clearing to hit the dirt hard and roll. He rose to one knee in time for a foot to slam into his chest and send him sprawling once more.

"No," Aq Qa'shal cried out in desperation as he spun to narrowly avoid a vicious stamp designed to crack his armor open.

"No?" Da'kath mocked. "You deny my right to kill you for your treachery? Or are you just a coward?"

Qa'shal scrambled away, yelling as another stamp pinned the wrist of his upper arm. Without warning, Da'kath whipped a wide blade from his lower back and reversed it to stab down and sever the trapped limb.

Qa'shal roared in pain and anger as he tried to roll away to his left. Da'kath kicked him hard in the back, rolling him over again where the blade chopped down in a brutally savage and short arc to cut through the other arm on that side. Qa'shal's howl of agony was higher pitched than before. The pain of losing another arm overtook the anger. Writhing on the dusty ground he received two more kicks from Da'kath and stayed down.

For weeks he had hunted this traitor, losing brave warriors to the human patrols, until they finally found him. He had delivered him for justice to be served, even if it meant surrendering to the humans to be allowed to return to the planet.

"Do any of you doubt that I am *Do-Ch'aal*?" Muq Da'kath bellowed, beating both right hands on his armored chest. "I am the First Warrior and leader of this expedition." As he yelled, he scanned the assembled crowd for anyone brave enough to think they could lead. "Do any of you challenge my authority, as this *kruh'chunn* has?"

None of them did. Da'kath turned his attention back to the only warrior to have offered him any rivalry in all the time they had been in the system. Since he had undermined the Muq's orders and subverted not only Va'alen loyal to the clan of Qa'shal but also those of lesser clans, he had removed the forces sent to protect one of their Hive Lords who had been subsequently captured by the humans. The usurper would pay for their betrayal as much as his own, and without a *Borka*, without any clan elders meeting to decide his fate, Da'kath would take his own revenge there and then in front of all of his people.

"You betrayed the expedition," he said as he delivered another brutal kick to his leg, which resulted in a loud crack. A split opened up in the carapace of his thigh. That injury alone would put the Aq into a regeneration tube for a week. "You betrayed your oath to me," he kicked him again, "and you betrayed all Va'alen."

Qa'shal rolled over to avoid another kick, exposing the remaining arms of his left side to invite another downward chop of the sword. The blade severed the upper arm and bit deeply into the lower. An agonized ululation rippled through the air to silence the crowd as all of them could feel the emotion of his pain and loss.

"We are trapped in this system," Da'kath called out. All must hear his conviction and sentencing. "The humans pen us in like vermin. The hated Kuldar have escaped us and we are *defeated*." The snarl of the last word cut as sharply as the honed blade in his hand.

"Br... brother..." Qa'shal croaked weakly.

Da'kath stopped and looked down at the defeated challenger. He sheathed the blade and grasped the only remaining arm on the other's body. Dragging him painfully to the center of the ring, he stopped and twisted the arm to wrench it away with a sickening crackling and ripping noise. He pulled the final arm off slowly, enjoying the excruciating pain he was causing the warrior who had cost them all so dearly, and held it aloft at arm's length to let it fall from his grasp and hit the dusty ground with a weak thud.

Limbless, with black gore pouring from the severed stumps, Qa'shal looked up at his attacker. Da'kath mercilessly stamped down on his ridged chest plate over and over until cracks opened up.

"Brother," he whispered up at the Muq when the attack had subsided.

Da'kath reached down to wedge the tips of his clawed hands into the largest crack. He tensed his body as the armor was slowly torn open, exposing the soft and vulnerable creature inside.

"You call me brother," Da'kath growled, "when you have no honor. You are *not* my brother."

He punched the spiked tip of his right arm into the chest of the true form of his rival, watching as his eyes slowly closed with a final breath.

A tortured scream of rage tore the air at the back of the crowd. Even though none of them had ever experienced the Path of Ending, they instinctively knew the sound. They knew what it meant.

A channel opened up from the scene of the murder to the female warrior, Qa'shal's mate, who shuddered in stricken agony and uncontrollable rage. She dragged the claws of both set of arms across her armored torso to score deep wounds. Da'kath stepped back, drawing his blade and taking a defensive stance as he prepared for her enraged assault.

A spear tip punched through her chest, stopping her shuddering and forcing her to her knees. As she dropped, Da'kath's mate was revealed standing behind her with all four clawed hands gripping the shaft of her short metal spear. He nodded at her, conveying more than mere thanks, and quietly turned from the gathering to walk away.

"Now," he hissed in a low voice to an aide who had fallen in beside him after a conspicuous absence during the fight, "we will talk to the humans and negotiate safe passage for all of us that remain."

CHAPTER 14

Dropship Crash Site, French Alps

"We have incoming," Brandt muttered into the radio mic.

She had tried not to draw attention to her position with poor noise discipline. Static was her only answer. The fear of whatever was falling on her team without warning was stronger than the fear for her own safety. She listened for a few seconds longer, gauging as much as she could from the noises and interpreting them in her fuzzy brain. She took in a long breath, finding a new pain in her ribs on the left side she hadn't noticed until then, and bawled out a warning.

"Incoming!" she yelled, drawing the word out.

The effort made her head pound. She dropped carefully past the jagged metal of the severed cockpit section. She hit the soft ground of the forest hard, standing up with a palm stabbed full of dark green pine needles. She brushed the hand against the leg of her jumpsuit to remove them, dragging off the high-visibility vest as she ran. She didn't need to be any easier a target than she already was. Sprinting around the far side of the wrecked dropship, she reached the tail ramp and the collection of troops looking confused.

"Zero?" she snapped, scanning the faces for her sniper.

"He went that way, looking for you," a voice said from the ramp.

She looked to the speaker; Kekoa walked down the twisted ramp carrying a grown man as though he was a child. He pointed around the other way with his chin.

"Alone?"

"No, he took the lieutenant and three others. All armed."

"Payne?" Brandt demanded as she fumbled with the two pistols and spare ammunition she carried.

"Here," the younger woman's voice came from behind her. Brandt spun and thrust a weapon and spare magazine at her.

"Incoming," she said, eyes wide as she pointed in the direction of the noises she had heard. "That way."

Payne snatched up the gun and checked the action before stuffing the spare magazine into a leg pocket.

"What do you need, Commander?" a rumbling voice asked from beside her.

She turned to find Kekoa towering above her, his burden of an injured squadmate now laid down gently beside the injured medic. She didn't hesitate, pushing the other weapon on the huge man and ordering them both to follow her. She stepped over the still forms of some troops, at least two of which had their smocks laid reverently over their faces. She didn't have time to consider what those losses meant.

"Wait," Turner said to her as she walked past. "You'll need these." He handed up a small black satchel. She reached inside, handing one item each to Payne and Kekoa.

"Spread out, left and right, advance twenty paces and take cover," she ordered. "Take cover from view and activate the mobile shields. Don't engage until I do unless you're compromised."

She went straight ahead, stopping slightly short of the twenty paces she had instructed the others and inviting any attack to walk into a kill zone. It was weak, but it was the best thing she could manage as far as immediate plans went.

"Zero," she hissed, hoping her marksman was within earshot. "Zero!"

An answer came from ahead, but it wasn't the NCO responding. The dense foliage fifteen paces ahead of her opened up to reveal something that took her a few valuable seconds to comprehend. Walking into focus was the unmistakable shape of a person wearing the last generation armor, like the set she had worn years earlier. Her derision at the old equipment facing them was short lived, as she realized that old gen-three armor was still more bulletproof than gen-one human skin.

Hold, she told herself, willing her nerves to keep it together. *Hold…*

One armored body became two. The two became three, all showing a worrying discipline by keeping their spacings and not bunching up. These three were evidently trained in combat.

By the time six of them had entered her view, she worried that their slowly advancing line would overlap her own pathetically small and rushed ambush position. Taking action to try and draw their attackers into their center—to do something that didn't force her to wait any longer—Brandt hit the button, activated her mobile cover and rose on one knee. She leaned around the side of the shielding and triggered off three rapid pairs of rounds. Almost every shot struck the reflective visor, cracking its outermost layer and throwing the wearer back to the ground. At once, the forest ahead lit up with a multitude of answering muzzle flashes sending rapid bullets back at her.

She ducked back under cover, feeling exposed. The bush in front of the shield was shredded by the incoming hail of bullets, leaving her cowering half in the open behind her mobile shield. A glance down revealed she had already used up over a quarter of the power stored in the emitter's base.

More shots came from each side, not penetrating the armor of their attackers but confusing them for long enough to stall their assault. Two of them withdrew, seeking cover instinctively. The one Brandt had dropped with her opening shots crawled for safety.

"Groin," Zero yelled from off to their left. He fell on the exposed flank to add his small firepower to their ambush. "The armor is weakest at the groin."

She caught sight of him as he shouted the last words before he ducked back out of sight behind a tree.

It didn't surprise Brandt that he knew that. Seeing that it was technically out of date intelligence, she had forgotten it. Of all the people she knew—on or off planet—it was Zero who would know the best way to exploit the weakness of any human enemy.

She spotted the crawling figure trying to regain his feet. She risked popping back out of cover to squeeze off a series of rapid shots aimed at the up-turned ass before they could stand fully.

A strangled cry of pain made her think that one of her rounds had been lucky and penetrated the armor. She quickly realized, however, that her luck was taking a turn for the worse.

As the armored attackers withdrew, an old first generation mech stomped awkwardly forward, waddling slightly like a duck. While the gait was funny to watch, the belt-fed 12mm cannons on both arms were not. It stopped, taking a wide stance, which promised an ominous onslaught. Brandt sucked in a breath to roar her orders.

"Fall back," she bellowed, dragging out the second word with emphasis.

She switched position, preparing to sprint back to escape the spinning barrels ahead of them spitting death and destruction. She acted on instinct, out of self-preservation. If she'd thought just that little bit harder, she would have asked herself what their purpose in attacking them had been.

By itself the attack would be meaningless. It could be chalked up to being in the wrong place at the wrong time, but given the recent attempt by hostile forces to capture her, Brandt would have expected they wanted her alive.

She was already running by the time that thought began to blossom. Instead of letting it bloom into a fully resolved belief, she was interrupted by a noise she didn't understand.

It was speech, a language she didn't understand. It sounded like a melodious war cry that was somehow both rousing and frightening. She dove for cover, rolling to her feet to see Kekoa twenty paces ahead of her standing tall and beating both fists the size of a child's head against his huge chest. It sent an echoing shockwave through the forest that she could feel from her position. She opened her mouth to scream at him to get down, to take cover and not do anything stupid, but any words she could have said would have been wasted. He started off running, lumbering at first but gaining speed at an alarming rate in his enraged state.

Afterward, long afterward when she had replayed the scene over and over, she could only liken what he did to the behavior of the Va'alen warrior who had lost his mate and flown into an uncontrollable state of violence.

Kekoa slammed his shoulder into the left leg of the mech side-on, dipping his body like a professional ball player before the hit. He lifted the limb off the ground with every ounce of his very substantial weight and strength. His arms tensed to fill the material of his uniform sleeves and threaten the seams with the swelling muscles as he drove his boots into the soft earth and slowly began to topple the mech that must have weighed close to a ton.

The driver of the mech took a couple of precious seconds to figure out what was happening. By then it was too late. He was already losing balance and beginning the slow process of falling down. He had time to react in one way, articulating the upper section of the walking tank to swing a cannon arm at the insane beast attacking him. The blow glanced off Kekoa's shoulder, temporarily stopping his keening bellow of a war cry as the air was driven from his lungs.

The mech went down, sinking down a foot into the soft, leaf-covered earth under the heavy tree cover. Kekoa was on his feet, tearing at the emergency release handle to fire the tiny explosive charges and pop the canopy open. His left hand gripped the opening and tore it the rest of the way as the mech rolled onto its back. Two gunshots rang out, making Kekoa stagger slightly, before he reached down into the cramped cab.

Brandt looked directly at his back; he tossed away a pistol easily wrested from the weak grip of his enemy like it was a toy. He stood, bringing with him the kicking and screaming form of a fully grown man who wailed in terror at being hauled about like a rag doll. Kekoa turned, throwing him down and jumping to follow; his face a mask of exposed teeth and wild eyes like he was truly in some psychotic state of detachment. His tongue protruded from his mouth in a way that would have been hilarious if it wasn't for the terrifying situation and the fact that the huge man had seemed to grow even larger like some uncontrollable animal broken free from a cage.

He reached down, grabbing his prize by his clothing and lifting him up with both hands as easily as if he was a bag of fresh linen. Kekoa held the other man out in front of his body in a display of inhuman strength and roaring further challenge in the direction of the attackers.

Unbidden, Brandt's feet returned her to the fight, making a run for Kekoa's cover before he had leapt out to fight like an enraged animal. She got her gun up and added to the weight of fire coming from Payne and the small group Zero had armed and led, effectively pinning down the attackers.

These people could not have been experienced troops, Brandt now knew. If they were, they would have known the way to break the ambush, even in spite of the bizarre and terrifying behavior of the biggest member of her squad, was to trust the armor and rush the position to overwhelm their unarmored victims.

Instead, their panic was their downfall. The sharp whine of retro-repulsers firing signaled the arrival of reinforcements, which turned out to be in support of Brandt and her team instead of their attackers.

Four bodies in dark armor dropped through the trees to raise weapons and drill accelerated rounds through the old armor of the attackers, ending their assault in an instant.

"Clear," Beale's voice shouted over his suit's speakers.

"Clear," Zero yelled from the flank.

"Clear," Brandt echoed as she stood. Beale ran toward her, cupping her chin with a gauntleted hand to inspect her cut eye and earning an annoyed slap of her hand. It had no physical effect on his augmented strength but made him release her anyway.

"No more in the area," he told her. "Any casualties?"

"Multiple injuries and at least two fatalities in the crash," Brandt said. She remembered the two pilots as soon as she had spoken. "Scratch that; four KIA minimum. What happened?"

"You got painted by a hidden missile battery off the north African coast. Our pilot went vertical when they opened fire and not even a gun to the back of his head changed his mind. We had to drop from the mid stratosphere, which is why we took a while to back you up."

Some shadow, Brandt thought angrily. She kept her fury to herself and her bloodied face devoid of emotion. It wasn't Beale's fault.

"I'll deal with the pilot when we get back," Beale promised. "If he's lucky he'll be flying a sub-light bucket of bolts to Mars with no grav emitter to replace their ass-wipe…"

He trailed off as the sounds of yelling and struggling came from behind him. They both turned to see Kekoa walking in their direction, carrying the captured mech driver around the neck with one hand like he was a chicken.

"What do you want me to do with this, Commander?" he asked seriously.

Brandt looked at Beale, nodding with her chin toward the struggling man and saying, "Cuff him."

Beale pulled the man's struggling arms down from his restricted neck and zip-tied them roughly behind his back. A nod from Brandt told Kekoa to let the man go, and the prisoner promptly proved he wasn't in full possession of a natural sense of self-preservation.

He was over six feet tall, noticeably taller than Brandt who was tall for a woman, and had to jump to line up the headbutt with Kekoa's face. The big Hawaiian saw it coming a mile off, simply lowering his chin and leaning forward, so the prisoner broke his nose audibly off the top of his massive skull.

Slumping to the ground unconscious, he became the subject of more than one confused stare.

Brandt changed the subject. "Medevac, if you wouldn't mind, Lieutenant."

"Yes, ma'am."

UN Base, Virginia

The final toll numbered almost half of the training squad and reached eleven dead including the two pilots.

Official declarations had been made to the remaining areas of the African territory and the entire Middle Eastern Alliance in protest of the unlawful military action. The claims were denied, blaming dissident factions in Europe for the attack. A counter-claim of airspace incursion was made against the American UN; part of their rescue mission involved the maneuvering of a pair of frigates in orbit over the crash site and ignoring the enforced no-fly zone. Their presence was met with the intentional test firing of orbital rail cannons intended as a show of strength. The joint UN forces from Europe, America and Australia escalated by moving troops and ships into tactical positions implying an immediate intention to invade.

All of that happened far above Brandt's pay grade, and she sat patiently waiting for her eye to be cleaned up and repaired. She had insisted that Turner's triage was followed, and he fought against her insistence that he should have his leg returned to its natural direction; he didn't want to be sedated. She knew he was fighting hard against the pain, trying to fix everyone else before he allowed himself to be treated, but a stern order from his commanding officer had to be obeyed.

Kekoa had been shot three times, though no one watching him would have guessed. Two of those rounds had passed straight through extremities but the third, a ricochet from what Zero suspected was one of his shots, was lodged in the thick meat of his upper chest and had to be forcibly dug out. The big man tried to refuse pain medication, not wanting to feel groggy, but a local anesthetic was administered whether he wanted it or not. Brandt suspected he would have made the same amount of noise had the injection not been delivered before surgery.

Brandt's comm device vibrated simultaneously with Beale's and both of them walked off into a corner of the medical facility.

"Crawford," she said. Beale's face appeared beside the UNID woman's on the screen.

"Commander," she answered. "Still alive I see?"

"No thanks to… whoever it was that attacked us, yeah." Crawford ignored the comment. She was a master at not being drawn into gossip or confirming the speculation of those not enjoying her high clearance level.

"We're moving you to a secure location with a no-fly zone. You've got Beale and his team, leaving you space for two more. Comm blackout will be imposed after this, so any questions you have you better ask them now."

Brandt knew not to bother asking where they were going. She suspected they would find themselves off world, but only after she had become either a terrorist target or separatist alliance enemy.

"How long?" she asked.

"Oh-five-hundred zulu," Crawford said. Brandt wondered where the UNID agent was to refer to time zones like they mattered, but dismissed the thought from her exhausted brain. It was irrelevant in the moment. Beale muttered to himself, working out how long they had out loud. The figure he came up with didn't allow much time.

"Confirm we'll have access to our equipment when we get there?" Brandt asked. "And a couple of mine have minor injuries, so we'll need recovery time."

"You'll have all the recovery time you need," Crawford said. "And yes, you'll be outfitted with some better protection than an obscure training detail." She scoffed to herself, looking at someone off camera her end and admonishing them for what she clearly believed was a bad plan. "Hiding in plain sight... pfft!"

She looked back at Brandt. "As the lieutenant has managed to count three fingers, you know how long until wheels up. Crawford out."

Their screens went dead at the same time.

"Your team solid?" she asked Beale.

"Solid, if a little unimaginative," he admitted. She glanced toward the doors of the med bay where the three armored troops stood guard.

"Who are you taking?" Beale asked.

"Zero, obviously. Turner and Payne but they're a little banged up so will need a rest."

"You taking the man mountain?"

"Kekoa? What do you think?"

"I think he's... I think he's insane to be honest. I mean, come on? Who tackles a mech without even wearing armor? Who gets shot three times and barely notices?"

"I'm taking him," she assured the younger officer with an amused chuckle, unsure if she was going to until that moment. "If anything he'll make excellent cover when we fit him with armor."

"Who else? The LT?"

"Beale," Brandt said in a slightly condescending tone, "if you learn anything from this, it's that junior officers are expendable but NCOs and characters like, what did you call him? Man Mountain? Are worth their weight in gold." She thought for a moment before finishing. "No, I'll keep my team small. Except for, you know, the guy who's double-sized."

The dropship wasn't the standard transport to anyone with eyes. It had no viewports and the pilots' screen was replaced with additional armor plating. The fly-boys inside could only get a screen view through wide-angle pinhole cameras mounted outside the ship. It bore no markings at all, and took on the human cargo of nine bodies, all but one of them walking under their own power. Turner protested loudly at being pushed on a repulser-powered wheelchair. The bird was on the deck for under a minute before it took off again, angling hard upward to confuse the passengers with the grav emitter working overtime. Breaking through happened almost immediately and the roar and orange glow subsided quickly to be replaced by the silence of the void. Brandt, as she always did, pulled down the headset to listen to the pilots' chatter as the rest of her exhausted and injured team slept.

Just as tired as they were, she closed her eyes and drifted off.

~

"Mayd... yday... freighter Lora... route to Mars in need of... sistance... ome in..."

The tone of the distress call snapped Brandt from her light sleep in an instant. In the moments of confusion after waking up, a bad habit she had slipped into since she had been back on Earth, she couldn't understand why the pilots weren't responding.

"Fold Drive energy signature detected," one said calmly. "Weapons array is online and seems to be masked as life support. No engine signature, running ID codes... no ID on record. False flag, repeat false flag. Power up weapons."

"Powering weapons, shields at fu—"

Three rippling impacts rocked the ship, prompting a cry of anger and surprise from Payne, who woke beside her to the unexpected attack.

"Direct hit to our stern, rerouting power to aft shields," one of the pilots reported. "Signal that we're under attack on sub space band three."

Two more hits shook the dropship, which wasn't equipped for fast space flight but for breaching atmosphere. It was a bus, for all intents and purposes.

"Gunner, standby to engage… *firing*."

The ship shook from the vibrations of their own pulse cannon rippling energy at their pursuers. Brandt recognized the telltale indication of advanced weaponry.

"Minimal effect on their shields," the report came, sounding a little panicked. "Any response on sub space?"

"Nothing yet, change course to three-fiv—"

Another heavy impact shook the ship; all of the human cargo was wide awake and feeling useless that they couldn't affect the fight happening outside.

"Jump signature dead ahead!" came the shout over the net. Another enemy had dropped out of an artificially created wormhole to block their escape.

Silence from outside. Nothing hit them. Nothing was fired from their dropship. But all hell could be breaking loose in the void and they wouldn't be able to hear it.

"Vessel destroyed, you have our thanks," the pilot announced with relief.

"Our pleasure," a new and familiar voice answered. "Clear to dock, and please pass my compliments to Commander Brandt to report to the bridge when she is able. *Hammer* actual out," Captain Craig Hayes finished.

CHAPTER 15

Bridge of the Frigate Hammer, Deep Space Beyond the Moon

"Jesus, Brandt," Hayes said as he looked at the officer walking onto his bridge. "You look like pan-fried shit that got stomped."

"Thank you, Captain," Brandt answered stiffly. She limped toward him and shook the offered hand. "I'd ask how you ended up here but—"

"But I won't tell you," he answered. "So save your breath for now. What the hell happened to you?"

"Got shot down," she told him. It was, admittedly, a stupidly simplistic description of everything she'd been through recently.

"Med bay," Hayes ordered. He held up one hand to staunch her expected barrage of objections. "No arguing; you just sit back and wait until we reach where we're going."

Her eyebrows went up and her mouth opened until he cut her off.

"Med bay!"

~

Brandt entered the med bay to find her team already being treated. Payne lounged on a fixed gurney beside Kekoa who had a young female ensign about a third of his size running a dermal treatment

144

probe over the three stapled holes in his massive torso. He was smiling broadly and was so immersed in trying not to stare at the woman fixing him up that he didn't even notice his new CO limping past.

Zero, having suffered only a gash to his head—easily fixed by a shower and some pain meds—wasn't present. He was probably seeking out an armory to make himself feel more appropriately dressed.

She walked straight for Turner who, with his badly dislocated knee manipulated back to the right position, was sitting upright on a bed. He wore shorts to expose the inflated isolation sleeve his leg was encased in. The top of his exposed foot was a livid purple, but his face was still smiling.

"Not as bad as it looks, Commander," he assured her with a slight slur to his words. "Three days and I'll be running marathons again."

"Take as long as you need, Turner," she said reassuringly. "Something tells me we're getting hidden away for a while now."

"…Not that I ever actually ran a marathon…" he muttered. "*So many dark corners of this solar system they could stick us in.*" Turner giggled mildly before gathering himself. "Sorry ma'am, it's the painkillers. They've made me… a little too honest."

Brandt laughed lightly as she tapped at the datapad attached to the end of his bed. Her eyes scrolled down past the stims and the anti-inflammatory meds, to find the artificial opiates, which were dulling his senses and loosening his tongue. Brandt decided, selfishly, to use the opportunity to gauge what the few people left under her command felt about her.

"I'm sorry you got caught up in this, Turner," she said as she pulled up a chair to sit beside him. "I'll see if I can get you transferred to a good unit when this is cleared up. Payne too."

"*NnnnnO!*" he slurred, his body jolting as dull light pulsed through the brace on his injured leg. He lifted a wavering finger toward her and whispered again. "No…" He smiled and dropped his finger to speak normally. "No, ma'am. We're with you… you get us involved in all the interesting stuff, Commander *Ssshit*-Magnet…"

"Okay, Turner," she said with a smile. "You enjoy your rest."

She reached out to pat his leg, stopping herself just in time before her hand made contact with his damaged flesh. She looked at the damaged limb, wondering how long injuries like theirs would have taken to heal before the advances in field medicine. Turner would be back on his feet in forty-eight hours but, despite his claims, wouldn't be running. Within a week, so long as he kept up with the electricity stimulus and ultrasound treatments, he'd be almost as good as new. The stretched ligaments, if left to their own devices, would take months to heal and would leave him with permanent weakness in the joint.

The young ensign who had been treating the massive trooper stepped into the small booth where she sat and fixed her with a smile.

"Commander," she said in an accent that was Alabama to the core. "I'm Ensign Curtis. I'm a junior doctor on the *Indomitable*, standing in on the *Hammer* for a while. This bunch all yours?"

"They are," Brandt admitted. "They all going to be okay?"

Curtis gave her a look—patient confidentiality, of course—but her maturity showed through her inexperience and youth as she told the commander what she could.

"They'll be fine," she assured her. "Just so long as they do what I've ordered." Brandt smiled, liking the young doctor's confident streak. "Now, I can tell from that limp you walked in here with that the slice outta your eyebrow ain't all that's bothering you…"

"Lower back," Brandt admitted. "Left ribs and right hip. Guess it's just my age…" She smiled self-effacingly as she unzipped the jumpsuit and sat back. The adrenaline coursing through her body when they had returned to the base in Virginia had masked the extent of her injuries.

She struggled out of the jumpsuit, stripping down to her underwear after accepting help from Curtis to remove her boots. The ensign pressed a dermal injector into her neck without warning; Brandt felt her body relax and the edge of pain fade away.

"Just a muscle relaxant and a mild painkiller, Commander. Nothing to worry about."

Brandt lay flat, enjoying being able to breathe without a tight pain in her ribs, as Curtis scanned a device over her body.

"Good news," she said. "It's all soft-tissue damage, except the ribs. I'll give you a vitamin and calcium booster, and some slow-release painkillers. You should be fixed up in a few days of rest."

Brandt sat up, reaching for her jumpsuit and groaning. She caught the look on Curtis's face. "What is it, Ensign?" she asked.

"Hmm?" Curtis responded, trying and failing to brush her off.

"The look on your face. What aren't you saying?"

"Commander, I'm not *not* saying anything I can or can't say. That's all I'm saying."

"Well that clears things up," Brandt said as she slipped her feet into her boots and headed to find coffee.

Mars Orbit

The largest vessel in the docking area was the natural meeting place for the crews and passengers of the various ships gathering from differing orbits of the red planet. That vessel was, easily, the carrier *Indomitable*—the technical flagship of the Ninth Fleet even though half of those ships were temporarily attached elsewhere.

Brandt, having had twelve uninterrupted hours of sleep, limped a little faster out of the airlock and down the long series of gangways.

Beale was beside her. He had relieved Zero of the second-in-command duties pressed on him. Zero didn't seem to mind, as the arrival of three other elite-trained troops made him feel more at home.

That wasn't to say that the CP elements under her command were keeping apart from regular troops. In fact, they had welcomed her NCOs who had kept their temporary promotions—the bureaucratic systems of the UN had missed demoting them in the rush of everything happening back on Earth. Kekoa's admission to the group was automatic. All of them wanted to know just what the hell he was thinking when he had rushed a mech and tackled the damn thing to the ground, ripping the pilot out of the cockpit like a savage.

Kekoa shrugged it off, though they reminded him that even an old mech fired new bullets. He mumbled his embarrassment away, saying that he wouldn't be able to look at himself in the mirror ever again if they had shot down his commanding officer.

Brandt, hearing that secondhand, blushed with a mixture of emotions she couldn't quite pin down.

"Attention on deck!" barked a master petty officer as they walked into the large briefing room near to the carrier's bridge.

Brandt stopped and returned the salutes of the officers and NCOs facing her. She stopped when a loud voice from behind her made her realize, embarrassed, that she had mistaken the call for attention to be for her.

"At ease," Dassiova called out over the top of her head. He walked around her and patted a quick but sympathetic hand on her shoulder. "No time for that. Let's get to it."

Brandt made a beeline for the nearest chair with Beale beside her. She was confused; she had assumed that the assembly of senior officers from other ships was gathered together to discuss what had happened to her and her team. As she tried to piece together the few bits of the jigsaw puzzle she had, a smiling face sat opposite her. She smiled back, realizing it was smiling face of the youthfully good-looking and confident Kyle Torres. He wore the same rank insignia as her own but with a captain's star over the name of his ship stenciled on his jumpsuit.

"Take a seat, shut up, don't ask when chow-time is, the head is out in the corridor and if you haven't been yet then that's just tough." Dassiova's words brought a few smiles to the table, mostly on the faces of people who didn't know he was being deadly serious.

"I'll be brief," he told the small assembly of important people. "This is what we know."

He was interrupted by a deliberate throat-clearing noise from a man with a hawk nose and small eyes who stood by the large display screen. Dassiova turned toward the noise of the interruption and glared for a second before he carried on.

"As I was saying, the facts ar—"

"Admiral," the man with the pointy face and a seeming aversion to bright lights said politely. "Should I not run through the set briefing package?"

"No," Dassiova said firmly. "Flight Officer Parker you should not. Like I was saying, this is how the world is."

"Galaxy," Parker corrected him, loudly enough for everyone to hear.

"We have military control of every part of the Centauri System with the exception of one planet, which happens to be the most valuable asset. It's got a bunch of big-ass aliens stuck there who like to pull our limbs off. They're stuck there because we blew up their only ticket home." His gaze fell deliberately on Torres and Halstead, Brandt saw as she followed the admiral's look.

"Add to that, we have a political situation on Earth that might burn our supply chain, human elements in the CS who *will* try to undermine our political and military standing given any opportunity. We've got untraceable persons making attempts on the Kuldar habitat as well as on key UN personnel who hold intelligence of value to our enemies, and we can't say for certain whether they are state-sponsored or if it's just plain old idealistic terrorist horseshit." He left off the fact that his troop commanders were supporting representatives of the UNID in 'questioning' the two prisoners captured after the attempt on Mars.

"Furthermore," the flight officer interrupted. Dassiova's face turned purple in seconds. "The 'roaches now want to talk, and they have invited the separatist Middle Eastern Alliance to join those talks—"

"Parker," Dassiova said in a tone one would use to control an obnoxious child. "Coffee. Cream and no sugar. Anyone else need coffee?" he asked the table in general.

Murmurs in the affirmative rippled around them as the admiral turned back to his executive officer.

"Just bring a pot from the galley and everything to go with it," he ordered.

It was Parker's turn to change color as he stalked from the briefing room with as much dignity as he could manage. Dassiova waited until the door hissed shut behind the retreating man and sat back.

"Ass," he muttered, earning a few stifled laughs that quickly turned into coughs. "As I was saying, we also had a situation involving the alien race who had been our allies up until the brass panicked and shoved them in a cage on Mars. Torres? Care to bring us all up to speed there?"

"Yes, sir," Torres said, sitting up and leaning forward to be seen. "The Kuldar, as you'll all know by now, were interned on Mars and removed from all joint research and development projects following the Va'alen autopsy that revealed their bodies were actually a biological exoskeleton grown over the bodies of what are effectively just shorter Kuldar."

He shifted in his seat as he gave his next words some thought. "We've established trust with the Kuldar once more, and we are of the firm belief that they did *not* know about the true nature of the Va'alen. Our best information leads us to believe that the two originated as the same species but have evolved separately under different conditions. One is a race of peaceful engineers and the other has evolved to be more territorial and war-like."

"More like us then," Dassiova interrupted with a mirthless smile before gesturing his apology to Torres.

"Both have telepathic abilities to a degree, and both are or have been controlled by other beings that exert an 'overmind' ability." He looked at Dassiova for permission to give the next piece of intelligence.

The admiral nodded his consent.

"We encountered one of these beings on the moon which has been assessed as a mining colony among other uses." He nodded acknowledgement at Brandt who returned the small gesture. "It's our belief that one more of these other aliens, what translates as the Hive Lords, are trapped on Gaia Neos with the remainder of the Va'alen."

"So," Dassiova said, "we're friends with our alien buddies again and they're going to be helping work on new toys and the like. In the meantime, we are heading back to the CS to continue R&D and conduct the negotiations, which we *will* be entering into. Yes, the hostile Earth faction with the new acronym I can't be bothered to remember will be there too, but the long and the short of it is that we're a bigger player than they are, and if push came to shove, we'll take them out."

Dassiova's eyes flickered to Brandt. She wondered for a second if her presence there was more than as a refugee to be hidden away.

Before Dassiova could speak again the door hissed open and Parker walked in ahead of two junior ratings bearing trays. It was totally against protocol to bring unauthorized crewmembers into a briefing, but his annoyance at being dismissed for a menial task made him brave to the point of arrogant stupidity.

Dassiova waited until the two nervous ratings, no doubt ordered from their duties in the galley so Parker didn't have to lift a finger himself, deposited their burdens and stood to attention waiting to be dismissed.

"Thank you, boys," the admiral said kindly. "Go on back to your stations now."

They saluted and left, eager to be away from so many senior officers and back to the anonymity and safety they knew. "Mister Parker?" Dassiova enquired, as the door shut behind them.
The flight officer smile at the respect shown to him.

"Admiral?"

"I'd like you to go and watch all of the Va'alen combat footage you're cleared to see, both in space and on the ground, and remember that you don't get to be derivative and call them 'roaches until you've at least been on the receiving end of their guns. Dismissed."

Parker seemed to boil with indignation but turned and walked out without a word. Nobody spoke as they all leaned in to get their drinks from the trays. When everyone who wanted a drink had one, the group settled back down.

"Forgive my unprofessionalism," Dassiova apologized, "but I don't like piss-ant little bureaucrats getting in the way of real soldiers… Anyway, that's our situation."

He invited reports from the various ship's captains as to their current state of readiness. Over the next ten minutes, he laid out the chain of command he had decided on and then brought the briefing to a close.

"Our next stop is *Omaha Two*. Any questions?" For once, there weren't.

"Dismissed. Commander Brandt? A minute?" As the others rose from the table to filter out, taking their drinks with them and leaving Brandt and Beale behind. Torres paused as he passed her, giving her arm a nudge as he went and winking at her when she met his eye.

"This your new number two?" Dassiova asked her, looking at Beale.

"My shadow, apparently, sir," she explained. "Admiral Dassiova, Lieutenant Beale."

"An honor to meet you, Admiral," Beale said, barely able to contain his excitement and seeming even younger than he had appeared before.

"Good to have you aboard, son," Dassiova told him kindly. "CP I presume?" He noted the special operations emblem on the young man's uniform.

Beale nodded with pride.

"So was I, some years back before I got my own unit command," Dassiova said. He turned to Brandt. "I ever tell you the callsign they gave me, Grip?"

"No, sir," Brandt answered, realizing she didn't know and had never thought to find out.

"Sandy," Dassiova said with a smile of reminiscence. "As in, I got my armor vents clogged up with sand during a training exercise and damn near suffocated."

Neither junior officer laughed at his misfortune. Beale shifted uncomfortably as though he was going to be asked for his callsign again, and this time he could hardly refuse an admiral.

Dassiova, luckily for Beale, furrowed his brow in thought. "You got a brother in the service I know?"

"Cousin, sir," Beale said. "Practically grew up together."

"He's a lieutenant commander in Tenth Fleet, that right? Transferred to the European territory on promotion if I'm not mistaken?" Dassiova asked, making Beale's face light up with pride.

"Yes, sir, he is," he replied enthusiastically.

"Good, good. Well, give me a minute with the commander, will you?"

Beale saluted and marched away leaving them alone in the briefing room. Dassiova poured himself another coffee and sat, inviting Brandt to do the same and eyeing her with concern when she winced with discomfort.

"Dropship crash?"

"Not to split hairs, Admiral," she said, "but it was more of a 'shot down' thing than a crash."

He took a tentative sip to test the heat of the drink. "Yeah, I heard it was rough." He frowned in thought and at the cold temperature of his coffee. "I also heard that some recruit had a stand-up fist fight with a mech, that true?"

Brandt chuckled.

"It was more of a linebacker's tackle, sir," she admitted. "But yeah, seaman Kekoa is built like a ground transport and hits about as hard. Tipped the damn thing over and ripped the driver out."

"Jesus H… You need to recruit this guy."

Brandt smiled. "Already have. How can I help, Admiral?"

"I just wanted you to know that while officially you aren't here, given the intel, I intend to put you and your misfits to good use, after you're rested of course. That okay with you?"

"Gainful employment at the sharp end of business?" Brandt asked with a smirk. "Count me in, Admiral. Count me in."

CHAPTER 16

Space Station Orbiting Proxima B

Omaha Two was the space station they had constructed in sections when they had jumped into the CS for the second time. It had been intended as a foothold, a docking platform for multiple ships, and the design was based on a smaller version of the shipyard frames orbiting Earth.

The station itself had a very small staff that primarily organized the docking and rotation of stores, but the presence of three huge cargo ships with advanced shielding and weaponry took care of most of the supply issues.

Their secondary purpose, which almost everyone posted there liked to believe was the priority, was the maintenance and operation of the heavy pulse cannons and multi-directional rotating singularity 'nuke' launchers. In effect, the station was a floating heavy weapons base, doubling up as a docking platform. They had six power supplies, producing more than three times what they needed. They maintained extensive battery banks to power the multiple layers of shields and rapidly replenish any depleted energy reserves of any docking ship.

In terms of propulsion, they only had maneuvering thrusters designed to perpetually adjust their orbital attitude to prevent it from decaying and risking the station.

There had been suggestions of converting one of the empty central cargo hold into a bar and R&R accommodation. Those suggestions only made it as far as the commander of the station; he had to remind his crew that they were on active service in a theater of war against a brutal alien race who would eradicate them given half a chance. The daydreams of having a casino melted away.

"Jump signatures inbound," the crewman operating the tactical station announced.

"Power up weapons, raise shields," the commander said as he turned to the communications station. "Who is scheduled to arrive?"

"Elements of the Ninth Fleet, sir," the comm officer said. "I've got the *Indomitable* transmitting now… ID codes and authorization matches the schedule."

"Power down shields and weapons," the commander announced, bored. "Send them our greetings and request schedule for sector departure."

He walked off the command and control deck without following protocol and declaring a handover of command. Instead, he walked directly to his spartan quarters nearby. He poured himself a lukewarm coffee and sat in the uncomfortable chair, pulling a small flask from the pocket of his flight suit. He poured in an unmeasured but generous amount of dark liquid for added flavor.

"Send me something to do," he pleaded with the plain bulkhead before him, "before I lose my mind entirely."

The bulkhead remained annoyingly silent, so he sipped his laced coffee and brooded.

Deep Orbit of Gaia Néos

The arrival of the *Indomitable*, with two heavily modified frigates and a light cruiser flanking her, prompted a stir in the arrayed ships of the Tenth Fleet. It comprised more than a few ships that had previously fallen under Dassiova's flag.

Formal pleasantries were exchanged, with Admiral Vernay extending her personal welcome to Dassiova and his crews.

"To put your mind at ease, Admiral," Dassiova said, "I'm not here to step on your toes at all. Just here for the negotiations. You have my word. If there's anything we can do for you or your people, let me know."

"That is appreciated, Admiral," Vernay said. She masked her dislike for the man she found overbearing; he seemed to have problems not being in control. "As much as I do not like accepting that offer straight away, I could make use of your warships for a few days if you can spare them?"

Dassiova glanced away from the display, evidently catching the eye of someone who had an opinion on the request. He looked back and smiled, albeit a little falsely.

"I can spare my frigates for a while. That work for you?" "It does, and you have my thanks, Admiral. Vernay out."

Dassiova turned to the comm officer, asking for a channel to be opened to both the *Hammer* and the *Vengeance*. When both captains reported in, he broke the news to them.

"You're under orders from the admiral of the Tenth for two days," he told them. "Get to it, but show them the benefit of being first on the field, understood?"

Both captains understood. The message was clear; play nice but demonstrate a higher ability if the opportunity arises.

"Get me the *Corvus*," he told the comm officer.

Moments later the viewscreen filled with the head and torso of Captain Torres.

"Our frigates have been *borrowed* for an indeterminate while, so I'm putting out my gun barges as a screen. Consider yourself released to the *Anvil* until the talks are ready to start."

"Understood, sir," Torres answered

He signed off and gave orders for his partly cybernetic pilot to ease their cruiser away from the behemoth carrier and to make for orbit of the forest moon to rendezvous with the forge ship.

"Open a comm to Captain Novak," he instructed the communications officer. When the call went through it was audio only and the Russian sounded harassed.

"How can I help you, Captain Torres? I am very busy man these days." He sounded like he was walking, and his voice had an echo to it making Torres suspect he had his personal comm device on loudspeaker as he multitasked.

"Don't mean to be a burden to you, Captain," Torres said. "Just a courtesy call that we're docking for a personnel refit. Let me know if you get any free time to catch up."

"I will, Captain," Novak responded, sounding for all the world like he wanted to add something that the bridge crew of Torres's ship shouldn't hear.

Torres cut the transmission and nodded to Rogers who was watching him expectantly.

"Take us in, Lieutenant," he said, glancing down at his console to his written orders. "Ventral docking platform twelve. It's closest to where we need to be, apparently."

The *Corvus* slid into position until the automated docking programming took over. As the *Anvil* had so many ships coming and going on different vectors around the clock, the system negated any risk of collisions between distracted or unaware pilots. Or cocky pilots.

Distraction and ignorance hardly accounted for every avionic crash in human history.

Rogers, being something of a purist, hated the sensation of being at the controls of a ship but letting it park itself. His left leg jigged incessantly in an unconscious tick. The automated system gave no verbal updates like a pilot and a control tower would exchange. He was tempted to close his eyes to wait the agonizing minutes it took for the docking clamps to engage to their upper hull.

"Hard seal," the tactical officer reported.

"Shut down propulsion," Torres ordered. "Run full systems diagnostics, then run them again." He tapped at his console to open a channel to Brandt who answered sleepily on the third ring.

"Sorry to wake you," Torres said, "but we're docked to the *Anvil* now, and you have orders to report for a refit. Deck four, section nine, cargo hold sigma six."

"Understood," Brandt said, tapping the comm device. She slumped back onto her rack and muttered to herself. "Just five more minutes."

~

"It's up ahead and on the left," Payne told Brandt. She swiped her finger along her comm to check the ship's schematic map against their orders. "That's section nine."

"Tell me this place ain't the armory," Zero complained. "You wanna try findin' this place in a hurry?"

"That's section ten," Brandt complained. "We were just in section eight so where the hell… Crewman!" She snapped at a scurrying jumpsuit ahead of her small team—small with the exception of Kekoa who somehow managed to look even bigger in the confines of the *Anvil's* gangways. He pushed Turner ahead of him in a re-pulser-powered wheelchair.

The jumpsuit stopped, turning and squinting at Brandt until he saw her rank insignia. His eyes went wide, as though he had never expected anyone of high rank to be this far into the belly of the ship. He held a cup in his left hand and a box under his right arm, hesitating in confused panic as to which item to put down so he could salute her. Brandt recognized this and saved him the obviously difficult decision.

"As you were," she said. "Direct us to section nine, cargo hold sigma six."

"Y'all are on the wrong side of the boat," he exclaimed, as though he found their predicament funny. "What you need to do is take yourselves back to section six where there's a crossway y'all can use to head to the starboard side—that's the side that ain't this one—then what you wanna do is head right, go toward the stern for a good long while and it'll be on yer left."

"Thank you," Brandt said, a little perplexed by the man and his directions. She decided that Payne should bear the brunt of her annoyance for her claims of being the best navigator.

"You know how embarrassing it is, to have to ask for directions and find out you've walked five minutes in the wrong direction, right?"

"Or," Payne said, her nose still buried in the small screen showing the schematics, "we go this way for another two frames and take another crossway starboard, then double back two frames."

Brandt looked at the wall beside her.

"You're saying that this," she banged the bulkhead, "is where we need to be and we're still facing half a day's walk to get there?"

"Five minutes, Commander," Payne assured her. "Trust me."

After going toward the stern and cutting across to the starboard side, they found that the reason the crewman hadn't sent them the quick way Payne had found was that the section ended at that crossway. It was physically separated from the forward sections of the massive ship as part of the breach safety protocol when being built.

Having lost another ten minutes turning around and retracing their steps, they bumped into the same crewman. He opened his mouth to offer directions again, realizing what they had done. He closed his mouth again and said nothing as they walked by, faces unimpressed and stiff, still-injured bodies limping with the effort of the unexpected exercise.

Eventually—after going back, crossing over to the starboard side again, turning right and heading toward the stern for a good long while—they reached a large cargo door simply marked 'sigma six.'

None of them spoke by the time they had reached their objective. They had lost almost forty minutes in the gloomy maze of the forge ship's belly. Brandt scanned her arm over the door reader to make it sweep open loudly. An orange light blinked in the gangway, indicting an open door, which must have access to space through another door. The light warned others not to open any gangway doors in that section.

What they saw when the doors opened was not what they had expected.

Brandt stepped in ahead of her battered team and was instantly hit by something familiar but surprising; it was like the echo of an emotion that wasn't her own.

She felt a wave of excitement, almost awe, and her eyes roamed the massive cargo hold until she found the tall shape of a Kuldar.

She saw them, two of them, standing with a tall human who was just under the aliens' height.

If she was surprised to see two aliens there, she was even more surprised to recognize the human they spoke with. From the parts of the face she could see, given that it was partially covered by a mess of wiry brown hair tinged with auburn, there was no mistaking the man underneath. He walked over to them, grinning wide with teeth showing and eyes crinkled up in a genuine smile.

"When I got the orders, I couldn't believe it," Paterson said. "Just wait until you see what I've got in store for you."

They followed the excited scientist, most of them accustomed to Doctor Jamie Paterson's sometimes odd behavior. They stopped at a massive workbench stretching longer than those in the cramped bars in the bigger establishments on the Lunar base; the ones where they served cheap liquor around the clock without judgment. As Kekoa stopped pushing Turner's chair and stood up straight, Paterson's beard cracked open with a smile of maniacal proportions.

"What the hell are you?" he asked, seemingly oblivious to the insult he had just issued to a man bigger than he was. Paterson was tall, but seeing him beside Kekoa put into perspective the Hawaiian's sheer hulking size.

"Name's Kekoa," their tame giant said, offering a hand that Paterson shook with trepidation.

"Leslie," he muttered half under his breath, "do you know what long-term effects there are to eating growth hormones like they're candy?"

"Play nice, Jamie," she said with a smirk. "Remind me to tell you what he did to a mark one mech with his bare hands."

Paterson swallowed, still eying the huge man who clearly had proportionately sized kahunas.

"What the hell is this place?" Brandt asked him.

"Sigma Six? It's R&D, Hyper and UN all the way. Almost everyone I had on the Moon first time around is here now. I shipped out over a month ago. Maybe two months. I'm not sure…"

"Let me guess, under orders that if you set foot on any alien planet that you'll get home to find divorce papers?"

"Almost word for word," Paterson admitted, recalling the venom with which his wife had berated him when she learned he had been a little too close to the fighting only months before.

"So what's your part in this?" Brandt asked. "I thought you were all about microwave emitters and shield harmonics and stuff. Isn't this weapons tech stuff?"

"You think the two are that far removed?" he answered.

Brandt shrugged. She hadn't given the semantics much thought, and since it didn't really affect her life, she didn't much care.

"Shield harmonics," he said with a wink. "I have a few prototypes I would just *love* to have some guinea pigs for—"

"Guinea pigs?" Zero asked skeptically.

"I mean human trials volunteers," Paterson said, digging an even deeper hole.

"Dude, not making this sound much better," Brandt warned.

"Irrelevant," Paterson said. "Just step in here one at a time. You first, Commander."

He offered Brandt an extravagant bow. She sighed and stepped forward, taking two steps up into a large booth. The door closed behind her and through the glass she could see Paterson's mouth moving but heard his voice through a speaker in the ceiling.

"Arms down by your sides, back straight and stay still," he told her.

She did, almost losing her balance and wincing at the stab of pain in her injured right hip from the jolt of unexpected movement. Red beams of light ran up and down her body. They ran side to side, forming a grid pattern and sweeping over her to give the sensation that the light was passing through her body. With the same amount of warning as it had started, the rotating platform stopped, and the door opened.

"Next," Paterson said.

Payne climbed up eagerly to go through the same process. Turner, seeing where this was heading, unstrapped the brace from his leg and had hauled himself to his feet by the time Payne was out of the booth. He climbed inside awkwardly, reaching out and placing a hand against the thick glass to steady himself when the platform started rotating. His process took much longer as he couldn't stay as still. The program kept working until it had mapped his body and he gratefully accepted help back into the chair where he fitted the brace back on the injured leg again.

"Still hurting you?" Brandt asked him quietly.

"Not really, Commander," he replied. "But it's frozen with an injection to the nerve cluster so I don't accidentally move it. Better that way."

Kekoa was the last to go. Being the new boy and trying to remain as inconspicuous as possible was difficult when you were larger than most living quarters on ships. He barely fit inside the booth, but still the program spun him as the beams of light mapped his body. When he was done, he emerged from the booth like a caterpillar breaking free of the chrysalis.

"That'll work overnight and have stuff ready in, say, eighteen hours?"

"Okay," Brandt said, still not certain what was happening.

Before she could ask, Paterson jumped and startled all of them.

"Ooh, specialisms! I forgot to upload specialisms." He turned to the console and began tapping away.

"Brandt, Commander Leslie, recon and close quarter combat..." Paterson spoke slowly as he hit the keys on the console. "Conrad, Master Petty Officer James, marksman... Payne, Petty Officer Class One Daisy, heavy weapons and support... wait. Hehe!" He chuckled like a schoolboy. "Your name is *Daisy*?"

Payne stepped up wearing a look of anger. "It's Payne," she said through gritted teeth. "Pronounced just like the thing you're about to be feeling a lot of, only spelt different."

"Moving on," Paterson said swiftly. "Turner, Petty Officer Class Two Steven, combat medic... Kekoa, Seaman Ik... *I-ka-ika*?" He turned to Kekoa to check if he was pronouncing his name properly, not wanting a repeat of upsetting someone especially if they were large enough to breach the hull.

"Ikaika Kekoa," the big man said proudly. "It means 'warrior, man of strength.'"

Paterson gave a high-pitched squeak before he spoke. "Heh! No shit... anyway, I've got no specialism listed on your UN personnel file. What's your bag, Kekoa? Heavy weapons? Breacher? Covert orbital drop insertion? Drinking the blood of your enemies from a skull? Needlepoint?"

"Put him down as a breacher and CQ," Brandt said as she eyed the big Hawaiian with a smile. "Would you want to face him in armor in close quarters?"

"Les," Paterson said absently as he typed, "I wouldn't want to face him if *I* was in armor, and he was asleep... Now, come back tomorrow when I've got something for you, and if you see Jake tell him I need him in for an oil change."

CHAPTER 17

Surface of Gaia Néos

"The humans have responded?" Da'kath asked. The subservient warrior turned from the console to bow his head to the supreme commander.

"They have, Muq," he said. "They have brought their people to negotiate with us. How shall we proceed?"

"Tell them to come to the surface," Da'kath ordered. "They are not to bring weapons and they must have only one person." The warrior bowed his assent and turned back to the console to input the message into the array. Da'kath knew the humans would not send a lone negotiator to them, but his pride and status dictated that he must demand everything on his terms. He could only relent when it would appear that he was being benevolent or simply humoring them.

~

One of the biggest factors in negotiations was understanding the culture and customs of your opponents. When the demand was received onboard the *Indomitable* it was relayed to the team assembled to conduct the negotiations.

Crawford read out the translated demand to Dassiova, and both felt a wave of amusement from their newly recruited advisor.

"Their arrogance demands that they do this," Asha said in his hissing voice. "It is an attempt to intimidate you, to dominate, to give them the upper hand in negotiations. It shows me that they do not respect you."

Dassiova grumbled his annoyance. "Get me a line to that Chakour guy from the other side," he said dismissively.

The comm officer began the process of hailing the rival fleet that was allied through a fragile necessity. They got the expected runaround—instructed to wait for long, unnecessary periods as the call was bounced around from terminal to terminal in a display of what Dassiova referred to with vulgarity as 'pulling his dick.'

Twice the communication link was lost, and both times the comm officer held his nerve and professionalism. He calmly made the connection again and pretended not to be pissed at them. Eventually the leader of the Middle Eastern Alliance forces came on the line.

"This is General Chakour. With whom am I speaking?"

"Chakour, this is Admiral Dassiova on the *Indomitable*," he said gruffly.

"Who?" Chakour asked.

Dassiova was accustomed to the game they played, suspecting that he was possibly more experienced at it and ignored the attempt at goading him.

"I imagine you've received the demands from the Va'alen?" he asked.

The silence from the other end of the comm confirmed that they had, but that his opposite number had yet to figure out how best to respond. Dassiova filled the silence for him.

"My suggestion is that we show a united front until we actually sit down at the table. I'd suggest we decline their offer and leave them for twenty-four hours until we answer them again. Do we have your agreement?"

Again Chakour hesitated; he had allowed himself to be painted into a corner by the UN admiral.

"You have my agreement, Admiral," he said, finally. "We will signal our refusal to comply with their demands, and give them a time that we will be able to receive further communications."

"Perfect, good talk. Dassiova out," he said.

Once the link was severed, he smiled, having played one side of their three-sided coin already. He asked for a message to be sent back to the Va'alen.

"What's their leader call himself again?"

"It translates as Supreme Commander First Warrior Muq, which is equivalent to a general or an admiral, Da'kath," Crawford told him with a hint of amusement in her voice.

"Well, inform First Supreme Warrior Commander Admiral-slash-General Kathy, that we decline his offer and will attend with a full protection detail and a team of negotiators. Tell him we will select a place on the planet which will act as neutral ground, and that we will establish a military presence on the surface throughout the negotiations. Remind him, with my deepest respects"—Dassiova put a humble hand to his chest as he bowed slightly— "that we are entering negotiations in good spirit as, militarily speaking, he is defeated. Tell him it's out of the kindness of our hearts that we are willing to talk."

An external hint of doubt tickled his consciousness, making him turn to Asha and look at him expectantly. "Something to add?"

"I would suggest," Asha said as he mimicked the bowing gesture the admiral had just performed, "with respect, that you do not make mention of human kindness. As a race of warriors, the Va'alen will see your compassion and your kindness as flaws in your nature."

"It'll show us as weak?" Crawford asked.

"Exactly this," Asha said, "But I would leave in the part where you so cleverly reminded him that he has already been defeated. As you would say," he added with a toothy smirk, "you have handed him your ass."

Dassiova nodded to the comm officer, indicating his approval to scrap the part about them giving a shit, and added one last order.

"Find me a place to set down this meet. And find me Torres," he added as an afterthought. "I'd suggest the first place to look would be in one of my senior troop commander's quarters…"

Sigma Six, The Anvil

Paterson, if Brandt had to guess, had been stuck inside for too long. His glee at having people to play with was palpable, and the flamboyant show he tried to put on was less embarrassing for her than it was for him. He didn't know that, though.

"Lady and gentlemen," Paterson announced. "Wearing this year's must-have item, Commander Brandt!" He clapped delicately as she stepped out wearing her new armor. Being a guinea pig, as Paterson put it, had some negative connotations but she had to admit that getting her hands on prototype armor was not an opportunity to turn down.

She stepped forward, feeling a little awkward driving a new rig that she hadn't grown accustomed to yet. It hadn't fully adapted to her individuality of movement, especially after being without a suit for too long. The others stayed where they were, distracted by their own armor, which didn't conform to any familiar designs.

"Okay, Doc," she said. She stood there and ran her eyes over the HUD interface inside her visor which was now a narrow slit and not a full-face as before. "What's new about it?"

"Much of the same," Paterson told her. "Only with higher output servos and an overboost system for bigger jumps and stronger limbs. I wouldn't recommend using that all the time though or you'll never want to come out into the real world."

Brandt turned to try and see the larger protrusion behind her helmet that ran out and down her spine like a woodlouse.

"And this thing?"

"Look at the top left of your HUD," Paterson told her. "Has the upload bar reached one hundred percent yet?"

"No," she said. "Ninety-one. What is it?"

"Something I cooked up with Althari's help," he said, glancing to one of the Kuldar tapping at a datapad. The alien smiled, flooding them all with the sense of her pride, as Paterson resumed his bragging. "It's a neural interface. Nothing invasive, just allows for one or two commands to automate reactions in the armor."

"Like what?" Zero asked skeptically. He wouldn't wear armor that would take over control and do something he didn't want it to.

"You'll see in a minute or two. Now, HUD controls are all as standard; it's just like when you got the last upgrade, which just made everything better. The wireless links to external systems will be noticeably faster and more secure, so you can access ship's systems, security camera footage, even remotely hack more things if you're that way inclined—"

"I'm at one hundred percent," Kekoa interrupted, making Paterson almost jump with excitement.

"Ha! Excellent! Okay, step forward, if you will," he said, shooing Brandt from center stage. "Now that your neural interface is loaded, a few… *feelings* for want of a more accurate term will prompt an automatic suit response. So, imagine yourself in contact and a Va'alen drops from above to whip out a big curved sword, for example."

"Okaaaay," Kekoa said uncertainly, looking down at his hands.

Paterson frowned and snatched up a datapad, which he tapped at furiously. His eyes went up to Kekoa's visor slit as his right index finger remained poised ready to execute a command.

"Ready?" He tapped the screen before the big trooper answered.

Kekoa flinched, throwing his arms up in response to whatever Paterson had projected onto his HUD. As he clenched his fists, the armor solidified and grew to make the gauntlets like metal boxing gloves, bristling with eight-inch straight spikes.

"Whoa," Kekoa said. He relaxed a little, watching as the hands returned to the normal, if rather large, gauntlets.

"And there's this," Paterson said, pulling a sidearm from a drawer and aiming it at him. He pulled the trigger, panicking most of those watching until they heard the report and saw the icy flash of near white light that denoted a stun bolt instead of a live round.

Kekoa, his natural instincts to protect himself surging to the forefront of his mind, radiated a shimmering orb of blue around him. The stun bolt hit that forcefield and dissipated all over it until the shield stopped glowing. Again, when Kekoa relaxed, the shield deactivated.

"Okay," Brandt admitted. "Color me officially impressed."

Paterson put the sidearm back in the drawer and shot a wary look at Kekoa to make sure he wasn't too pissed.

"Shielding as standard," he told them. "It taps directly into the body's automatic flinch reaction, which you'll know from your unarmed combat training can't be overridden. The armor also comes with specialisms to match your own skills. Close quarters have the overboost facility and melee weapons—" He stopped talking as Brandt tensed her arms in a fighting pose and two short swords shot from the forearm greaves. Paterson carried on as though it hadn't happened.

"Heavy weapons," he said turning to Payne, "have the option of a waist-mounted gyroscopic cradle for accurate fire on the move as well as additional ammunition carrying capabilities. Medics have suit interface diagnostic tools," he said to Turner who was enjoying standing upright for the first time in days as the armor moved his damaged limb for him.

"Already got that," the medic said.

"But you don't have it wirelessly and you don't have it this fast," Paterson said without skipping a beat. "There are a few other tricks but you're better off reading the manual."

"What about me?" Zero asked, sounding a little peeved at being left out.

"Dampening field emitter, shielding, and a little buddy to keep you company."

"A buddy?"

"Not enough space to work properly in here but check your suit subroutines for a program called BARTDIS."

"...*Bart's?*" Zero asked. His eyes scanned the menu inside his visor until he found the program. "The hell kinda name is... oh... oh *hell* yeah."

"The Battlefield Assistant Recon Targeting Drone Information Subsystem... Stupid name... It's a microdrone linked to your suit's HUD with automated or direct neurological control. Real quiet and hard to hit they reckon, and it paints a battlefield for you up to a mile in all directions. Fully programmable for icons and preferences, it'll basically give you a god's eye view of your combat space."

"Nice," Zero said. "I like Bart already."

"If anyone can use that gear to take heads like there's no tomorrow, it's you," Brandt said, meaning every word and sounding a little cheesy. She turned the conversation around. "Ahem. Prototypes, huh? That means they'll glitch and break down, right? Just when we need them the most?"

"It's all based on existing tech," Paterson answered seriously. "Did Jake's shield ever fail? Did your old suits let you down?"

"You mean other than getting shot to shit?" Brandt countered.

"Apart from that, yeah."

Brandt thought about it. "I guess you're right, but we're still the human testing phase, right?"

"Right," Paterson agreed with a grin. "Which is why you get the best offense to go with your defense. Can I trouble you to follow me to the armory?" he added with a smile bordering on a little manic.

CHAPTER 18

Surface of Gaia Néos

The area chosen for the meeting grounds had been assessed from a military point of view, which half of the advisory team sent to support the negotiators failed to comprehend.

Most of those advisors remained safely onboard the *Indomitable*, watching through the live links established with the hastily built base.

It was built in a hurry, mostly comprising of prefabricated sections of buildings linked together on the ground and powered by the dropship that remained as the emergency evac.

The area was a wide plateau with only two approaches: one to the northwest and one long road heading south to the lower ground in the direction of the Va'alen camp.

They had previously declined any offer of aid or resources extended by either human faction. It was still unknown how they fed themselves. In fact, very little was known about the Va'alen, and part of the negotiations was designed to gather as much intelligence as possible.

The meeting place was set up as two camps, one for each side, and neutral ground in between where the negotiations were intended to take place. Should either side wish to tactically withdraw or storm off in a display of being insulted, they had a space nearby to go to.

This way, hopefully, they wouldn't lose days on end with the Va'alen travelling back and forth to their camp.

Of course their area was bugged, and those listening and recording devices could likely be found, but the humans gambled on not all of them being discovered. The men and women in charge guessed that the Va'alen would be offended if their opposition didn't at least try to gain an advantage.

That was what one of their advisors had told them—them being Dassiova, Torres and Crawford.

"They are a hostile race who thrive on confrontation," Doctor Laura Church, the British psychologist on the advisory team explained. "They would see any obvious and immediate willingness to talk as a weakness, as though they already have the upper hand. Incidentally, that is how they will probably act when they first arrive. You need to see past this and not get offended."

It had all seemed like good advice, had she shut her mouth at that point.

"Alternatively," she went on, "they may get depressed at being defeated and imprisoned as such, and you could find yourselves facing split factions who want to negotiate their own individual surrender agreements. They may come across as being the supplicant, and be grateful for everything you would offer."

"So which is it?" Dassiova asked, not mincing his words. He never had before. "Are they coming to kiss our asses or are they coming to tell us to get the hell off their planet and go home?"

Doctor Church smiled kindly, as though she was trying to explain quantum mechanics to a toddler.

"It could be either," she said annoyingly. "Or it could be a third or fourth approach which we haven't considered yet."

Dassiova had cleared his throat at that point and excused himself from the meeting, before he said something which resulted in a formal grievance being lodged with UN command back on Earth.

"I'll be getting a coffee," he explained to the others, "or I might hit the head. Maybe both, or maybe neither..." Smiles and fake coughing covered the amusement of the others as the admiral retreated. "Useful as an ashtray in zero-G," he muttered to himself in barely audible exasperation on his way out.

As the three of them sat at the large table under the open-sided cover to await the arrival of their enemy, Dassiova grumbled to them both.

"This feels wrong," he complained.

"Wrong how, Admiral?" Crawford asked quietly.

"Wrong in that we're sitting here while the coffee's going cold waiting for them to show up." He stood abruptly, tucking his chair in after himself. "Judgment call. We come to the table when they arrive. Not before."

Torres and Crawford followed his lead and walked back to their base a hundred paces to the north.

"You coming, Chakour?" Dassiova said as he turned to the confused general still sitting with his own two advisors. Without a better plan and unwilling to risk the negotiations in a display of infighting, the representatives of the Middle Eastern Alliance followed suit.

"Negotiators coming back in," Brandt said into the open channel with her new team.

Beale, as her official second-in-command, acknowledged her words and checked with the three troops who had been assigned to him when they left Earth in a hurry. They reported that the smaller approach to the northwest was clear.

"Zero," Brandt said as she turned to the metal scaffolding built to support the observation nest. "What have we got?"

"Dust cloud," the sniper answered. "A little over five miles out and coming in steady." His line of sight from the raised platform, coupled with the naturally high ground, gave him a clear view for a distance farther than he could shoot.

Brandt corrected her thought, recalling the new toy he had set up on a fixed bipod in the nest. The concept of a rail cannon was not a new one, but the ability to shrink and condense that technology into a man-portable platform had previously not existed.

The gun was still too bulky to go running around with, but Zero had a new marksman weapon to fill that gap.

"Roger that," Brandt acknowledged. "*Corvus*, confirm you have visual?"

"Confirmed visual," Ivanov's voice returned through the open channel. "Finger on the trigger and eyes on the enemy."

"Standby," Brandt shot back. "All personnel: confirmed arrival of Va'alen negotiators in…" she checked the projection on her HUD, "two minutes. Stay sharp."

She didn't add that the approaching Va'alen could be a war party, or worse still a pack of crazy-ass aliens intent on blowing them all to hell.

She didn't need to reiterate their orders. She didn't need to tell Zero to take a shot if he had an airtight threat. She didn't need to tell the man in command of the light cruiser in a tight, low orbit to eradicate the aliens' transport if it passed the designated barriers.

It wasn't just their lives and the negotiations at risk, they realized. Everything they had brought to the surface was either firewalled or protected and purged of any technology that could assist their enemy. They couldn't risk the aliens upgrading their threat assessments of the human or earning their secret of faster-than-light travel.

As far as bargaining chips went, the ability of the combined fleets to return the Va'alen to their home worlds was the ultimate offer.

The Va'alen gaining the ability to construct their own Fold Drives was, by contrast, what Dassiova called a goddamned shitstorm of a nightmare. That would allow their enemy to pop up in Earth orbit whenever they felt like it.

The desired outcome, agreed upon behind closed doors by the various UN territories and the MEA, was for the Va'alen threat to be removed peaceably from the system. The humans also wanted the habitable planets in the system to be divided on a relatively equal basis, allowing for colonization and expansion of humanity regardless of the flag their individual members followed.

To that end, the MEA had demanded an equal presence at the negotiations, but agreed to display a united front to their joint enemy in order to achieve those aims without unnecessary human bloodshed.

War, Chakour had told his people, was only profitable until a certain point. After that, it required an economy and a carefully built infrastructure to support the growth and expansion of their people until, ultimately, they would build up to another war and begin the whole cycle again.

"Thirty seconds," Zero called out. "Five—correction *six* Va'alen and another…" He hesitated for a second. "They've brought one of their overlord dudes. Advise."

Maintain radio discipline, Brandt thought to herself. Her mind bounced around in her skull like an antique pinball machine.

"Wait out," she ordered. She had half expected something like this. "Let's see if they follow the instructions."

Zero watched through his scope, the wide torso of the massive Va'alen at the head of the group filling his sight so much that he had to dial back the zoom. He watched as the group stopped, reading the large sign written in the Va'alen hieroglyphs. New weapons and armor weren't the only advances in assimilating complex alien technology; the translation software was a boon as well.

The huge warrior at the front turned and ordered with pointed claws two of the smaller ones to remain. He escorted the hooded figure toward the no-man's land in the center of the negotiating field.

"All units," said a breathy, low voice over the channel. "Should any of you experience any sensation of manipulation or find yourselves considering doing something you should not, I recommend that you terminate the Hive Lord immediately."

Silence filled the net. No one on the team acknowledged Asha's words from his position up in low orbit.

"Understood, Asha," Dassiova said as he led the procession of humans to the table. "Sniper?"

"Here, Admiral," Zero answered.

"You see me start twitching and you rearrange that alien into one without a head, you hear me, son?"

"Five by five, sir," Zero said smoothly. "Five by five."

~

"You will leave this planet immediately," the massive warrior demanded, banging a clawed hand on the table so hard that a couple of cups bounced back up to spill their contents onto the surface. The man to Chakour's left leapt up, desperately brushing the hot coffee

180

from his burning crotch and stealing the moment as all eyes turned to him. "Your ships will leave orbit, and you will go from this system."

"Good afternoon," Dassiova said formally. "I'm Admiral Dassiova. This is Captain Torres, Ms. Crawford from our United Nations."

An angry rattle of throat clicks emanated from the beast standing before them, but Dassiova carried on.

"General Chakour of the Middle Eastern Alliance and his entourage," he added, diminishing the importance of their presence blatantly but politely. "And you are?"

"You will go, all humans will go," demanded the Va'alen warrior.

Dassiova was far more frightened than anyone would ever know. Even so, he bit back his retort that 'you will go' was a strange name and thought better of asking the alien if his parents liked him. That kind of humor probably wouldn't translate very well.

He decided to rise to the challenge and act offended, just to give his opponent the feeling of having got to him.

"Your name?"

"I am Muq Da'kath," he said. The translation software ran audio through their earpieces but failed to match the pitch and tone of the words spoken. "I am the Va'alen *Do-Ch'aal*." The phrase didn't verbally translate, making the humans look down at their screens for the long-winded written approximation.

"You're in charge then?" Dassiova asked. "You're the leader of your people?"

"I am the first warrior of my kind," Da'kath growled back in English. 'First' seemed more to mean 'best' than anything to do with sequence.

"Do you speak for all of the Va'alen?" Chakour asked, annoying Dassiova. He seemed to be one of those people who enjoyed asking obvious questions just to hear himself speak.

"I… all Va'alen follow my…" He made a noise in his native language, and the humans looked down again for the approximate translation.

INSPIRING GUIDANCE BY INFLUENTIAL LEADERSHIP AND BRAVERY, the translation told them, adding SUPREME COMMANDER to simplify things.

"Your people follow your lead because you're the best?" Torres guessed.

Da'kath's substantial torso seemed to swell with violent pride.

"They do," he said, "or they pay the price with their bodies."

He turned to the other Va'alen who stood stock still, holding what looked like a heavy canvas sack. Behind him stood the other creature and not one human had felt the faintest glimmer of mental interference from them.

"This is the price paid by the coward who betrayed my orders and attacked your fleet," Da'kath said. "By doing this he disobeyed my commands and directly challenged my right to lead our people. This is the reward he earned for that disobedience."

He tipped the sack up onto the table and let four severed claw arms the same size as his own fall out to smear drying, black gore onto the tabletop. The action elicited yelps of alarm and disgust from some of the negotiators.

Dassiova was annoyed to find that one of those noises came from the UNID agent to his right. He was gratified, however, that the other yelp came from the annoyingly well-groomed officer with Chakour.

A little harsh, Dassiova thought. *A court-martial and some prison time definitely, but ripping a guy's arms off?*

"That's all very impressive," the admiral said blandly, "but is that supposed to make up for the lives we lost fighting this traitor's warriors?"

At the mention of treachery all three officers from the MEA shot hostile glances at the UN personnel, feeling the rub of his words on their raw nerves. Dassiova kept his face very still. His former flight officer Suranne Massey was likely still aboard Chakour's ship; he found himself imagining carrying out her death sentence personally.

With a wooden bat.

He shook the thoughts away and looked up at the Va'alen expectantly.

"I lost many warriors to this *kruh'chunn*," he snarled.

Dassiova glanced at the screen beside him, which showed the words, MINOR SEGMENT OF FECAL MATTER.

"My intention is to inform the humans that we have been betrayed also"—he glanced at Chakour—"but that we now follow one voice." He slammed a hard claw into his ridged breast to make a head-splitting crack ring over their conversation. "*My* voice."

"Okay," Dassiova said. "So let's get to the point. We're not leaving this sector of space. We're not relinquishing the worlds here, we're not handing over the Kuldar and we're not vacating the system for you to spread out again and be a problem for us."

Da'kath made as though he would bang his claws hard on the table again but he stopped suddenly. His hard-shelled body quivered for half a second before he dropped his hands and stared in silence at the admiral.

"You have nothing to bargain," he told them. He looked left and right, preparing to break terrible news. "If you want the other one of *those* back then I suggest you comply."

They followed the direction of his finger. It passed by the other Va'alen warrior and to the figure behind which, for the first time anyone noticed, was hovering half a foot off the ground in total stillness.

It slid around the warrior, gliding forward without any sign of how it moved. It came to rest beside Da'kath with its head and face hidden under a heavy shroud.

Da'kath spoke again in a quiet voice different from the angry demands he had led with. "We will hear your demands, but My Lord will need to have assurances before that."

Dassiova, for the first time, felt a hint of a tug at his consciousness. It was like a tiny, fleeting sensation, like that of a passing fly distracting him for a split second. In that small time he hadn't been concentrating, *something* had crept in silently behind his eyes. He flexed the finger of his right hand, squeezing the nails into his palm one by one until he was sure he was in complete control of his body, before answering.

CHAPTER 19

Dropship En Route to Gaia Néos Orbit

"Why didn't we know you had captured an alien overlord?" Chakour demanded angrily.

"We've formally asked for you to turn over Massey and you declined," Crawford snapped back. "Care to rethink that now?"

"She is a political refugee and the Sovereign State of the Middle Eastern Alliance has granted her asylum from persecut—"

"Ah, cut the shit, *General*," Dassiova barked. "She's a goddamned spy who was working for you all along. The only persecution she's at risk from is legitimate prosecution for war crimes and espionage."

Chakour smiled and folded his arms.

"It sounds to me, *Admiral*, like this is more of a personal vendetta by you. Did Colonel Massey mean something more to you than just your flight officer, perhaps?"

Dassiova used every ounce of self-control not to stand up and throttle the little bastard. He stared hard at Chakour, recalling the intel package on him and trying to keep the derision from his face as he did. The general was connected to the private corporations through blood and marriage; he was part of the old breed who had entered into the new era of clean energy after amassing billions in old currency off the sale and control of fossil fuels. Dassiova had thought that would put men like Chakour's great-great-great-grandfather out of business, but if he knew one thing it was that money bred money.

The family invested their not-so-hard-earned elsewhere to stay floating at the top of society. Men like Chakour had never suffered restraints or hardships, had never had to follow the rules to get by. Even when the money backing in his own territory had all but undermined the UN, the job of leading the new fleet into uncharted space fell to him because his father had personally funded much of the costs of the fleet.

Dassiova hated him for that part. He had given almost every day of his life to the UN since he was a boy and had worked hard to land a position that was likely to be blamed for any failure. He would be branded unworthy or too inexperienced. Every day was a battle for him, and the suave little prick eying him now had everything handed to him by a servant.

"What she represents to me, General Chakour," Dassiova said formally, "is the greed and duplicitous nature of humanity and, as such, everything that I think is wrong with our species."

"You seem to feel very strongly about this, Admiral," Chakour said, enjoying getting under his skin. "But it has nothing to do with why you kept a prisoner of war of an alien race from your *allies* in that war. Need I remind you that you would have been annihilated by the Va'alen if we hadn't arrived when we did to offer assistance?"

As much as Dassiova wanted to grab the gaudy lapels of his uniform, a uniform that already bore two medals—not UN-issued, he noted—and drive a knee up into his groin, he kept his cool.

"Would you have told us?" he asked simply. Chakour's face dropped, betraying that there was no way in the galaxy that he would share that information with a superior enemy, even if temporarily called an ally. He couldn't do that if it meant a tactical advantage at some point down the line.

"Exactly," Dassiova said. "We're telling you now, because the thing itself is useless without cutting it up while it's still alive."

"What do you mean?" Chakour asked.

"It's gone into a kind of hibernation coma," Crawford said, "and no, it hasn't managed to control our minds like it does the Va'alen."

"This... this is information we did not have," Chakour complained hesitantly. "You have harmed our ability to negotiate."

"Has it harmed your ability to try and capture the UN troops who encountered the alien?" Crawford asked pointedly.

"Preposterous!" Chakour exploded. "Who are you to make these accusations? The Middle Eastern Alliance has engaged in no such unlawful activity on Earth. I will lodge a formal complaint about your actions today and—"

Torres laughed darkly, interrupting and earning the full attention of the separatist general. "Nobody mentioned that they were on Earth, General. Do yourself a favor, sir, and never play poker."

Chakour and his entourage were dropped off at his ship, the grandiosely named *Weapon of God*. The engines of the dropship ramped up to full to get the negotiators back to the almost equally boastful *Indomitable*. The general's last words were suspect, as he informed the admiral that he would attend the following day's negotiations in his own dropship and with his own security detail.

Dassiova didn't think that Brandt would like that much but was also fairly certain it wouldn't cause her any issues.

"Are we going to talk about what just happened?" Crawford asked pointedly.

"What happened, Ms. Crawford," the admiral said flatly, "is that we just let the enemy know we both offer their only hope for salvation and also possess an alien that they revere as some kind of god. Did *you* see what happened?"

"Yes," Crawford snapped. "You made the Va'alen angry, revealed state secrets without authority and alienated our supposed allies. Did I miss something, *Admiral?*"

"You missed a pretty big thing, Crawford," Torres said from his static position behind them in the airlock. "You missed what the other Hive Lord did when it found out we had one of them."

"Well?" Crawford asked as both men were silent. "What did it do?"

"It took control of the Va'alen and left, because my guess is they had no plan for what do to in that eventuality," Dassiova said. "We hold all of the cards, Ms. Crawford. Just go with it."

The airlock door rolled shut with a hiss, leaving the admiral and the UNID agent alone.

People working for Dassiova, especially those like the Chief who felt obliged to worry about his personal safety, were concerned that he insisted on going everywhere like he was still a unit commander in armor and carrying a rifle. As much as the world—the galaxy to be more precise—had moved on, the admiral tried to stay firmly anchored in his past.

Crawford left him, going to her securely locked suite of rooms to talk with the other shady intelligence types who accompanied her. The admiral walked on alone.

He didn't return directly to the bridge, but instead headed for the lower decks near his engineering core where he hoped to find the person he needed to speak to.

He greeted each soldier, sailor and officer he passed, acknowledging them with a nod and a smile. He gently admonished the two young crewmembers who panicked and saluted him. He asked questions of a few, those he recognized and knew something about, which made them feel as though the admiral cared about them personally. He did, he always had, but his gruff manner led many to believe that he wasn't the considerate father figure he was actually becoming more and more each day.

He insisted on showing respect for rank, making the distinction that even if the person wearing that rank wasn't respected then it still had to look like it. He had that curious and natural ability of true military leaders; his crew, his *fleet* even, would follow him on a mission with a low probable outcome for success in a heartbeat because they *wanted* to work for him. They wanted his respect, they wanted him to see them, and the reverence he commanded seemed oblivious to him.

The admiral never acted like an important man. He never pushed the envelope of his arrogance or success to use it as influence or leverage. He remained humble, but at the same time his crew knew he would lead them in the best interests of their planet with his dying breath.

They loved him for it—not that Dassiova would recognize that—and the change in him since he had first been awarded command of the Ninth Fleet was as big as the change for humanity having discovered new worlds and new species.

Stopping outside an innocuous door, he straightened his uniform and hit the call button, feeling an instant flash of excitement edged with a little panic from the occupant of the room before Asha mastered his emotions and opened the door.

Chakour stalked angrily through the narrow gangways of his ship until he reached the bridge. Every sailor and officer in his way scattered to press themselves into the bulkhead and stand to attention holding salutes which the general neither acknowledged or returned. He yelled grand threats at the officers flanking him, their legs scurrying fast to keep up with the angry general. No one wanted to upset the man who was so narcissistic he made sure that nobody in his entourage was taller than he was.

He demanded to know how the UN knew of their involvement in the attempts to capture the team who had experienced direct contact with the alien overlord.

None of them had answers that would satisfy the general; none of them offered any information or opinion in case it earned them derision or punishment. Chakour, in as great a contrast with Dassiova as possible, was a terrible leader who demanded respect based on fear of consequences instead of trust in attitude and abilities.

Chakour had not earned the respect of his crew or his fleet. Among the captains of the other ships there were at least ten men and women more capable to lead the fleet with far greater success than he was having. Political and financial dominance, however, dictated that he should be in charge although he had never led troops into a full battle in his life.

He had commanded operations against criminal organizations in his former UN territory; he had served as expected to the rank of commander on rapid promotion until such time as the right political position opened up. Because of this, he thought of himself as a great military leader and didn't want to step down. When the coup happened, he pleaded with his father and uncles for command of the fleet, which was given freely. The political environment dropped him into water far beyond his depth. His father reminded him of the only time he had ever seen real combat, bringing up the recent embarrassment of his son's poor leadership during the terrorist activity on the Lunar surface. Chakour explained that away, as he always did, by blaming other people. It was the cowardice of the men and officers under his command, he assured his father. It was the incompetence and the substandard equipment and weaponry which was to blame for them escaping and taking the new technology desperately coveted by his territory.

He had been shamed by that defeat, not in combat but in failure to steal the prototype ship. It had been pursued into deep space before it vanished, confirming they had faster-than-light travel capability. In the end, his people had used another method to secure the designs, but his failure had cost them months of development. They had to wait to begin constructing the right shield arrays and the Fold Drives to allow their fleet to jump outside of their own solar system.

"Get me a secure comm line to command," he snapped at the signaler on his bridge. He jumped in terror and hastily hit the icons to comply. Chakour ignored the standing deck crew and their salutes, and didn't bother asking for a report on his fleet while he had been on the surface. Instead, he went to his opulent private quarters to complain at length over subspace to his father about the unfairness of everything in the galaxy.

~

The dropship slowed and spun in a single, smooth movement to line up on the small docking bay of the *Corvus*. With the matching shield harmonics between the dropship and the cruiser—a recent upgrade from a young engineer on the *Indomitable*—the dropship slid through the energy barrier without difficulty. The tweak made the whole process and far quicker than it had previously been.

Torres stepped down the ramp, exchanged a greeting with the deck boss pleased to have the ship's commanding officer grace his deck, and headed straight for the most important place on the ship.

Sitting down to enjoy a sandwich of fresh bread, slices of peppery, cold meat and a generous helping of salad, Torres tried to ignore the awkward glances from the crew trying to relax in the small galley. He felt like turning around on his stool and calling out for everyone to relax. He wanted to tell them that there was no rank on a crash deck—even though the galley technically wasn't a crash deck, and the crew wasn't separated by a UN commission. He didn't. Instead, he tried to act natural and oblivious until he had finished his sandwich, or his crew started to relax.

Like Dassiova, Torres preferred a more informal feel onboard a ship unfathomably far from home. Everyone called him Sir or Captain, but he too insisted on no saluting whilst at sea.

"Save the salutes for the parade ground back home when they give us medals and a weekend pass," he would tell the younger, less experienced crewmembers when they inevitably would forget and throw up a salute when he passed. People began to like him for it, and even though very few of them had served under him previously, he began to suspect that he was earning their trust as much as they had already earned his.

Finishing his sandwich—he complimented the chef and asked for just a little more mustard next time—Torres left the galley and headed away from the bridge. He walked quietly through the ship until he reached the unmarked door in a seldom-used section of the cruiser. Opening it with his bio chip, he stepped inside and waited for the door to close behind him. There was another door inside. It acted like an airlock, but Torres knew this airlock was intentionally deadly. No one should be able to breach the first door and not be authorized to go through the second.

In addition to the scan of his implant, he was required to speak for voice pattern identification. He would also have to go through a biometric body scan to confirm his identity and authorization. When the system was satisfied, he stepped through the second door and spoke to the only conscious occupant.

"Any change?" Torres asked Specter.

"No," his cybernetic friend replied. "No movement, no mind control, nothing."

Torres felt something from the hovering, seemingly comatose alien before them. It stayed still, wrapped up as though it hugged itself. Its head was bowed as it floated a few inches from the deck of the cell. The *something* was like an itch of static electricity in the back of his brain, like a very faint comm signal that just couldn't be cleaned up.

The alien had been transferred from the *Indomitable* to the *Corvus* in secret, appearing on no manifest anywhere in the galaxy. Any communication regarding it had been done face to face so the record could not be hacked or traced.

UNID had control of it, choosing Torres to command the mission and appointing his second-in-command to ensure oversight. Ivanov knew of the alien's presence, and was fully authorized to access it, but he remained at arm's length from that side of their mission intentionally should there be any compromise.

"What are we going to do with it?" Specter asked.

"Eventually," Torres said, "give it back to them and send them all on a one-way ticket out of this system. It's ours now, and as much as they want to make noise, they have no way to regain dominance."

He chuckled, prompting Specter to ask what was so funny.

"Ironic really," the captain explained. "We hold the key to their release with technology reverse engineered from the alien race they tried to eradicate, perhaps not even knowing that they used to be one and the same."

"Yeah," muttered Specter. He was more Jake Santana than superhuman cyborg in that instant. "I guess aliens are as screwed up as we are, right?"

"Right," Torres agreed. "Anyway, stand down for the rest of the watch and let the UNID guys handle it. I want you to come with us to the surface from now on."

"Expecting trouble?" Specter asked.

"Only on days that end in Y," Torres answered. "And on every other day we have to pretend to be on the same side as the separatists."

CHAPTER 20

Gaia Néos, Negotiation Site

"Here comes our relief," Brandt told her small team.

She watched as the dropship breached atmosphere to give off a small orange flare in the darkening sky high above them. Moments later the team comm channel transmitted the voice of the pilot giving a three-minute ETA. Brandt acknowledged

the call, giving a report of no activity and a clear LZ.

Her team had remained in position until all of the negotiators and allies—a word she tried hard not to pronounce in air quotes—had left the surface. The Va'alen envoys had left long before, prompting her to call a full standby in readiness of any attack.

As the dropship landed, kicking up light red dust from their plateau, the tail ramp lowered and a familiar figure stepped down it. Like Brandt, she had her helmet retracted, the air on the planet was remarkably breathable and fresh. Her smooth skin bunched ever so slightly around her eyes as she smiled in greeting.

"Viper," Brandt greeted her as the two touched gauntleted fists.

"Grip," Eze responded.

"How're you liking the promotion?" Brandt asked quietly, her suit's mic muted to allow for a private conversation.

"It's... *different*," Eze admitted.

Brandt smiled in answer, knowing exactly how the younger woman felt. There was always more administration than expected.

When she had been made lieutenant commander as part of her fast track promotion program, she had served in that rank for almost three years. During that time she put her armor on perhaps once every three months to re-qualify on her weapons. Luckily for her, they moved her around to give her experience in different roles, but when her promotion to commander came due she elected for special operations. She hoped to escape captaining a supply bucket doing red runs to Mars.

"What have we got?" Eze asked.

"Raised plateau," Brandt answered, all business again. "Heavy weapons to the north road which is blocked, marksman in the tower watching the open southern road. That's where they come from. Single ground transport; if they breach the barriers past their section then open up with everything you have before they reach the negotiation table."

"And air superiority?" Eze asked.

In answer, Brandt brought up the toughened screen built into her left forearm greave and transferred comm channel access codes to her.

"The site is covered by orbital guns around the clock," she said. "Check the data I just gave you for preset targeting locations and the ordnance splash, so you don't paint your own team."

Eze thanked her, tapping at her own screen to save the information and change the command authority to her own settings. She turned, watching her team as they filed off the dropship to form two ranks. There were twenty, an entire squad, and all of them carried singularity-charged weapons.

All but two hefted the big squad support guns firing the heavier ammunition.

"You brought all heavies?" Brandt asked, not in criticism but with genuine interest.

"Not all," Eze replied. "I brought a sniper team from my recon squad too. Let the heavies run a lottery to see which two get the night off."

Brandt smiled again. A small gesture like that was a surefire way to become liked and remain popular among the unit she was second in command of.

"Hogan, Williams," she said, earning the instant attention of the two armored figures carrying long rifles. "Relieve the sniper's nest." They nodded and broke formation to comply. "Lieutenant Laforche, take six gunners and command the north approach. Signal me when you're in position."

"Yes, ma'am," Laforche answered sounding excited as he detailed off the three pairs on the right side of the formation to follow him.

"Boss Ryers?" A very tall suit of armor stepped forward with the rank of master petty officer stenciled on the right side of his breast-plate. "Deploy two fireteams to the south road to take position under the NCOs and retain the rest here as a reactionary force with you."

The master petty officer nodded, and set to work. Eze turned back to Brandt with a look in her eye that almost pleaded for reassurance.

"Forget *different*," Brandt said. "You're doing great."

Eze smiled and relaxed a little, relief evident on her face. Beale joined them, looking from Brandt to Eze expectantly. "Lieutenant Commander Eze," she said, "this is Beale. He's a bit of an eager beaver, this one…"

The lieutenant shot Brandt a sudden look of angry panic but turned away and offered gloved hand for her to shake. Brandt connected the dots in her head but kept her thoughts to herself.

"An honor to meet you," he said with a boyish grin of adoration.

Eze shot Brandt the subtlest of looks and reached out to shake his hand.

"Good to meet you," she said, a little awkwardly before turning back to Brandt. "Are you staying here or heading back up?"

"Going up," Brandt told her. "Be back down by oh-seven-hundred. Try not to wreck the place for us!"

Eze laughed at her poor joke until her eyes widened looking over Brandt's shoulder.

"Is that... is that a mech?" she asked.

Brandt turned to look, then turned back laughing. Eze had, understandably, mistaken Kekoa in armor for a piece of heavy ordnance.

"No, it's just my..." She hesitated, searching for the right words to describe him. "That's Kekoa. He's... *big*."

"I can see that," Eze said. "But what the hell is he driving? And what the hell is on your back?"

"We're just the crash test dummies for some new tech," Brandt told her nonchalantly.

Eze wasn't fooled. Her keen, intelligent eyes roamed over the new armor that she hadn't yet noticed. She looked more closely and could see the changes.

"Yours is thicker," she said suspiciously as her experienced eyes scanned the new equipment Brandt wore. "And that thing on your back is what?"

"Shield emitter," Brandt said quietly as she leaned in closer.

Eze's eyes went wide and her mouth opened to begin a heavy bombardment of questions. "What's the battery life? Is it like the mobile cover devices? How many uses does it hold?"

Brandt held up both hands to stop the onslaught.

"I can't tell you any of this," she said quietly. "You know that. This is research tech and has the smell of Hyper all over it."

Eze tamped down her excitement reluctantly. If there was anything that got troops excited it was new equipment. She changed the subject. "You taking our ride or calling down your own?"

"I'll call one down," Brandt said. "The authorization code file holds the evac plan, and that involves orbital strikes glassing everything here. You'll want to leave the dropship powering everything behind if you have to go in a hurry."

Eze's forehead wrinkled slightly as she thought. "So how were you getting out if something happened?"

"That's what I've been thinking for the last few hours since the high-ups left," Brandt mused darkly. She stepped away a few paces to her assembled team. "Take five, I'm calling our cab."

Eight minutes later, Rogers's voice came over the comm to her.

"Been wondering where you were hiding," she told him.

"Kickin' ass, takin' names and flying spacecraft, Commander," he responded in his flat, deadpan voice that still somehow sounded cocky.

The ship came in fast, turning and leveling out in one smooth movement as the downward flight was arrested in stylistic fashion. They loaded up as soon as the ramp hit the dirt and the craft began to rise before it lifted to seal the cargo area.

"Good seal," Brandt said over the ship channel.

The team stood, grabbing handholds to ride the short distance back up to orbit. All except Kekoa, who had yet to grow accustomed to being outside of the normal stiff discipline structure of the UN. He tried to wedge his large and armored form into a seat, which was designed to fit an average human wearing a suit. Since he was over-sized already without armor, he wasn't enjoying any success.

"Did you not learn from the trip down this morning?" Zero asked.

The whole team watched his attempts with amusement. Kekoa stood, abandoning the attempt and awkwardly grabbing a handhold with the thumb and forefinger of one huge gauntlet. He kept his helmet activated, following procedure for any non-atmospheric flight. The others, however, preferred to not feel claustrophobic. They trusted that their suits would automatically activate the protective seal if any breach of containment occurred.

"Did you see them checking out our new gear?" Payne asked, the big gun running vertically down her back over her right shoulder. "It's not like they're rocking old gear or anything either."

"What do you reckon one of these suits costs?" Turner asked. He had spent most of the day looking over the additional functions of his advanced medic's equipment.

"In credits?" Zero said. "I doubt there's a number. Value to those who don't have it, like our *allies*, is priceless. Value to the UN? Probably more than a whole bunch of expendable ground pounders without any armor at all." His cynicism lowered the mood a little until Rogers came back on the channel to interrupt.

"Docking in thirty seconds," he announced. "Thank you for flying one-armed airways. We know you have a choice when it comes to travel, and as always, we appreciate your custom. Please ensure you take all of your belongings from the spacecraft when you depart. On behalf of myself and the cabin crew, we wish you a very pleasant remainder of your day."

"Jackass," Brandt muttered with a smile.

As the call for a ride came from the surface, Rogers's duty shift was coming to an end. His relief pilot was an eager female lieutenant who, he had to admit, wasn't without considerable skill. She stood hovering a whole half-hour early under the guise of taking a handover briefing.

"Hey," he said. "Mind taking over a little early so I can run that dropship to the surface?"

"Sure," she said, desperate to get her hands on the controls and her butt in the seat.

"Sir?" Rogers said to Ivanov who tapped at a datapad in the command chair.

"What is it, Lieutenant?"

"Mind if I run that transport request to the surface? My relief's here and good to go. I can clock off straight after so I won't go over."

Ivanov didn't look up, but he did stop tapping for a moment to think. The regulations, which the Russian insisted on following to the letter, stated that each pilot must have a full ten hours stood down between rotations. He was clearly calculating whether Rogers could make the run and not cause his scheduling and headaches.

"Go on," he said eventually. "But if you are late ending your shift, I don't want to hear about it, understood?"

"Five by five, sir," Rogers said as he jogged for the door.

He carried on his run the rest of the way to the shuttle bay. He had placed the call from his personal device to the standby pilots to let them off the hook for flying. They didn't seem concerned, merely surprised that someone would volunteer for work.

The lone petty officer acting as crew boss had little to do as he ran over the checks—the dropship was kept on two-minute notice day and night. Rogers jumped into a ready suit, ran the last second checks, called for permission to launch from the deck boss, and pushed the dropship out of the bay and through the shielding a little faster than he should have.

He rolled the ship over, pointing its nose at the planet and continuing the spin for an additional, unnecessary turn before cranking the engines to a full burn into the atmosphere.

He carried on burning hard for the surface, following the waypoint on the HUD displayed inside the screen. The rules dictated that he should have cut thrust at three thousand feet and descend slowly but he decided to declare the pickup an active engagement. That meant that he could pretty much do whatever he needed to in order to get the job done.

He hit the comm, hoping for a response from Brandt and feeling happy that she didn't disappoint him.

Rogers flew them back, delivering a cocky speech on landing, which he hoped hadn't sounded like he had rehearsed it. He powered down the ship and climbed down, thanking the bored crewman who barely acknowledged him, and went to his quarters.

He had no appetite for food. He hadn't for a few months since he had last been in that part of the galaxy. He took a ration pill just to maintain his body's technical needs and stripped off his flight suit. Next, he stood up tall on his tiptoes and dropped forward to the small patch of clear deck in his small quarters.

Rogers pumped out fifty push-ups straight, counting out loud and barely slowing down even toward the very end. At fifty he bounced to his feet, stepping to the door frame to the small bathroom and reached for the lip to hang from it. He dangled, lifting his legs at the knees to prevent them from hitting the deck, and began to do full-arm chin-ups, lowering himself slowly to the full extent of both limbs. He had to concentrate, to force himself to try and use both arms equally and not cheat to rely on the arm that wouldn't tire. When he began to slow and fail he gritted his teeth and carried on until he hit thirty before straightening his legs and standing. His bare torso glistened with fresh sweat that ran in rivulets over muscles he never used to know existed.

Stripping off the remainder of his clothing he stepped into the shower and scrubbed himself clean fastidiously. Once out of the shower, he put on fresh garments and lay down on his bed. He had over thirteen hours until his next bridge duty, and he lay flat on his back searching for sleep.

It didn't come. He entered that terrible state of nothingness, hovering between asleep and awake where nothing was real and everything was heightened. He was trapped inside his body, unable to do anything but tense and thrash without any control.

Then the dreams came.

The crash. The Va'alen warrior, huge and terrifying, bursting into their position and slamming him to the ground. The beating, the warnings from his armor flashing up on his HUD over and over. The brutal and sickening sensation of his limb stretching and popping before it began to tear. The pain. The agony. Then the dull ache of nothingness as the hot blood poured from his shoulder before the suit pumped him with coagulants and painkillers.

Rogers woke with a start, his mind filling the gaps in his memory with vivid constructs, each worse than the last.

He felt the wet sensation of his blood all over his body. Rogers felt a flash of panic until his confused mind pushed through the fog and he realized he was soaked with sweat worse than after he had exercised.

He rose and checked his comm device to find that he had been out for a total of five hours. He stepped into the shower again to try and wash away the stress.

CHAPTER 21

Shuttle Bay of The Corvus

"To what do we owe the honor?" Zero asked, bumping his armored gauntlet into Specter's.

"Captain Torres is letting me out to play." He returned the curious looks of the three armored troops in dark armor. "Fellas," he said in greeting. The synthesized twang to his voice resonated around the open ramp of the dropship as the three troops stared at his bright green eyes. He turned back to Zero. "Love it when the new guys stare. You'd think they'd never seen a cyborg before."

"It's not that," Zero said with a rueful smirk. "It's just they haven't seen anyone as ugly as you are before."

"They've seen you, haven't they?" Specter asked innocently.

"Alright, listen up!" Torres said as he stepped onto the ramp. "Everyone grab a spot and hold on. RV with the admiral's dropship in two."

Dropping their grab-ass routine, Brandt's team filed in ahead of Torres. The captain seemed half dressed in a flight suit without armor and only a sidearm on his thigh. He walked to the front of the dropship and pulled on a headset to mutter a conversation with the pilot. Something about his attitude and demeanor put Brandt on guard. Something was wrong, something she wasn't read-in on. She pushed it aside and activated her suit's helmet to bring up the fully interactive HUD. Using her eyes to navigate the menu she checked on the status the vital readings of each of her team members.

"Specter," she called out over the team channel. "Want to share stats with me?"

"Sorry, Commander."

Specter instantly granted her authority to monitor his brain activity; it was the only measure of his health she could decipher quickly. The software in his armor didn't conform to the standard settings, and her command authority didn't allow her to override his software as she did all the others. He had to physically let her in to add him to her squad readouts.

"Gotcha," she said to herself. "Kekoa, sound off!"

"Here, Commander," he answered instantly. His tone held a hint of fear, reminding Brandt that he was new, albeit physically impressive and undoubtedly brave.

"Your suit warning you about dehydration?" she asked, annoyed.

"Yes, ma'am," Kekoa answered. "I already drank loads this morning. It's being in space; it just dries me out!"

"That's true," Payne confirmed. "He chugged like, a quart of juice at breakfast."

Turner, with his own limited access to the readings of the team's suits, waded in.

"Kekoa, you been experiencing any dizziness or lethargy?"

"No."

"Got a dry mouth?"

"No," he said again. It was as though everyone was watching him get told off for not washing his hands after using the bathroom.

"Experienced any vomiting, excess sweating or diarrhea in the last forty-eight hours?" Turner went on as though they were enjoying a private medical consultation.

"Dude!" Kekoa protested before trying to reply under his breath over an open comm channel. "There's girls listening man, come on!"

"Answer the question, Seaman Kekoa," Zero snapped as he tried to keep a straight face.

"Yeah," Payne added with a hint of cruelty. "Have you had a poorly tum-tum, Kekoa?"

"NO!" he replied, a little too loudly. His protest forced their suits to compensate and lower the volume as if responding to sudden gunfire.

"Well that's okay then," Turner said deadpan. "Just keep up your fluid intake and try not to tell everyone your personal business. Show a little professionalism, okay?"

Zero changed the subject, pointing to the guns on Specter's armored thighs. "New toys?"

Specter knew better than to start showing off a new weapon inside a dropship flying through space. He described it instead of showing the marksman.

"Yeah. My old twelves got vented into space when that thing on Mars happened. These are pulse blasters."

Brandt was only half listening to the conversation as she scrolled through briefing documents and continued checking her team on her HUD. She stifled a scoff at the comic book description of the weapons. She knew the technology was no joke, and even though she had yet to try out the short-barreled rifle mag locked to her back, she was glad to have it.

Since she had been forced to give up the captured Va'alen rifle on her return to UN control, she had lamented its loss, missing the tech longingly until she got to test out her new suit with the new weapons.

Essentially, the rifle she now carried was a blend of advanced human technology combined with the destructive power of the alien weaponry. The rifle looked like an Earth weapon but the double sockets for singularity charges didn't just up the power of standard projectiles. They fired condensed bolts of energy created by the device at the core of the Va'alen weapons. She doubted if anyone fully understood the science, much like the perpetual energy source of the spinning metals they found on the forest moon nearby.

Fortunately, though, the reverse engineering had allowed humans to replicate the device and meld it to their own technology to create what she carried now. Her waist was ringed with a magnetically fixed series of pouches containing more charges for the weapon; they had yet to find a way to combine the weapon with an endless energy source.

The others were similarly equipped with the standard rifle she used, with the exception of Payne. She carried a far bigger version in combination with the heavy charge pack and built-in stability rig for firing it on the move. Zero was different as well. His rifle was longer for greater accuracy, but he still preferred the new rail rifle for his chosen skillset, killing at a great distance.

All of them carried the enhanced sidearms as they had before. They hadn't seen the new technology condensed into a small enough package to use one-handed. Until Specter stepped onboard, that was.

Brandt guessed that the pistols he carried were too difficult for mere humans to use, even though the armor was a great leveler for strength. They were basically, from what she could see at least, the compact version of the rifle she carried in oversized handgun format.

She noted with approval that Specter still carried a rifle over his right shoulder.

"Alright," Torres's voice cut over the channel. "RV with the admiral's dropship in one minute. Standby."

"Zero," Brandt said, "ventral gun. Specter, dorsal gun. Pilot? Prepare to release gun turret control."

"All yours, Commander," the pilot's voice came back. He was happy to relinquish control of their rear defenses and maintain responsibility for the gun in the nose. Not all dropships had defensive capabilities like that, but the UN was all about modifications to standard build platforms.

"Locked in," Zero said as he took control of the guns via his suit.

"Likewise," Specter said after his helmet activated to allow him full use of the interior head-up display.

The rendezvous with the other dropship went without incident. It was set in an area of space through which no other ships had a reason to pass, making the identification of any threat easier.

Dassiova's ship fell in beside theirs as both headed for the surface. Once there, however, they found the contingent of Middle Eastern Alliance already waiting.

Bridge, Weapon of God, One Hour Earlier

"I understand, sir," Chakour said, "but…"

"But what, General?" the other man demanded with barely disguised hostility. He was Chakour's uncle and clearly felt that their pawn in the Centauri system should not be doing such foolish things as trying to think for himself.

"It is just that…" Chakour straightened himself and cleared his throat. "How certain are we of this information?"

"We are certain, General," the other man said confidently. "Our intelligence operatives have confirmed it, and you yourself have told us that the UN have agreed to hand over custody of the overlord to the enemy."

Chakour folded. He lacked the experience as a leader and the natural authority of a man in his position to argue, to demand more answers before acting blindly.

"I understand," he said solemnly. "Tell me what is required of me?"

"It is all in hand. Continue with the dance of negotiations so the UN suspects nothing. Be ready to create a disturbance and leave the surface."

Chakour sat in silence for a few moments after the screen went black. He naively thought he might have had an opportunity to legitimize the MEA's claim to sovereignty, to act in a manner befitting the high rank he had been awarded through influence and family connection. Now he knew he would not.

He stood, smoothed down the uniform that was still very new, and left to board the dropship waiting for him. It would take him to the surface where he had to pretend like the good little puppet he was.

Gaia Néos, Va'alen Camp

"Are we certain that these humans are to be trusted?" Muq Da'kath demanded of one of his subordinates.

"They are not from the same clans as the other humans," the warrior said as he bowed his head respectfully. "Their claims ring true. Might I enquire, Supreme Commander, what we have to lose by agreeing to their plan?"

"Nothing," Da'kath answered. "The risk is all theirs if they fail. The gain is ours. It is the cost of their race-betrayal that concerns me, and what they would do with access to our technology."

"Imagine," said his mate from behind him, "what *we* could achieve with *their* technology, my mate."

"We could dominate our home worlds and our clan would rule over all Va'alen," Da'kath admitted. "That would lead to conquering more worlds beyond the reach of our gateways…"

"And if we ignore their offer of alliance?" the subordinate asked. "Or tell the other human clan of their treachery?"

"Then we cannot guarantee the return of the Hive Lord and we cannot acquire their ability to move between the stars without gateways," Da'kath responded. He leaned all four upper limbs on the large desk. Before any answer could come they all felt the cold veil of control descend over them; the Hive Lord entered ahead of its guards.

There is nothing to decide and nothing to discuss, it told them directly into their brains. *We cannot recover the Lord without their help and I cannot control the primitive minds of these humans to make them comply. You will signal this smaller human clan and agree to their terms.*

"But, My Lord," Da'kath pleaded. "We cannot guarant—"

WE CAN GUARANTEE DEATH AND FAILURE IF WE SKULK IN THE SHADOWS, the Hive Lord roared into their brains painfully. *You will do as commanded.*

The Hive Lord floated out of the room, leaving no opportunity to contest its orders.

Da'kath glanced at his mate as the two of them shared an emotion like concern bordering on fear. The Hive Lords never directly involved themselves in the daily matters of Va'alen clan command. They had always preferred to remain aloof from such primitive squabbles and consider the larger picture of galactic domination, but then these were unprecedented times.

"We go," Da'kath said. He turned to his mate. "You stay here and handle the negotiations with these smaller-clan humans. Signal me when we have confirmation."

She nodded, bowing to accept her orders and acknowledge the trust he placed in her above more senior male warriors.

Da'kath picked two junior warriors of little to no standing in their clans, but who were large and seemed capable. They were ordered with their mates to accompany Da'kath. The supreme commander turned to his aide at the doorway of the transport.

"Prepare every ship capable of space flight to launch," he ordered. "When we have confirmation that the Hive Lord is safely under Va'alen protection, they are to destroy any human ship from this clan of United Nations."

"And the others, Supreme Commander?"

"The others are to defend this site and the Hive Lords to their deaths," Da'kath said simply. "And I want a battalion of warriors to advance on my position and crush the humans there. We will take their knowledge and equipment for study just as we will take that of the smaller human clan."

CHAPTER 22

Negotiation Site, Gaia Néos

"Here they come," Zero said from atop his sniper tower.

"Okay, people," Brandt called out over the comm. "Look alive; we have eyeball on Chatty Da'kathy and his backing singers." She nodded to Dassiova, Crawford and Torres as they

started walking toward the neutral ground. The three representatives of the MEA followed, and Brandt's face dropped to become a mask of unreadable distaste.

Much as it had gone the day before, the aliens parked their transport and walked up to begin talks.

"Three 'roaches," Zero reported. "No ghost this time." He added a low mutter, "Comm discipline…" which went ignored. Ghost was what they had dubbed the floating overlord

aliens who were able to control the big, dangerous warrior caste with their minds.

Something nagged at Brandt's consciousness. She tested it to see if it would go away by pushing it back. Instead, the feeling forced its way to the front of her mind like an angry person with a thirst elbowing their way to the front of a packed bar. She tried to understand why she was on edge but nothing came to her. The commander satisfied herself by reminding Zero to keep a close eye on the aliens.

They maintained their watch, waiting patiently but with an alertness as the talking started. They had no idea what other moving parts were working high above them.

~

The shuttle, a smaller model of dropship, flew a wide, shrouded loop through deeper space so that it approached the UN orbital positions from the right direction. The resupply routes were predictable, and it was no difficult task to plan their mission a few minutes ahead of the rostered ship.

"UNS *Corvus*, shuttle Alpha-two-five on resupply," hailed the pilot over the simple to hack UN communications channels. "Request docking clearance, over."

On the bridge of the cruiser, the comm officer checked the shuttle's identification and origin against the schedule. He didn't dig any deeper than the facts in front of him and granted docking authority.

"Two-five, *Corvus*," he said lifelessly. "Cleared for docking."

The pilot acknowledged, sounding as bored as the comm officer, before turning to nod behind him to where the resupply crates should have been. In place of the food supplies, a black-clad armored shape returned the nod and held up two gauntleted fingers to the other suited troops crammed into the small craft. Nobody said a word, not even when the ship shuddered passing through the docking bay shielding and bumped to the deck. The leader, identifiable only through their actions —none of them bore any markings on their armor—stepped toward the rear ramp and waited as the others formed up behind him in anticipation.

The ramp lowered slowly, letting in the new environment of the cruiser's shuttle bay, and the conversation of the two crewmen waiting for the supplies.

"...yeah, but if you *absolutely had to*," one insisted. "Like, your life depended on it, who would it be?"

"Come on, man," another laughed. "I'm not answering that. You're backing me into a corner!"

The first crewman never got his answer. The dropship ramp lowered just enough to bring their heads into sight of the leader in black armor. The pistol in his hand coughed twice, the fat protrusion from the barrel masking the report of the gunshots as it lowered their velocity. The reduced firepower didn't matter; the 6mm rounds easily penetrated their skulls from that short distance. The ramp continued lowering, allowing the team of murderous infiltrators to file out and sweep the remainder of the small shuttle bay. They quietly dispatch two more unsuspecting crewmembers. The pilot stayed in the cockpit, keeping the shuttle a foot from the deck as she slowly rotated it to face outward. The blast door operators were leaking blood and brain matter onto the metal deck where they had fallen.

The leader stopped at the exit door again as three of his team lined up behind him. Two stayed in the hangar bay to keep their escape route open, and four armored shapes slipped into the *Corvus* to bring more murder to the unsuspecting crew.

They swept through the wider corridors leading to the shuttle bay as the leader kept his gun pointed ahead; those who followed behind him swept into doorways left and right to fire single shots if anyone presented themselves. After forty paces, they reached a ladder going down and dropped to the lower deck. They worked back toward the stern in search of an unmarked doorway, the waypoint objective displayed inside their HUDs.

215

They found the door and the leader stopped, waiting for the other three to fall in behind him. He placed a small device the size of a coffee mug onto the locking mechanism. The leader activated it, hearing a gathering whine as it powered up, then his suit cut the external feed of sound to protect his eardrums. In seconds, the micro grav emitter created the small area of strong gravity to rip the locking mechanism clean out of the reinforced housing.

When the team had been given the schematics for the seemingly innocuous light cruiser, they could tell immediately that this was no standard ship. Someone had gone to great lengths to design a state-of–the-art fighting ship and hide it away inside the body of something innocuous-looking.

The heavy lock, one that had no business being on a supply storeroom door, fell away with a heavy clang. The leader flew through the door as it swung in, meeting the trooper who was rising from his seat and trying to bring a rifle to bear on the doorway.

He should've forgotten the rifle and gone straight for his sidearm, the leader knew. He should've drawn a blade from somewhere. Though, the leader knew, neither weapon would do the trooper any good. Not even the rifle had the firepower to penetrate his new armor. But still, poor training for close quarters work was still poor training.

He grabbed the business end of the rifle, squeezing with his augmented strength and bending the metal of the barrel away from him. The trooper was powerless to stop them, not without armor or better weapons and not without better training.

Instinct was all, and before he consciously thought about what he was doing the leader was withdrawing the big tactical knife from where it had been buried into the dead trooper's chest cavity, leaving the heart and lungs a bloody ruin. He let the trooper go, his corpse sliding down the wall. The leader turned to his team and flicked the knife away from him to shed the gore before sheathing it on the chest plate of his armor.

He didn't need to give his team orders. They had drilled this precise scenario over and over for days. The one at the rear pushed forward, taking something off his back and opening it out. It was an emergency gurney, extending poles on both sides and small repulsers to keep the casualty level.

The leader waited for the nod that he was ready and tapped at the toughened screen on his forearm to play a sound clip. He didn't know what it meant, but his suit automatically translated the Va'alen words onto his HUD as he stood before the containment cage in the corner and let the sound carry to the floating alien.

The shield dropped from the cage, deactivated by another of his team. He didn't know if the alien had heard the words or not; it gave no response.

Very carefully, the leader helped the others move the floating, sleeping alien onto the gurney where the auto straps engaged to hold it safely in place. Priority one was to secure the alien overlord. Priority two would be achievable as they had yet to be discovered.

Inside his helmet, he allowed himself a cruel smile.

⁓

"Tactical," Ivanov enquired pedantically as he tapped and swiped at a datapad in his hands. "The resupply shuttle is taking a very long time unless I am mistaken."

The way he said it—*unless I am mistaken*—was a clear reprimand that he had noticed something that others had not. His tone made it clear that they were all unworthy of his presence. The bridge was a chilly place to be when Captain Torres wasn't onboard.

"Yes, sir, they are," the ensign at the tactical station said. He moved to an internal ship comm line. "Shuttle bay from bridge," he hailed.

No response.

"Shuttle bay, come in, this is the bridge, over."

Still nothing.

"Sir," the comm officer reported casually. He hadn't heard the conversation happening behind him. "We have a scheduled resupply shuttle inbound, requesting docking clearance."

The ensign spun to stare at Ivanov. The lieutenant commander froze in his usual pacing for a moment before erupting into action and throwing himself into the command chair, hitting icons on the console beside it and barking out orders.

"Battle stations, send out a fleet alert that we have suspected hostile boarders on the ship. All ready troops to the shuttle bay. Tactical? If that shuttle launches you are to destroy it, is that understood?" He didn't wait for answers but punched another icon and called out over the comm channel he had opened to the reinforced cell holding their unusual prisoner. "This is Ivanov, are you receiving?"

No answer again.

"Shit," Ivanov cursed. "Priority response team to deck four, aft section, compartment twelve-bravo. Confirm." His order was acknowledged and confirmed. Lieutenant Commander Ivanov prayed that he had reacted in time to save the ship.

~

Rogers sat bolt upright in his bunk with the sheets stuck to his bare chest again. He hadn't slept all night and was due to rotate onto the bridge for the afternoon shift. But he had slept through breakfast out of sheer exhaustion.

It took him a few seconds to figure out that the warning klaxon wasn't being sounded inside a suit of armor. His hands wiped feverishly at his face as he tried to scrub away the error messages displayed on an imaginary HUD.

He looked around the small cabin as he tried to understand what was happening. Suddenly, he realized the alarm was real and it was sounding battle stations.

He reached for a shirt and pulled it on over his sweaty skin before stuffing his feet into his boots. Rogers hit the door release button but hesitated before continuing. As he was a pilot, his place was on the bridge, but in his current state and given the suddenness of the alarms he doubted he would make it there in time to be of use. He decided on the next best thing: the shuttle bay where their dropships sat.

Dropship, he corrected himself. *Singular*.

His brain caught up bit by bit as he remembered the other would be on the surface with their troops and Brandt. He ran for the ladder half a section back from his quarters and slid down it to the deck below. There he picked up his run once more as the door of the shuttle bay came into sight.

Only it wasn't just the door. It was four armored soldiers running with a field gurney, just like the one he had been strapped to when he lost his arm.

He couldn't place one single element of this that signaled the full truth; he couldn't site a particular evidential fact. In spite of this, he knew in a heartbeat that something very wrong was happening.

Rogers opened his mouth to cry out, stopping before he could paint a huge target on his white-shirted chest. He clammed up as the intruders—they could be nothing else—disappeared into the shuttle bay.

As they went inside, the one at the rear turned and raised a rifle to quickly sweep the corridor. Rogers ducked inside an open hatch to be out of sight. His boots slipped on something in the dark just as his nose picked up the metallic tang of blood in the air. He didn't turn on the light in the cabin. He didn't want to see who it was. But he knew he was sharing a room with a dead body.

"Intruders in the shuttle bay," he said into his forearm device, alerting the bridge.

Rogers ducked out of the room and followed the path of the armored killers to open the door of the shuttle bay. He was unarmed, dressed in sweat-drenched PT gear with his boots unlaced, and he had no idea what he was going to do if he caught up to them.

~

"Intruders in the shuttle bay," announced the report over the bridge comm speakers.

Ivanov said nothing, having already dispatched a team of troops there, but the next report threw him into total panic.

"Sir! MEA frigate dropping shroud at five thousand kilometers to our stern... Weapons are powered. They're firing!"

"Shields to maximum and engage a half-second emergency jump on my mar—" He couldn't finish his orders as the bridge took a shattering concentration of heavy pulse fire. It seemed like everything happened at once, but in his last moments Ivanov knew the sequence of things.

First, the shield emitter, that was routinely activated to protect against the space debris, overloaded and fed back through the power relays to knock out power to all bridge systems. That blacked out the bridge and removed all control they had over the *Corvus*. The second impact was much different. It wasn't a burst of pulse bolts each the size of a small dog that hit them this time, but the solid slug charged to hypervelocity by the railgun on the enemy frigate.

The slug punched straight through the bridge, opening up the control center through the roof like a tin can that had burst in a fire.

The vacuum of space sucked at the flash frozen bodies of his crew, yanking them into the void before they knew what was happening. Ivanov, strapped into the command chair, was locked in an eternal and everlasting rictus of anger as he shouted an order that would never be issued. The few remaining bodies of his bridge crew bounced lazily around the vented space.

Rogers felt the impacts of the first volley and saw the lights flicker in the gangway. The second impact made his heart sink though the deck; he could feel the subtle vibrations of the ship venting atmosphere through rips in the hull. He didn't know where, but anywhere venting atmosphere wasn't somewhere he wanted to be.

He returned to his original plan and ran into the shuttle bay in time to see a black-armored trooper lob an item the size of a dinner plate into the open ramp of their remaining dropship. He then piled into the shuttle as it took off and passed through the docking shields as if they weren't there.

A metallic *crump* noise sounded from inside the dropship. Instead of the smoke and ruin he expected, Rogers could only stare in horror as the center section of the vessel buckled in toward the deck like it had been hit by a small meteor.

The ship rocked again as more heavy ordnance fire hit it. Rogers did the only thing he could think of to do and ran into the ruined ship. He climbed over the twisted wreckage of metal in order to reach the cockpit.

He knew the ship wasn't capable of flight and certainly couldn't hold an air seal any longer, but he also knew that the dropship's cockpit was still in one piece.

Throwing himself into the co-pilot's seat he hit a few controls and sat back to press his body straight into the seat. "Activate emergency ejection sequence."

The MEA ships were unshrouding all over the UN's fleet positions and opening fire with everything they had. Then the cowardly traitors shrouded again and jumped to avoid any counterattack by their unsuspecting victims.

In all of the panic and confusion, nobody noticed a small dropship ejection module rise vertically up out of the dropship's cockpit roof and fire straight out through the collapsed shield of the shuttle bay to spin away from the doomed *Corvus* as it broke apart.

CHAPTER 23

Negotiation Site, Gaia Néos

"And where does the Alliance fall into this great vision of the UN, Admiral?" Chakour asked peevishly, interrupting Dassiova who had been laying out the non-negotiable terms of the Va'alen's total surrender.

"On behalf of the *combined* Earth fleets," Crawford said carefully as Dassiova just held Chakour in a death stare, "what we mean by *we,* is just that. The minutia of what forces conduct which part aren't set in stone." Her political smoothing seemed to work, only Chakour stirred himself as though he had intentionally taken offence to nothing in particular.

"I must consult with my superiors," he said as he stood. He offered a small but respectful bow to the three Va'alen seated opposite. On his way out, he draped a withering glance over the three UN personnel with his entourage scurrying in confusion to follow him.

Unimpressed with the childish display, Dassiova returned to the negotiations as though the MEA's presence was irrelevant.

"What the hell...?" Brandt muttered as the MEA contingent suddenly stood, walked away from the negotiations and went directly to the rear of their dropship. The ship powered up engines without warning, an action downright discourteous and dangerous to anyone on the ground not protected from the dust and debris.

She watched as it took off and worked through the active comms inside her helmet by using the HUD interface.

"*Corvus*, Brandt, come in," she said over the channel. It was supposed to always stay open to their air and artillery cover high above their exposed position. "*Corvus*," she tried again. "Commander Brandt, ground team, acknowledge transmission, over."

"What'ya got there, Commander?" Zero asked over the squad comm. He'd seen her nervous pacing below his position and recognized it immediately.

"Don't panic just yet," she said. "Just having a little trouble raising the *Cor*—"

"Look!" Beale shouted. He was out of sight and nobody knew what he was telling them to look at. As though realizing this, he activated a squad waypoint marker on his HUD, which gave them all a direction to look.

The squad radio lit up with various curses and noises of disbelief as the sky far above them looked like a meteor shower. They all knew there was no chance it was a meteor shower; concentrated space debris like that could only be a damaged ship breaking apart on uncontrolled atmospheric entry. Brandt, locked in slow-motion as though every action and thought took place underwater, turned back to the negotiations.

Da'kath watched the race-traitors, as he called them, leave the table and stood.

"I must report this to my Lord," he said, interrupting Dassiova. "My warriors will stay here; I will return momentarily." He left without waiting for permission or acknowledgment, pacing quickly toward the area they were allocated, and nodded once to the senior warrior he had left there with the mates of his fellow negotiators.

The warrior returned the nod. He pulled two long stiletto-like blades from his back and plunged them simultaneously into the backs of the females standing before him, killing them instantly. Their deaths sent their mates at the negotiation table into a blood rage the humans could not even begin to cope with.

"Zero!" Brandt cried out. They had worked together long enough, she hoped that just the tone of her voice would convey her orders.

She ran, Payne and Kekoa beside her, and brought her gun up, just as the table inside the negotiation tent was flipped over and obscured her targeting view. She ran faster, stretching out an instant lead over the others thanks to her enhanced armor servos, though she still had no clear target to engage.

The distance was a short one to cover but it would mean getting up close and personal with a Va'alen warrior. Coming so soon after the last time wasn't a prospect she relished.

The table splintered as a Va'alen burst through it. Brandt almost stumbled as she recognized the deep scratch marks running diagonally across the beast's chest in an X. The berserker rage, the name for when a bonded mate dies, made her instinctively know what she was up against.

Did they sacrifice their own warriors to gain a tactical edge and assassinate the negotiators?

She didn't put it past them, not one little bit. The Va'alen were bloodthirsty animals totally without mercy. The only way to deal with something that brutal was to kill them before they could kill you.

The warrior who emerged roared and swung its left arms viciously to throw a body-sized shape hard into the side of the tent. She squeezed the trigger and hit it with three shots in the right side of its ridged torso. One arm hung limply as it turned to face them. It took a step forward before crouching like a bull about to charge. It started its forward momentum as more pulse rifle shots struck the hard armor and blew non-essential chunks of it away. Brandt realized that it could cross the gap to them too fast to bring it down. As her body tensed ready for that threat, both forearm greaves shot out their wide blades and her shields burst to life in anticipation of the fight. Her armor was reacting to her... her what? Her *fear*?

The creature never made it to them. Instead it was snatched back like a parachute was tethered to its back and had opened mid-flight. Brandt glimpsed a snapshot of the hole the size of her armored fist appearing almost dead center in its chest. The shot had torn the hardened carapace capable of withstanding weapons fire and the smaller, softer alien nestled inside, like a baby in a fixed womb able to control the mother, into black-gored ruin.

Zero's railgun would be charging a second slug already, hoping for a glimpse of the other Va'alen warrior.

It was an easy thing, she thought to herself, to demean the aliens by calling them 'roaches. But when faced with a Va'alen warrior in full berserker mode, she couldn't think of a single derisive thing to say; they truly were terrifying killing machines evolved to perfection. Only the humans' superior technology gave them even a chance of surviving contact with them.

A scream, a guttural bellow of rage, tore her out of the thought as she ran forward. The enemy was still inside the tent and trying its hardest to eviscerate the unarmed humans trapped there. Brandt caught a glimpse of it and raised her rifle just as another roar of challenge came from around the side of the tent.

"One more incoming and one bugging out," Zero reported quickly. "Targeting the one on the run."

The report of his railgun sliced the air again as Payne stood her ground and activated the support bracket that popped out of the waist of her armor. The big gun came vertically up and over her right shoulder before it descended and locked in, then connected to the battery bank acting as an ammo reservoir on her back.

As the roar of challenge became a physical entity, her gun fired up, the intensity and rate of pulses spitting from the barrel increasing to hit the torso of a large warrior who came in shooting. Three blasts from its gun hit Payne, each shot staggering her backward and threatening to drive her down to the dirt. Her shields held just long enough to keep her in the fight until her gun blew off the alien arm holding the weapon.

It kept coming but Payne didn't let up, keeping the weapon barrel depressed toward the alien. She hammered it back with the sheer weight of her fire.

Brandt wanted to veer off and help Payne, but she couldn't let up her advance toward the unprotected officers she owed more than just her loyalty. There had been no other screams from inside the tent. That was a reassurance in some ways but a total confusion in others.

Behind her, Zero's railgun still boomed, sending electric crackles through the air in an attempt to destroy the transport fleeing the plateau.

She burst into the tent, gun up, and drilled three short bursts into the enraged Va'alen warrior with fresh blood—red *human* blood—splashed across its face. The thing stayed on its feet, something a warrior in berserker mode wouldn't manage, and lashed out with a sharp claw tip. It impacted her shielding and threw her back out of the tent. She rolled with the blow, rising up to her feet and bringing her rifle back to her shoulder in one fluid movement. She stopped, as her shot was blocked by the runaway locomotive Kekoa.

He saw Payne hit but remain on her feet. He saw the slumped shape against the inside of the tent and the blood seeping into the pale canvas. He heard the shout, the cry of injured agony, and watched as his commander was thumped hard out of the tent to fly past him.

Something in Kekoa snapped then, just as it had when he had seen the mech lining up to stitch Brandt's position with heavy fire. His armor reacted to his rage, and as he entered the tent at a dead run with his fists balled up, the wicked spikes shot from the knuckles of the gauntlets.

His first blow, an instinctive right hook to the jaw, flattened one side of the beast's head into black gore and crushed carapace. The second blow, a left rising up to the body, was more effective; the spikes penetrated deep under the thickly ridged breastplate of the bio-armor and did internal damage. The Va'alen, enraged and feeling no pain, was unable even to recognize that it was physically damaged. It just kept on fighting. Kekoa felt the spiked claw of one of the Va'alen's left hands raked savagely over his helmet and down his chest.

He pushed the thing away from him, grabbing the claw and yanking it hard as he spun his body in an attempt to throw it to the dirt. There he could pound it into the dust and kill it.

This was what he was there for, he knew. He was the blunt instrument, the wrecking ball to complement the surgeon's scalpel that was Zero's rifle. He was the hammer to Payne's anvil, the damage to Turner's healing and the brawn to the commander's brains. His brawn didn't recognize what had happened, however, when the arm he was trying to use as a lever to throw down the alien snapped off at the elbow. It left the thing with open access to his back.

It grabbed him, wrapping three and a half limbs around his body as it lifted Kekoa in his armor and tried to crush him. He had no doubt that without the protection his torso would be a ruined bag of mixed bone fragments and mushy organs by now. Even so, he couldn't trust the armor completely. He fought like he was in a bar brawl. He stamped down on clawed feet, and threw his helmet back to connect with a head that couldn't be concussed. What happened next took him by surprise. His armor emitted a kind of electrical pulse like a shock round or an old-fashioned taser, breaking him free enough to half turn and wrap his left arm around the shoulders of the creature. He freed his right fist.

His weapon forgotten, his body becoming the weapon, Kekoa pounded the arms and shoulders of the alien repeatedly with the spiked fists of his gauntlets until it could no longer physically hold him. His armored feet met the dusty ground again and he turned to face it, punching it repeatedly until it fell backward. Kekoa leaned over the downed alien, ready to beat it to death, when it kicked out to send him sprawling. It flew to its feet faster than anything had a right to move with a torso riddled with deep wounds that poured black gore. With the remaining right claws it pulled back a savage blow, winding it up to punch clean through any material in the known galaxy.

Brandt's shots came in steady, controlled double-taps, thumping into the creature where it was most damaged and forcing it back. Its armor absorbed more punishment than it could withstand, making the thing falter.

"Stay down!" Specter yelled.

He appeared in the entrance at a dead run, barreling into the alien like it had stepped in front of a fast-moving ground transport. It disappeared out of the other side of the tent as the two figures rolled to their feet. Specter ducked under the first wild blow that seemed capable of decapitating him even through his armor, rising up as the blade activated from his left greave to sever the claw that had swung at him. The blade pulled back as he leaned away from the answering backswing. Specter dropped to one knee as he swung his right arm in a wide arc, activating the other melee weapon and cutting through the leg with enough force to make the Va'alen warrior fall and lash out with the other leg. Specter stepped back out of range and drew both pistols before unloading them in rapid-fire bursts from a devastatingly short range.

The Va'alen warrior didn't last long. The combined fire from their weapons had cooked the thing inside the armor. Black, oily fluid bubbled out of the holes the Hawaiian had punched deep into it. It dropped backward, knees bending as the heavy torso flopped over to leave it lying in the dirt at a grotesque angle. In the sudden silence the team heard a shout that chilled them all.

"Admiral!" Torres yelled. "Dassiova, can you hear me? Dammit, Elias, stay with me!"

"Get the hell outta my way," Turner yelled out as he piled in. He swapped rifle for emergency medical kit, as he slid to his knees beside the wounded officer.

"How bad?" Brandt demanded. She pointed two fingers at her eyes in front of Payne before gesturing for her to watch the hopefully dead alien.

"Bad," Turner said. "Deep laceration to the abdominal area. Intestinal ruptures… everywhere… I think damage to the liver, too. Commander, I can't treat this here; he needs surgery RFN."

"Torres, you hurt?" Brandt asked as Turner was pumping the admiral full of various drugs. He unsealed what looked like industrial grade plastic wrap to keep Dassiova's guts where nature intended them to be.

"N…no," he stammered, fresh blood streaked over his face and hands. He had been tending to the admiral's wounds in the most basic way possible: simply applying pressure.

"Good," Turner said, taking command. "Help me get him to the dropship. I need a medevac gurney." He didn't stop what he was doing; he was applying field medicine and controlling the HUD menus with his eyes.

True multitasking.

"I'll bring one," Beale answered.

"Agent Crawford?" Turner called out without moving his head to search for her. "Sound off!"

Brandt turned to the collapsed section of the tent and lifted the canvas before dropping it quickly.

"God dammit," she cursed.

"She hurt?" Turner wanted to know. "How bad is she? Can you describe the wound to me?"

"KIA," Brandt said quietly.

"You sure?" Turner asked. "She breathing?"

"She's KIA, Turner," Brandt said in a firm, low voice. She knew something was horribly wrong when she lifted the canvas and saw an upturned palm beside the woman's boot. Though similar to the injury Dassiova suffered, Crawford had taken a much harder hit and was cut in half.

Literally cut in half.

Beale burst into the tent carrying a folded-down field gurney, which Turner snatched and began rigging up. He directed the lieutenant and the commander to assist him like they were junior listings.

"I need that dropship fired up and ready to fly direct to the *Indomitable*," Brandt ordered over the net. "Zero, cry out if you see anything heading our way." She didn't need to tell him what to do but she said it anyway to reassure the others that the vaunted sniper was their overwatch. "We're working on the assumption that we've lost the *Corvus* and have no orbital firepower. Payne?"

"Commander," Payne acknowledged.

"Get me a comm to the flagship. I don't care how." Dassiova, barely conscious, came out of the tent on the floating gurney. His wounds dripped blood onto the dusty ground only for it to be swallowed up instantly and leave a tiny dark mark wherever it fell.

"Torres," he grumbled weakly. When he coughed, he showed the younger officer what that did to a person's internal organs.

"Here, Admiral," Torres said reassuringly. "You just hold on, sir."

"Torres," Dassiova grumbled slightly louder. "Shut your mouth a second and listen. Don't trust…"

"You'll be alright," Torres told him again before the older man's hand gripped his arm with surprising force, given that his stomach was merely held together by a clear film.

"Command… authority override," Dassiova said into Torres's comm device as his own was lost somewhere inside the ruined tent.

"Transfer command authority to Torres, Captain Kyle…" He uttered his words carefully with a labored breath in between each. "Authorization… Dassiova… Lunar… twelve… four… six."

"Command authority transfer accepted, Admiral Dassiova. Captain Torres, command authority of the carrier *Indomitable* has been transferred to you. Would you like to review the current mission status and crew rost—"

"Cancel," Torres interrupted the automated voice so that it stopped talking to him.

Torres looked at Dassiova, trying to figure out why he had given the fleet flagship to him when he had two subordinate commanders already serving there in addition to the flight officer. He wouldn't get any answers; a combination of the drugs Turner had pumped into him along with the stress and the severe blood loss had knocked the admiral into unconsciousness.

"You need to go with him," Brandt said, pushing Torres along with the gurney. "Send us down an extraction bird. We'll hold the fort until we can burn the tech and the intel here. Go." Torres hesitated. "Go!"

He went, sitting beside Turner who was keeping the admiral alive. He took one last look back as the ramp closed to see a woefully small band of troops holding a flat hilltop.

CHAPTER 24

Deep Orbit of Gaia Néos

"Multiple contacts unshrouding," cried one of the French tactical officers onboard the bridge of the *Neptune*.

"Weapons armed," another officer shouted in French-accented English. "Inbound jump signatures detected!"

"Shields to full," Admiral Vernay said. She spoke in a cool voice that was the polar opposite of how she felt inside. "Launch all gun barges into defense pattern Omega, orders to target everything not broadcasting UN identification."

Those treacherous bastards, she thought, feeling the slightest bit justified in her thoughts of 'I told you so'. It had to be them, the so-called Middle Eastern Alliance, and she saw no way they could survive the conflict. Not unless the separatists had recruited the full support of the Va'alen.

"Any contact from the negotiations?" she asked her comm officer.

"Nothing," the younger woman called back, pausing as the ship rocked slightly. They were suffering the impact of ordnance against the outer layer of their retrofitted shields. "I can't raise the *Corvus*, which was providing planetary bombardment cover to th—"

"I know what the *Corvus* was doing, Lieutenant, thank you. Tactical, target and engage any ship firing on us. And I want to know where their flagship is."

"Admiral," another officer answered, "the *Weapon of God* is on the far side of the planet."

"Understood. Comm? Get the *Hammer* and the *Vengeance* back here immediately to join the fight."

Her order was acknowledged and the admiral silently cursed herself for sending away the heavily armed warships to do deep reconnaissance patrols.

"Outer shields just absorbed three singularity warhead collapses, Admiral," an officer at the weapons station reported. "They're gone. Down to seventy-five percent shields."

"Return fire, railguns and pulse cannons only. Give them hell."

The battle raged for a few minutes until the shielding and thick armor-plated hulls of the MEA ships were eroded and the enemy vessels were destroyed or driven away. Maneuvering a carrier in a dogfight was an irrelevant impossibility; the ship was so large it couldn't hope to evade anything unless it jumped. The gun barges moved in concentric figure-eights around the mothership, drawing fire and sending out vicious streaks of cannon fire at the enemy in return.

As the red icons on Vernay's display satisfyingly reduced in number, a shout made her heart drop.

"Incoming signals from the surface!"

"How many?" the admiral snapped, speaking more harshly than she intended. She had a sudden realization and fear that the Va'alen were a fundamental part of this betrayal.

"Too many to discern individual targets," the tactical officer said.

"Get me fleetwide," Vernay said, waiting a heartbeat for the nod of confirmation. "All UN forces in the Centauri System, this is Admiral Denise Vernay in command of the Tenth Fleet onboard the *Neptune*. I am declaring all MEA forces to be hostile. Destroy or force the unconditional surrender of every MEA asset. All Va'alen elements are hostile. Repeat: I am ending the ceasefire with the Va'alen. All orbital ships commence bombardment of Va'alen base and withdraw to engage enemy ships in fleet formation. Vernay out."

The temperature on the bridge of the *Neptune* dropped. Their senior officer had just declared war on not one group but two, one of them human, in a single announcement. If she was wrong about any of it the consequences stretched much further than simply the end of her career.

"I want an update on Dassiova and his ship," Vernay ordered. "And while you are doing that, send a dozen heavy payload nukes to the Va'alen base as a personal thank you from the crew of the *Neptune*."

—

"Clear a path," Turner yelled. "Gangway, dammit!"

Torres watched as the medic, minus his helmet, scattered crewmembers aside in his bid to get Dassiova into an operating theater some time last week. It was a fight he couldn't affect, couldn't influence in any meaningful way, so instead Torres made his way to the bridge.

His bridge.

He walked fast but didn't rush in a panic. Panic had a tendency to multiply in confined spaces with people under stress. He felt muted vibrations under his feet as the massive ship's shield absorbed hits. He was absorbed coming up with the best way to walk into the nerve center of a flagship carrier and announce to a crew who didn't know him that he was now their commanding officer.

Dassiova's words shook him still, resonating inside his head like an untethered datapad in zero gravity. Who was he not to trust? The

MEA? The Va'alen? That much was obvious, but what if he meant someone else? Torres had to hope that the admiral would pull through, that he would survive whatever emergency surgery he was enduring. In the meantime, Torres promised himself—he paused to look at the dried blood on his hand as he scanned his way onto the bridge—he would do his best to keep the ship intact and in the fight.

He stepped onto the bridge. The nearest officer noticed his bloodied appearance with sudden fear and twitched a hand to his sidearm instinctively.

"Stand down, Lieutenant," Torres said.

"Sir?" The lieutenant squeaked weakly. Before he could say any more, the commander in what Dassiova always called 'the big chair' turned to regard the dust-and blood-covered stranger walking onto his bridge.

"Commander Torres?" he said. "Can we help you?"

Torres decided that plain facts were his best tools. "Commander, the admiral is injured, and has transferred interim command authority to me." He added the concept of 'interim' as a placatory measure, hoping that the bridge crew would accept his appointment during a battle. None of the crew seemed concerned, but the officer running the bridge wasn't having it.

"No, sir," he said as he turned back to the displays. "This is my bridge. You're welcome to observe if you insis—"

"Mainframe," Torres interrupted firmly. "Confirm transfer of all command codes to me."

"Confirmed," the synthesized voice responded immediately. "Full command authority has been granted to Captain Torres."

The officer now relieved of command stared open-mouthed as the shabby new captain stepped closer to the chair and raised an expectant eyebrow. The commander stood, hesitantly at first, and stepped aside.

"The bridge is yours, sir."

Torres sat, feeling the weight of the chair on his shoulders instead of the other way around, and glanced at the console beside his right arm.

"Tactical, report."

"Shields at eighty-six percent," the officer answered. "Barges in a holding pattern. Currently under attack by two MEA cruisers and sensors have a frigate inbound."

"Barges into defense pattern beta," Torres ordered. He needed the eight gun ships orbiting the carrier to fly two concentric circles around the length of them and fire on anything not friendly. "Cannon batteries to target the cruisers but no warheads to be fired inside a fifty-thousand kilometer radius of our outer shields. Target all forward railguns on the approach vector of the frigate and prepare to fire…"

His orders were followed, and he sat back, blood-crusted hands brushing more flecks of dark red from his face as he waited to destroy their enemies.

~

"Prep theater immediately," Ensign Curtis said quickly. The coolness in her voice was instantly reassuring, "Turner, you want to assist?"

Turner did. He was ordered to lose the dirt-and blood-covered armor. He stepped to a corner of the medical bay and hit the emergency release function with the forearm screen. He stepped down out of his suit and instantly staggered, the weakness of his injured leg forgotten by the augmentation his suit had offered. He hissed in pain, snatching up a dermal injector from a tray and twisting the cap until the right dosage of pain inhibitor could be injected into his hip. As he continued to surgery, the dose would seep through the tissue to the nerve cluster and dull the pain he felt.

The flight suit he wore under his armor, standard clothing for personnel onboard, was clean despite his hours spent inside the suit. The older generation of protection he had worn previously would have left him sweaty and smelling stale at best. This prototype suit was so efficient at maintaining the right temperature that he was fresher than many of those who hadn't been to the surface.

"Okay," Curtis announced confidently. "I need all non-essential personnel to clear this room immediately." Faces looked at her blankly. She clapped her hands and ramped up her intensity. "Come on, people, let's go! Move!"

Turner stayed; he assumed he was essential personnel in this case, even though he was a combat medic and didn't have much experience with the nice, clean, sterile operating theaters onboard nearly new fleet carriers.

"Mainframe," Curtis said when only four of them remained inside the room, "seal us in."

The sound of a heavy mechanical lock sliding into place was both unmistakable and ominous. Turner wanted to ask just what in the hell was going on, but Curtis had more important priorities in mind.

"Activate first-stage Nanomites," Curtis instructed

She was passed a large dermal injector nearly double the size of a standard one. She applied the injector to various points of Dassiova's body through the clear plastic wrap as Turner watched closely. Innumerable questions ran through his mind but the intensity with which the young doctor worked made him hold his breath as he watched. Curtis stopped injecting and waved her gloved right hand in a gesture that brought up a projected screen showing imagery of the patient's abdomen. Tiny red dots the size of pinpricks moved over the image as they flowed like insects along the natural pathways of the body.

"First stage accepted," she said as her eyes flickered over the display. She glanced at the medic and offered an explanation. "There's no guarantee it works. Sometimes the Nanomites fail to activate for no obvious reason."

"But they're working now, right?" Turner asked with concern. He vaguely wondered why that was his first question and not asking what the hell Nanomites were. He knew enough to assume it was some kind of microscopic medical bot technology and just went with it.

"Appears that way," Curtis said. "But there's a helluva ways to go yet. Prep me some antivirals and rig up more fluids; he ain't outta the woods just yet."

"You want antibiotics too?"

"No need," Curtis said. "Just the IV and antivirals." Turner did as he was instructed. As a combat medic he was geared for this almost on autopilot: preventing shock through a loss of blood and making sure that wounds weren't at risk of infection. The problem with open wounds was that they had a habit of attracting the nastiest little particles of just about anything and seemed hell-bent on getting infected. Infection would mean a slower and far more painful death if left untreated than simply bleeding out while unconscious.

The flip side was that so many people in the past had relied on antibiotics unnecessarily. This had created entire generations of people with natural immunities to the drugs so only a few of those medicines still worked effectively.

After being one of the greatest discoveries in the history of medical science, humanity had overused and abused that power to render it almost pointless.

"The Nanomites will break down and remove any foreign object via the renal system. That takes the infection risk down to below five percent if they're applied fast enough, which I think they have been here. No need to waste antibiotics unless there's a secondary infection. What in the hell caused this wound anyway? Looks like he went through a turbine engine."

"Va'alen claw," Turner said simply.

Curtis showed no reaction. "Any other casualties?"

"One," the medic answered flatly. "Straight KIA." He rolled his shoulders and adjusted the weight on his still-injured leg. Curtis noticed and dismissed him.

"You need to rest. Go sit down and monitor the progress from that console." She nodded with her chin as her eyes stayed glued to the holo-display in front of her.

"Waiting game now, boys," she muttered half to herself. "Just a big ol' bag of wait and see."

⁓

Deep in the protected bowels of the carrier where the med bay was located, they could barely detect the signs that a battle was raging outside in the empty void of space.

MEA ships of all variants, even some previously unknown, had jumped into the system, appeared out of Fold space or dropped their shrouds to unleash hell on the UN fleet without warning.

The battle was in the favor of the ambushers at first, given the advantageous edge of a surprise betrayal. However, as the more combat-experienced crews of the UN ships, with the greater numbers, got their heads into the fight, that tide turned heavily against the separatist alliance.

That was when their new allies joined the fight.

Those Va'alen ships that could no longer fly, those that had been damaged or cannibalized to keep vital systems running on the planet's surface, had their guns combined and pointed at the skies.

It was hardly as devastating as the orbital railguns they should have used, but any attempt to build one even under cover would have resulted in orbital bombardments by their jailers.

If nothing else, the constant fire from the surface, no matter how weak, served as a distraction while over two hundred Va'alen ships left the surface.

Swarming was their style in combat. Every ship hit by pulse cannon fire or sucked into a collapsing singularity and crushed into nothingness prompted another ship. Each new arrival would turn its nose to the nearest human vessel and accelerate hard in search of revenge and salvation from the severed link to the pilot's lost mate.

One attack wing of aliens flew up to find a huge human ship appear out of nothing directly ahead of them. Their awe at the magical technology was short lived. Streaking cobalt blue bolts of railgun slugs the size of a Va'alen warrior stuck the ship. Its shields shimmered and flickered out before subsequent shots ripped through the hull of the ship at impossible velocities. The ship was torn apart without mercy.

The scattering debris of the ship took out two Va'alen vessels, but the others turned to the origin of the shots and burned hard to find humans to kill.

The orbit of Gaia Néos and the deeper space surrounding it had become a firework display of death and treachery. Among that confusion, a lone dropship docked with one of the three huge carrier ships. A dozen alien vessels approached at slow speeds, indicating it wasn't an attack run.

They maintained a steady velocity and four of the ships towed a large cube adorned with rolling scrolls of hieroglyphs.

~

"You have the alien overlord?" General Chakour demanded of the black-armored shape as it stepped down the ramp. The shape nodded once, showing less deference and respect than Chakour liked but the situation hardly dictated he could issue a reprimand or punishment.

He turned his attention to a subordinate officer instead. "Are our new allies arriving?"

"General," the officer answered with a small bow. Such display made Chakour feel a lot happier. "They have been diverted to docking bay four as they are towing something larger than their ships."

"It will be their other overlord," Chakour announced loudly, trying to impress everyone listening with his sharp intellect. It didn't occur to him that such intelligence was just a repetition of facts he had been given by someone else.

"We will greet them there." He turned to the leader of the strike team who intimidated him with a blank, helmeted stare.

"Bring the other one. They will want to see it immediately to know that we have kept our side of the agreement."

He fought down the thought that his superiors had forced a deal with the devil on him and led the way.

CHAPTER 25

Docking Bay Onboard the Weapon of God

Chakour told himself he would not bow. As terrified as he was by the sheer size and brutal violence promised even by their still form, the general forced himself not to show fear or repulsion in front of his crew when the Va'alen stepped onto his deck.

The arrival of the ships made the air on their side of the shielding fill with excitement and trepidation. He could almost smell it.

The outer blast doors closed and the air inside re-pressurized. The shielding separating the humans from their new allies flickered out when deactivated.

Chakour paced forward, his face displaying an arrogant pride that was almost entirely false to mask his fear. He stopped in front of the lowering rear ramps of the bulbous, insectoid ships.

A loud hissing sound came from the large cube, which hovered just above the deck. From a circular opening the Hive Lord descended without touching the ground. Its wide, dark eyes scanned the massive hangar deck until it zeroed in on the floating gurney amidst the black-armored humans. It turned its head slightly, making no sound but prompting four Va'alen warriors to run forward and scatter the humans with a flurry of yelps and shouts of alarm.

The lead warrior stopped in front of the one armored human who hadn't moved. He stood directly in front of the gurney hovering still on the tiny repulsers and looked up, craning his neck to look directly at the warrior.

The alien stepped around him, still keeping a careful watch as multiple limbs of the warriors reverently moved the comatose alien back toward the other Hive Lord.

Chakour cleared his throat. "On behalf of the Middle Eastern Allia—"

He stopped speaking as the biggest warrior, their leader, turned on him and issued a clicking growl. Chakour swallowed, his face still trying not to show fear and failing under the malevolent gaze of an ally he would not have freely chosen.

If he had his way, if his recommendations had been listened to, the general would have bombarded the interned aliens into dust and picked out any useful technology from the wreckage. His superiors, safe in their palaces back on Earth and making decisions with no regard for either the lives or the deaths of those making that sacrifice, had denied his request and insinuated cowardice on his part. He knew it had nothing to do with bravery or cowardice, but as the MEA were denied extra-terrestrial knowledge, they were eager to gain their own technological edge by any means.

Their option had been to ally themselves with the Va'alen and offer to rescue as many of their kind as possible before returning them to their home system.

The MEA still had no idea where that was—the aliens would not share the location of their home worlds until their Hive Lord was safe. Chakour couldn't help feeling as though they had made too risky a commitment just for the promise of new technology.

They watched as the captured alien was pushed toward the floating overlord who descended and raised both long, bony arms. It began

245

waving its limbs in some form of ritual. The air was utterly devoid of sound; not silence but almost the absence of any auditory feed like being in the void of space. Chakour glanced around and saw members of his crew using their hands to try and clear their ears as they would following depressurization. His own ear began to ring with a high-pitched whine and he worked his jaw subtly to try and achieve the popping sensation that he hoped would restore his hearing.

The sleeping alien's arm jerked, then a leg. The Va'alen warriors all knelt and bowed their heads to the deck in the direction of the two tall, floating aliens. The jerking limbs moved faster until, with an almost explosive effect, it sat up like a victim of drowning taking a deep gulp of air.

The sound of normal silence returned to the room, only to be replaced by a low, rumbling clicking noise emanating from the bowed Va'alen. It was as though they were praying. The alien who had revived what Chakour somehow knew was its mate half turned again and the warriors all stood to draw the wicked curved blades from behind their backs.

Rifles were raised and shouts of alarm filled the docking bay before the biggest warrior turned to Chakour.

"We do not threaten you," he hissed in English, which confused many of the nervous humans. "My warriors are showing their fealty to our Lords."

"Lower your guns," Chakour croaked in abject fear, hoping that his voice sounded normal. "These are our allies now."

Without a word, the warriors all stood and sheathed their blades after few more moments of tense silence. The large warrior turned to Chakour again.

"My people will take this area as our own," he said, taking control. "There will be more ships coming, and my engineers will have control of the docking bay controls."

"I... I..." Chakour stuttered. "I cannot allow that. My people must retain control of vital ship systems at all times."

"This is no longer a negotiation," Muq Da'kath said simply.

"Consider it a demonstration of trust that you will not vent my warriors into space. Do this for me and I will show you where our home worlds are."

Chakour, backed into a corner and forced to make a decision on the spot, snapped his fingers for an aide to run to his side.

"Isolate controls for the outer docking bay shields and doors only," he instructed in his native Arabic. It was his only way to converse in private before he switched back to English. "Show our new allies how to operate the controls. This docking bay is now the temporary home of the Va'alen, who we are proud to call our friends." He turned to Da'kath and smiled.

Da'kath, shocked at how easily the humans were manipulated, gave the small man a respectful bow and smiled to himself.

~

"Can we raise anyone left on the surface?" Torres asked of the comm officer he had tasked to get Brandt on the line.

"Negative, Captain. Too much interference."

"Tactical," Torres said as he tried another idea. "Can we launch dropships?"

"Negative, sir," the tactical officer said. "Not without deactivating the automated point defense cannon system and with this many enemy around I wouldn't recommend that. A dropship would be a sitting duck out there right now."

Dammit, Torres thought before another report snatched his mind away.

"Incoming wave of Va'alen fighters!"

"Screw this," Torres said. "Comm, standby to recall all gun barges. Helm, prepare a micro-jump one hundred thousand kilometers into the nearest patch of empty orbit." He waited until his orders, as bizarre as they seemed, were acknowledged. Jumping a carrier was no small feat given its size, and doing micro-jumps was a tactic for small recon ships and cruisers, not capital flagships.

"Sir," the helmsman said.

Torres looked over at a man he recognized, tall and well-built with a shaved head and clever eyes.

"What is it, Mister Moon?"

"I've found a spot, but it won't give us the time and space to launch dropships. Suggestion?"

"Speak your mind, Lieutenant."

"I can jump her in as close to the atmosphere as possible within reach of the target site and hold us there just long enough to get off a combat drop."

Torres thought about it hard for a few seconds.

"Get me the Chief of ground troops," he ordered one of the comm officers.

"Channel open," she said a second later.

"Chief, this is Captain Torres in interim command of the *Indomitable*. Do you copy?"

"Chief here, sir," the man answered, his voice taking Torres back years in an instant. "I was apprised of your command authority automatically. What do you need?"

"How quickly can you prepare personnel for an atmospheric combat drop to reinforce troops isolated on the surface?"

A long pause followed the unusual question.

"I have only twenty personnel rated for such an operation. I can have them ready in… four minutes."

"Understood," Torres shot back. "Four minutes. Torres out." He turned back to his pilot. "Four minutes, Lieutenant. Make it happen."

"Aye, sir," the pilot said. He rolled his neck on his shoulders to limber up for some highly unrecommended moves.

~

"We've got incoming," Zero warned from his elevated position. "Multiple ground transports and two fighter ships. Not flying at altitude though."

"Start sending our compliments," Brandt ordered. She heard the huge booming twang of the railgun as it fired rhythmically toward the approaching enemy attack.

"Contact rear!" Beale cried out a little too loudly over the channel in his surprise and fear.

There was a pause that should have been filled with enemy numbers and their disposition.

"Report?" Brandt snapped.

"Multiple contacts advancing on foot. Approaching fast!"

"I'll go," Specter said. He instinctively knew that Brandt needed the rear position bolstered with a level head and more firepower. She nodded her thanks. Beale and his three CP troops, no matter how well-trained and experienced, would feel better with the UN's secret super soldier backing them up.

"Payne, strip that dropship fast and get us ready to fly," Brandt instructed.

"Who is going to—"

"Specter can fly it," she interrupted her. "Now go."

"Zero," Brandt called, "put up your drone so we can all take a look." He gave no acknowledgement. He never spoke unless he had to. It was one of his best attributes. In a moment, the HUDs on all of the team's suits gave them a pop-up window in the lower left side as he shared the drone feed.

"Go do your thing, Bart," Zero muttered to himself. The drone activated and popped up from the pod on the back of his shoulder.

The drone flew fast, heading upward out of the back of their sniper's shoulder as it began painting targets on the battlefield. Those targets, outlined and recognized in an instant, gave everyone small glowing targets on their view inside their helmets. Brandt immediately regretted the decision to link the drone to the squad feed as she spun a slow three-sixty.

"Aah, crap," someone muttered.

"There appears to be quite a few of them," Zero reported dryly.

Their commander took in the mass of infantry behind their position and the vehicular assault approaching from the front.

"Could really do with that orbital bombardment capability right now, huh, Commander?" Payne asked in a surprisingly calm tone.

"It'd be nice," Brandt admitted. "But nice wasn't what we signed up for."

"Speak for yourself," Specter answered, suddenly more Jake than his cybernetic soldier alter ego.

A strange calm overtook them then. That calm was punctuated by the steady firing of railgun slugs from Zero's big rifle until a warning flashed over their feeds.

INCOMING ORDNANCE. RECOMMEND HARD COVER.

"Mortars," Zero yelled. The whistling sound screeched through the air to impact the dropship and engulf it in a blossoming gout of flame and black smoke.

"Payne!" Brandt shouted, looking at her HUD and confused by her vital signs.

"Daisy!" Zero echoed. "You still with us, kid?"

"I swear," Payne's voice came back strained after a pause. "You call me that again and you'll find that gun of yours giving you a rail-slug enema."

"She's fine," Zero announced over the comm.

"I'm in one piece," Payne confirmed. "But the dropship is toast."

Nobody got the chance to answer as another whistling round began to shriek in its descent toward their flat hilltop.

"Cover!" Brandt yelled.

The commander heard and felt the impact a fraction of a second before a much larger and more distant series of thudding booms echoed out over the dusty plain.

~

"Jump," Torres ordered. Instantly he felt the lurch of the ship's grav emitters working overtime to compensate for appearing back in real space too close to a planet.

"Bridge to drop team. Launch."

"Launching now," a familiar voice answered. Torres ignored the pang in his chest as he realized his order had just sent Eze to the surface to face whatever hell was happening down there.

"Tactical, report on the ground situation."

"Multiple vehicle contacts converging in convoy on the site, sir."

"Safe targeting solution?" Torres barked the question, agonizing over the few seconds it took to get the answer.

"Yes, sir."

"Ten seconds," Moon called out from the helm. "Then we either jump or get torn up in the atmosphere."

"Fire a salvo, target the vehicles with pulse cannons. Do it now!"

"Aye, sir," the tactical officer reported. He typed furiously to complete the targeting solution.

"Chief reports all jumpers away, Captain," said the comm officer.

"Acknowledged," Torres said.

"Salvo fired!"

"Jump us now!"

~

"Report!" Brandt said as she stood to shake the rubble and dust from her armor.

"Targets destroyed," Zero answered. "I only see one ground transport moving but it's damaged."

"Understood," Brandt said, grateful for whatever divine intervention had just saved them from being bombed and overrun. "Report rear?"

"Concentrated enemy infantry," Beale's voice came back, slightly calmer than before. "Still ahead of maximum range."

"Zero, care to address that?"

"I've got three rounds for the railgun, Commander."

"Dammit," Brandt said. She allowed the pressure of the situation to temporarily lower her leadership standards.

"So, I should target the leaders…?" Zero asked as a suggestion.

"Do it," Brandt answered. She spun to survey the panorama and figure out where best to counter the unstoppable arrival of too many red outlines. As she spun, a green arrow appeared on her HUD pointing up. She dismissed it; she thought it was detecting Zero in his tower. But when she carried on spinning, she saw their sniper outlined in green in the prone firing position. The arrow was still there, but now it was joined by three more. Then five. Then the entire upper limit of her display was bristling with moving green arrows until she craned her neck back to look up.

Just then the comm crackled into life. "Grip, Viper. Come in."

CHAPTER 26

Bridge of The Indomitable

"Sir," interrupted the tactical officer. "Long-range sensors are showing... uh..."

"Showing what?" Torres asked, trying not to sound frustrated.

"I'm... I'm not sure, sir."

Torres hit the console beside him. The sensors showed the MEA flagship, Chakour's carrier, seemingly in contact with Va'alen fighters. The red dots of the enemy ships approached the larger, green icon of the MEA ship that hadn't yet been reprogrammed to turn red for the transition from ally to treacherous assholes.

The Va'alen weren't attacking, though. If they were, their signals would be darting about in seemingly random patterns and not flying in neat, straight lines.

Torres briefly thought it must be a mass suicide run, but if that were the case why weren't they flying at maximum speed?

"They're... docking," a voice said from beside him.

He turned to see the commander he had relieved only minutes ago pouring over the data feed.

"Bastards," Torres spat. "Lieutenant Moon plot a jump ahead of that carrier. Comm, recall all barges. Tactical, prepare a full payload of warheads and standby all guns and rail cannons. Those bastards aren't jumping out on my goddamned watch!"

"We must leave before the UN target our ship," Chakour's aide insisted.

"Not without docking all of the aliens first," Chakour exploded angrily. He repeated his orders to the junior officer. The man had been assigned that role due to family and financial connections despite his young age and low rank. The general knew the aide was speaking out of fear but giving orders to his general should have been the greater concern.

"They're aboard, General," an officer shouted.

"Prepare to jump us out of here," Chakour said as he took his command chair, his throne. He suddenly felt he lacked the authority to sit there.

"Where to, General?"

"Anywhere but here!" Chakour erupted again. Any patience he had had with the unthinking fools that now made his life infinitely more difficult eroded to nothing.

"Jump plotted," he heard.

He relaxed slightly.

"Incoming jump signature!" shrieked an officer manning a sensor station. "It's the UNS *Indomitable*. They're firing on us!"

"Jump now!" Chakour roared, closing his eyes.

"Enemy in range."

"Open fire!" Torres cried out. He watched on the large viewscreen as the magnified image of the ship so similar to Dassiova's. To *his*.

As the ship shuddered under the combined might of the destructive power launching, he watched in horror as the *Weapon of God* disappeared in a muted, dull flash of light.

Silence filled the bridge.

"They've…" The officer trailed off.

"I'm aware, Tactical," Torres said flatly. "I'm aware."

He stood, turned to the commander beside him and asked if he would take command. He gave the instructions to get them back into the fight and mop up every last Va'alen and MEA ship left standing. He turned for Dassiova's quarters and called out to the comm officer.

"Get me Admiral Vernay, please."

~

"I'm a little busy right now, Commander," Vernay said, as she ran a series of battles from her bridge. Her losses were devastating, and far worse than she would have imagined. They hadn't expected the inclusion of the Va'alen ships. Their intelligence had clearly been incorrect as to how many of the alien ships were still operational as fighters.

"It's Captain, Admiral," Torres clarified. "I've been given command authority of the *Indomitable*."

Vernay said nothing. She wasn't sure how to respond; her initial thought was that the man young enough to be her son. And now his bony backside sat in the command chair where an admiral's more befitting behind should be.

"I need to update you about the MEA flagship," he said.

"Then speak, *Captain*," Vernay responded, more icily than she meant to.

"They've docked a bunch of Va'alen ships and jumped away. We were seconds from engaging them when they escaped—"

"You have no time to dwell on this, Captain," Vernay snapped in her smooth voice. "As the ranking officer of the UN forces in this sector, I am assuming command of all ships."

She didn't wait for agreement. It wasn't the place for a junior commander who had fallen into gaining control of a ship far beyond his experience to disagree.

"I want all Va'alen forces destroyed, including any opportunistic shots you can make on the surface, and I want MEA forces captured alive. Is that understood, Captain?"

"Five by five, Admiral," Torres answered, cutting the comm and striding back out onto the bridge.

His bridge.

"New standing orders," Torres announced confidently as the commander vacated the chair wordlessly on his return. "Alien forces are to be destroyed and separatist ships are to be disabled and captured alive wherever possible."

"How do we do that, Captain?" the officer at tactical asked.

"Target their engines, shield generators, and Fold Drive emitters, at a guess, Lieutenant," Torres answered patiently. He made a mental note to replace the man with someone who possessed a second brain cell to keep the other one company.

"Aye, sir. Adjusting targeting parameters."

"Incoming flight of four Va'alen fighters, port side!" called out another member of the bridge crew.

Torres looked at the display beside his chair. He saw the four red dots; they were really just little icons attributed to the enemy ships but too small to make out within the larger picture.

Torres said nothing. He had to steel himself to the mindset that he wasn't onboard a small recon ship or commanding a light cruiser. He trusted his now-enormous crew—not that he knew them or that they knew him—to do their jobs well.

"Number three and number seven barges engaging enemy…"

He watched as one of the red dots blinked out and another accelerated away from the undamaged, surviving pair. Torres's eyes mapped the trajectory to the upper level of orbiting ships around his carrier, the number three barge, as the red dot lined up a suicide run. He almost called out an order until another voice cut over the tense air on the bridge in a calm tone.

"Adjusting battery fire to compensate for the kamikaze," she said, almost unconcerned.

Torres saw the breakaway dot blink out, small and insignificant against the sheer size of the weapon of war he now commanded.

"Target destroyed," the woman's voice announced. "Adjusting fire to target remaining 'roaches."

Yeah, okay. Torres thought. He recalled Dassiova's words to the flight officer who annoyed him when he had last been aboard, *You get to call them 'roaches with a stone-cold, hard-ass demeanor like that.*

"Get some!" he called out, as the remaining two red dots vanished from his display.

Instantly realizing his outburst was unbecoming of a carrier captain, Torres straightened himself in his seat and muttered an apology to his bridge crew. His chief pilot chuckled.

"Nah, we're cool with that, Captain," Moon said. "It's just good to know you give a shit like us regular people!"

"Oh, I give a shit, Lieutenant," Torres answered.

He was suddenly more relaxed at the pilot's words; hopefully the crew would learn to trust him quickly. He knew the pilot's words had been a gamble. Torres might have been the kind of asshole officer who didn't allow other ranks to speak to him informally no matter what the situation. His response went a long way to letting his new crew know exactly the kind of officer he was.

"Four jump signatures detected," the officer on sensors called out.

"Ours or theirs?" Torres asked. He realized he hadn't heard or seen anything of the *Hammer* or the *Vengeance* since getting back from the surface.

"Standby," the officer on sensors announced coolly. "Dropping into real space now. Two of ours and two of theirs. Enemy firing on us."

"Sir, we're being hailed..." called the comm officer.

"On screen," Torres said. A second later the screen ahead of him came alive with side-by-side windows showing both Hayes and Halstead. Both seemed shocked not to see Dassiova there, and Torres's heart sank.

"Dassiova's hurt bad," he told them quickly. "He's given me the *Indomitable*."

"What about your cruiser?" Hayes asked.

"She..." Torres sucked in an emotional breath. He had learned the tragic facts from the battle report when he first sat in Dassiova's chair. "She's gone."

"Destroyed?" Halstead asked, real pain in her voice.

"Yes. Anyway, we've got these two. Reckon you can glass the surface for us? Brandt and her team are still down there in contact."

Both captains glanced away from Torres as they caught the eyes of each other in their respective views. Both said they could.

"Be safe," Hayes said before signing off. "Call us back if you need us." Torres nodded and cut the feed before returning his attention to his bridge crew.

"No warheads, pulse cannon batteries only. Disable those frigates," he said.

He knew with absolute certainty that it would be done.

He knew such heavily armed and armored ships wouldn't fold against the might of his carrier as quickly as the relatively miniscule Va'alen ships had; their strength was in their swarm-like numbers. The enemy frigates were too well armored, too well equipped to go down quickly. He was counting on that.

"Target their Fold Drive emitters and forward shields first," he ordered.

He watched on screen as pulsating waves of bright cannon fire impacted the lead frigate directly on the nose. There was a ripple effect moving back through the ship before it exploded spectacularly.

"Disabled," Torres reminded the crew. "Not annihilated with extreme prejudice."

"Sorry, sir," the officer on one of the gun stations said. "I… I don't know what happened."

"Their shield harmonics weren't calibrated correctly," said a female voice from a duty station to his left.

"And you are?" Torres asked.

"Petty Officer First Class Judge, Captain," she responded. "Shield harmonics engineer."

"Explain it to me like I'm a guy who spent the majority of his career ground-pounding."

"Sir," Judge said patiently. "If their shields were wired up right, the energy absorbed from our weapons impacts should dissipate through heat syncs and rechargers. I'd guess they hit a feedback loop directly into the singularity power generators and overloaded them, which is easy to do, and that's why they went boom. Either that or the energy fed back through a series of failed capacitors into their battery banks and started a cascading overload, which would achieve the same eventuality. Boom."

"Thanks," Torres said. "Way to simplify. Tac? Target engines on the other one; let's see if we could *not* make them go"—he shot a slightly amused look at the shield engineer—"boom?"

"Aye, sir," the tactical officer said. "Targeting main engines of the second frigate."

"Incoming warheads!"

This time Torres couldn't help himself but take over control.

"Divert power to forward shields," he shouted. "Helm, all stop and take us back."

He knew a stop and reverse maneuver wouldn't be a huge success in a ship of that size. He couldn't help it, though. It felt better to do *something* than to do nothing. Torres felt the ship shudder and saw his display blink out of focus and back in a position very different from what he had expected.

"Mister Moon," Torres said carefully. "Did, err... did you just micro-jump us ten thousand kilometers?"

"Nine thousand, Captain," Moon said coolly. "It was quicker than changing direction."

"Well... alright then," Torres said. "Target their engines and shut them down."

His orders were carried out and he watched the display screen in satisfaction as the ship tumbled end over end. "Captain Torres to Chief," he called on the comm.

"Chief here, go ahead."

"Chief, prepare a boarding party to secure that dead frigate."

"My pleasure, Captain," the Chief said; his tone promised violence.

CHAPTER 27

UN Held Plateau, Gaia Néos

"I'm out," Zero announced flatly. He lay down the railgun with the barrel angling upward on its bipod. He rose to one knee and picked up the smaller battle rifle to start picking out other targets.

The sniper didn't have to look too hard; three warriors were already breaking out of the pack to sprint ahead, all three enraged at the deaths of their mates. Rifle fire began to sound from the rear position as Beale, Specter and the three others opened up with carefully aimed shots.

"Viper, Grip," Brandt said over the radio as she craned her neck back even further. She tried to see the green outlines of friendly troops dropping in. "What the hell are you doing here?"

"You're not pleased to see us?" Eze quipped. "You have a large concentration of enemy closing on your position from the north east."

"We know," Brandt said. "We're engaging them. What's your drop ETA?"

"No, another wave behind that first attack in dead ground. Forty seconds," Eze said.

She read directly from her HUD as the countdown to her suit's retro-repulsers fired automatically to arrest her descent. That would give them time to arrive and get into position before the Va'alen made the climb up to the plateau. The commander pushed the thought of a second wave aside until they'd figured out how to survive the first.

"Count twenty?" Brandt confirmed.

"Count a hell of a lot more than twenty," Eze answered.

"I meant reinforcements," the commander said. "Twenty of you?"

"Affirmative," Eze responded. "All of our trained drop troops."

Brandt cursed silently at the dearth of troops certified for orbital drop. She had gained her qualification as part of CP training, as had Zero and, she assumed, Beale and the three troops he had brought along. She had to assume that Eze's contingent of reinforcements were either former or current CP or maybe just a collection of soldiers who enjoyed atmospheric re-entry for thrills, though she sure as hell didn't find the process pleasant.

"Station your team at the north approach," Brandt said. "I'll meet you there."

"Who will cover the southern approach?" Eze asked.

"We got a lucky hit from orbit, didn't we?"

"As I can see from the wreckage," Eze shot back. "But you have more incoming behind them. There is infantry but also some kind of large gun from what I can see. My targeting software does not recognize it."

"Aaahhh shit," Zero called out, after looking past the wreckage of the attack convoy. "She's right, Commander. My guess is some kind of dismounted ship's cannon they've rigged up as an artillery piece."

"Can you take it out?" Brandt asked.

"Not from here," Zero told her regretfully. "And not without the railgun."

"Williams, Lorenzo," Eze's voice snapped over the channel. "Adjust attitude to occupy the tower. I need effective railgun fire on an improvised heavy weapon being transported on the southern road."

Eze relayed the facts to Brandt's team.

"Commander, I have a two person sniper team angling for the tower. They have a railgun."

"With all due respect, Lieutenant Commander," Zero interrupted in between taking shots with his long-barreled pulse rifle, "might I suggest that team resupply me with their ammo and join the defenses?"

Brandt didn't think it was the time to compare appendage lengths. In spite of how gifted Zero was with a weapon, any trooper on Eze's, or the Chief's, detail who had earned their marksman badge would be more than competent.

"No, Zero," she said. "I want you on me. Payne too. All units, listen in. We have inbound friendlies on orbital drop arriving in ten seconds. They will take the north approach and engage the enemy. When relieved, all of my team to form up on me. Sniper cover will be re-established. Eze? Can you spare me a few troops to bolster the south?"

"Attention drop team," she announced on both channels. "Sniper team to take the tower, all other units to me at the northern approach to relieve existing forces."

She went on to detail four other names and instructed them to report to commander Brandt at the southern approach. Brandt thanked her and zoomed in her view on the growing ball of dust that signaled the approach of even more Va'alen intent on tearing them apart. A panicked noise over the channel snatched their attention away.

"Blackburn!" Eze yelled. "Activate repulsers. You're coming in too fast!"

Brandt flickered her eyes over the comm channels and connected herself to the drop team. Her HUD showed the green outlines of their meager reinforcements slowing down.

With the exception of one.

Shouts filled the airways and the overriding growling, screaming noise of the panicking trooper came through with disturbing clarity.

"Repulsers won't…" He grunted again in terrified frustration. "Repulsers won't fire! I can't… aaaaarh—"

The percussive thump of an armored body hitting the hard-packed dirt at terminal velocity resonated over the still air of the plateau. It was audible even over the incessant sound of weapons fire.

There was no time to dwell on the loss. The echo of the impact was replaced by the whine of repulsers firing en masse and with enough intensity to slow the fall of the remaining nineteen troopers. Boots hit the ground hard; more than one trooper pitched forward to support their landing with an outstretched gauntlet.

"Superhero landing," Brandt whispered to herself. She shot a sad glance at the patch of orange-streaked sky where Rogers and others had been.

"Commander?" Payne asked.

Three troopers ran directly toward Brandt; the rest congregated out of sight behind the burning wreckage of the dropship.

"Roebuck," the first one said as he pointed to his chest, adorned with the two vertical stripes of a petty officer first class. He half turned to indicate the other two joining him. "This is Roberts and Stevens." The two troops, a male and a female, joined them.

Stevens and Roberts both carried heavy items on their backs, which they removed and began to break down.

"Who has the spare barrels?" Roebuck asked them.

"Blackburn did," Stevens replied. She met the NCO's gaze. With an inaudible sigh, she turned and began running over the dusty ground to find the body of the trooper to retrieve the spare barrels for the heavy mounted gun.

Roebuck slammed down the central spike of a contraption that forced the three outer legs to drop down and automatically spin a wide screw from each foot into the ground. Roberts fitted the heavy cannon with three barrels onto the fixed tripod and both men began unloading the spare ammunition crates that were mag-locked to their bodies.

Stevens came running back carrying a set of spare barrels for the gun. The fact that she laid her hands on them so readily spoke to the savagery of the firing the gun underwent or highlighted a propensity for catastrophic failure. Brandt couldn't be sure. Either way, it was sheer luck that Blackburn had landed face down and not on his back to destroy the equipment.

"That thing gonna do much to the 'roaches?" Zero asked as he joined them.

"Twelve-millimeter exploding ordnance, boss," Roberts answered with bravado. He placed the first belt of bullets into the feed tray and slapped down the top cover to lock them in. Finally, he pulled back on the charging handle to prepare the whole process.

"I'll take that as a yes then," Zero said. He turned and assessed the battlefield. "Commander, might I suggest the right flank behind those boulders to offer an oblique firing position to the main gun here?"

Brandt turned and looked, assessing the same battlefield in an instant and coming to the same conclusion.

"Do it," she said before turning back to the three surviving troops who had been allocated to her position. "You got mobile cover on that thing?"

In answer both Stevens and Roberts held up the heavy base plates of the mobile shields.

"Great. We're taking your right flank so don't strafe beyond fifty degrees, got it?"

"Understood, Commander," Roebuck answered.

"Brandt to Eze," she said over the channel.

The deafening sound of heavy firing came back through her helmet until the software automatically dialed it down.

"Here," Eze said. "The enemy cannot break through. For now."

"Hold them," Brandt urged.

The heavy, thumping twang of a railgun slug seared the air above her head. She turned and zoomed again, watching the slug strike the makeshift gun heading toward them and ricochet off at a slight angle to punch through a Va'alen warrior. The alien stopped running alongside the gun, as others coming from behind flowed around it like water avoiding a boulder in a stream. As the Va'alen looked down at the gaping would in its abdomen, it saw the black oil like blood pouring down its legs. In a moment, the creature dropped to the dust and slumped over.

"Keep up the fire, sniper team," Brandt called out.

The relieved troops of her squad joined her. Something somber and unspoken passed between them in their relative silence, along with a shared feeling of resolve.

"Assessment of enemy numbers?" Brandt instructed Zero. He had the telemetry data from his drone where others just had the live feed.

"Ninety-eight Va'alen inbound our position," he answered stoically. "Twenty-four of us."

"Four to one," Brandt said. "Everybody kill four 'roaches and we can go home, got that?"

"That still leaves two," Eze answered, just as another metallic twang thumped the air.

"Negative," the voice of the sniper said coolly. "That leaves one."

Brandt smiled, knowing there was very little chance that any of them were getting off the planet alive. Even so, she was grateful that the arrival of a few reinforcements meant that the fight would last much, much longer.

~

Lieutenant Nathan Rogers kept his eyes shut to try and prevent the spinning pod from making him throw up. The grav emitters in the pod weren't functioning, or at least not functioning well enough to fully compensate for the spin.

"Hold on," he said out loud as his body lurched sickeningly. "This thing shouldn't even be spinning!"

He was overcome with the confusion of waking to find that hell had paid his ship a visit and the stress of having to make an instant decision. Though it had ultimately saved his life, or at least extended it a while longer, his choice had played havoc with his senses.

He shook his head as he tried to get his brain to function again. He thought. He forced himself to open his eyes and instantly regretted it as the edge of the planet swung violently in and out of view. He focused on the control panel, trying his hardest to ignore his empty stomach and other internal organs as they screamed out in protest as being flung around forcefully.

"Life support… functional…" he said out loud. He struggled to direct a single finger onto the small screen before realizing that he could use his prosthetic limb. It was far stronger. "Reboot… systems…"

It took him over a minute to hit the four commands to access the emergency reboot sequence. He almost passed out before he heard the harsh-sounding and authoritarian female voice bark a question at him.

"Manual reset is not advised when pod is deployed," it snapped, like a disappointed mother berating a child. "Do you wish to continue?"

"Yes!" Rogers said, the word sounding like a sob. "God dammit, yes!"

The computer beeped its confirmation. He felt the pod's interior go suddenly cold, so cold that it took his breath away.

A cloud of steam blew from his mouth like smoke from a fire only to freeze the instant it hit the inside of the glass viewport.

The pod slowed a little then stopped its spin so abruptly that if the grav emitter hadn't fired up at the exact same moment he would probably have suffered a broken neck. He looked at the control panel and saw everything functioning in the green before finding the nearest friendly waypoint and setting the pod's tiny engine to propel him toward it.

He activated the comm.

"*Indomitable, Indomitable*," he said as he hailed them. "This is Lieutenant Rogers of the *Corvus* in a dropship life raft. Do you read me?"

Crackling static was his only answer, so he tried again.

And again.

He tried on a different frequency as he looked at the distant shape of the behemoth carrier creating a silhouette against the backdrop of bright stars.

He stopped talking when the carrier jumped and disappeared from view.

"Give me a battle summary, Tactical," Admiral Vernay said. She typed a written command to re-route auxiliary power from non-essential decks to bolster the forward shield array; it was down to a little over thirty percent. The forward shields were always the most vital, and she didn't like the thought of being stranded mid-battle with a damaged Fold Drive emitter

because she couldn't keep her forward shields at optimal levels. Vernay loved running a fleet carrier, but the lack of maneuverability made her feel sluggish and frustrated in battle. For a senior ship commander who had come up as a pilot, her frustration was palpable. It was better with the smaller Va'alen ships buzzing around them like flies, but when faced with well-armed frigates she shuddered every time their warheads slammed into the shields. She fought on the retreat. She had the helmsman back the carrier away from the most prevalent threat in order to give her gunners more time to target the singularity warheads fired at them.

"All UN ships are engaging MEA forces," the tactical officer told her. "All Va'alen ships in the sector appear to have been destroyed and there are still four MEA vessels actively engaged with our forces."

"Are we winning, Ensign?" Vernay asked with a degree of patience she did not feel.

"I. Y... yes, Admiral," he stammered. "I think so."

"And all of our support ships are safely back at the station?"

The young officer glanced down at his console again.

"I think so," he said again lamely.

"Comm," Vernay sighed, "contact the station and ask for confirmation that the support vessels are safe."

"Aye, Admiral."

There was a pause as the comm traffic was relayed and the concerned operator turned back to face the admiral.

"Admiral! *Omaha Two* reports all support ships docked, but they have three enemy signatures approaching their position.

They are not responding to hails."

"Order them to defend themselves and the fleet at all costs," Vernay said calmly. "Remind the station commander that they are very well armed and should use that to their full potential."

"Cruiser destroyed!" the tactical officer cried out, facing the admiral and wiping the grin of terrified glee from his face instantly.

"I would like to take at least some members of the MEA alive for questioning," she reminded him gently but forcefully.

"The *Indomitable* has disabled one of their ships," he told her. "They are no longer in combat and are sending boarding troops."

"Order the fleet to converge and disable or destroy the three remaining traitor ships," she said. "Jump…"

She paused as she looked at the wider map of the battle. "Jump the remaining ships of squadron two back to the station, and get us over to the *Indomitable*."

CHAPTER 28

M.E.A. Frigate Sabya

"Magnetic lock in three, two, one… mark," the dropship pilot said. His hushed tones were indicative of the nature of their clandestine work. Two other dropships were doing the same in the other two hangars of the dead frigate as it spun slowly end over end to tumble through space.

"Preparing to vent all atmosphere," the pilot warned, in case any of the armored passengers seated behind him had decided to pop the sunroof on their armor to see what the vacuum of space smelled like. "Atmosphere venting… *now.*"

A violent whooshing of air sounded. The rear ramp cracked open to let the pressure equalize but not enough that they were all blown out into space. The pilot had landed the dropship, rear ramp facing inward, through the open hangar bay doors as the crew of the frigate trusted the shielding to keep them sealed in safely.

The Chief shuddered to think how many people got vented along with the atmosphere when the power went down. He shoved the thought aside as he unclipped his restraints and floated out of the dropship to lead his team through the zero-G interior.

It took them close to ten minutes to restore power by rerouting the coupling from the fried ship's system to the working singularity generator of their ship. When the shield reactivated, they all bumped hard to the metal deck. No one could figure out what was wrong right away.

They had restored a seal to the hangar deck, not power to the ship's main grav emitters.

The roll of space outside the open hangar bay slowed and stopped before the view of the planet began to shrink almost imperceptibly.

"They have engines," Chief announced to his team over their channel. "Bravo team secure the main power sources and sweep deck by deck, Charlie team to receive prisoners and consolidate on the main hangar. Alpha team, follow me."

The Chief's order given, the team made their way through the main doors. They had equalized the pressure enough so that only a cold rush of air passed through.

They all knew their way around; the ship's design was based on a UN vessel, before it had been retrofitted with the additional technology stolen by their spy in the Ninth Fleet.

The Chief led the way, weapon up and feet moving fast. The manual for ship boarding operations was woefully out of date and was only ever employed against civilian freighters. He had taken it upon himself—following the surprise arrival of the separatist fleet—to plan for the contingency of boarding the various types of ship in their own fleet. He was gratified that his paranoia and obsessive nature had paid off. The operation would have felt far more intense had they not trained for it.

Four times they encountered crewmembers and all but one of them submitted without any resistance. They surrendered their sidearms and had their hands bound with automatically tightening wrist restraints behind their backs.

One crewmember—young but big and stupid—rushed the Chief who stood stock-still in his armor. As the crewmember made contact, the only result was the sickening sound of crunching bones, firmly implanting itself in his memory.

Hand broken from the instinctive but ill-advised punch he threw at the Chief's helmet, the crewman wailed in agony as he tried to draw his sidearm with his off hand. A rough grab of his flight suit hauled him back to his feet. He was held against the bulkhead, with the weapon being stripped from his grasp.

"Foolish boy," the Chief said as he let him drop. The rearmost members of his team would deal with him. "You should have stayed at home with your mother." He walked on toward their goal.

The outer door to the bridge was sealed. Not locked electronically, but literally sealed. The metal still glowed faintly from the welding torches used in a hurry, but the rushed work held fast.

"Breach," Chief ordered gruffly.

One of his troopers push ahead through the stacked armor to reach the door. He set up six thin sticks against the door, two vertically on each side, one top and one bottom to complete the shape of a doorway inside the doorway. The Chief stepped back and assessed the shape of the gap, making a mental note to have the engineers onboard the *Anvil* manufacture some slightly longer breach rods.

He nodded, turned his back on the door and called the warning to his team. "Breach, breach, breach," he said, taking a firm grip on a grabrail.

The rest of his soldiers similarly secured themselves in case the room on the other side had lost atmospheric containment.

There was no loud bang. No sharp crack of explosives. Instead, the gentle crackle and fizz of chemical agents reacting with one another superheated the metal. In an instant, the introduction of another substance froze it.

No whistling air rushed through the minute cracks caused by the process. The Chief drew back a boot and stomp-kicked the center of the door, breaking the weakened joints easily. He prepared himself for a gunfight on the other side but he only heard the clanking noise of metal hitting more metal. He peered through to see another door identical to the one they had just breached.

"This is new," he said to himself. "Breach the inner door. Prepare the new shock devices."

More breach rods were fixed to the inner door, which was a couple of meters ahead as though a small personnel airlock had been retro-fitted to the bridge. Chief pulled two of the new devices out of a pouch on his armor and rolled them over in his gauntlets. They were another recent invention from the prototype armory. When he had paid it a visit courtesy of his still valid UNID credentials, he had made sure he hadn't left empty-handed.

The room they were thrown into was flooded with a blanket of gas, which hung low to the ground like fog. When the activation remote was pressed, a pin was pulled from the device to arm it like an old-fashioned hand grenade. When activated, it did... *something*. The device reacted and sucked all the oxygen from the room in an instant. Not like venting the area, but converted it to be completely unbreathable.

It acted like a sudden flash fire without the fire. When Chief had asked for a demonstration, he had to be satisfied with watching video footage. On the video, four people wearing neck braces and padded helmets were standing around watching the blanket of thick smoke spread out rapidly. When the smoke disappeared in a flash as it rose faster than any human could react, all four of them dropped to the deck instantly unconscious.

Chief had liked that, and had left with half a dozen of them in return for a promise of a full debrief if he got the chance to use them.

The breach rods fizzled and did their thing again. This time he got someone else to kick the damaged panel through so that he could toss two of the devices into the room personally.

Why two? Because I like to make sure, he thought, smiling as he pressed the buttons with both thumbs simultaneously.

The sounds of multiple people dropping to the deck as though fallen asleep echoed in the metallic confines of the airlock. Chief stepped through the gap onto the bridge. The sight brought a broad smile of satisfaction to his face; every one of the enemy crew was slumped at their duty stations. With one exception.

One crewmember was wearing armor which, with the helmet activated, rendered the device harmless to him. A handful of bullets impacted the Chief's right side. He turned toward the shots and raised his right hand, wrapping it around the grip of the rifle locked onto his back.

His attacker wore the same new armor that the Chief and his team had, but what the MEA hadn't gotten around to issuing was uprated weaponry. Chief's pulse rifle flared once, the streak of orange energy hitting the separatist trooper dead center to scorch and ruin the outer layer of armor and throw him down hard. It didn't kill him, though, and when he looked up into the muzzle of the rifle he raised both hands to surrender.

"Secure these stations," Chief ordered. "Get this prisoner out of his armor and detained with the rest. Signal Captain Torres that we have secured the bridge and will sweep the other decks. The ship is ours."

"Ammo count," the petty officer in charge of the now three-trooper gun team called out.

"Down to the last one," came the response.

The big support gun was left with a little over two hundred rounds before it ran dry and the Va'alen took the long slope leading south from their flat hilltop.

The situation to the north wasn't much better. Brandt had winced hearing the shouts of pain and alarm when they began taking casualties. Her own small team poured disciplined fire into the on-coming ranks of enemy, but what they had simply wasn't going to be enough. She muted her comm to the others and sent out another desperate request for assistance on the orbital monitoring channel.

"Mayday, mayday, mayday," she called. "UN forces at the nego-tiation site in immediate danger of being overrun. Any orbital forces able to assist, please respond." She gave it a few seconds before trying again, just as the big gun went dry and panic infected the besieged troops.

Brandt unmuted the comm and called out orders for their final stand.

"All forces, converge on the base of the tower and activate any remaining mobile cover. Let them bring the fight to us," she said grandly. "Then we end it."

She almost felt bad activating her personal shielding as she checked the battery life on her prototype pulse rifle. All around her young men and women knelt behind the sparse protection of layers of mobile cover as they checked and reloaded their weapons. The seemingly archaic exploding ordnance rounds they were using, she had to admit, were crude yet highly effective against the biological armor of the Va'alen.

"Make 'em count," someone called out.

It drew small laughter and Brandt smiled to herself. That these soldiers were making jokes right then was astounding and, she had to admit, pretty cool.

She was okay with dying down there, as long as whatever was happening above meant that her side would win. As long as the assholes who caused all the drama got what was coming to them.

She looked at the others who had fallen into her orbit. At Zero, gun to his shoulder as he took steady shots at their enemy; he wouldn't want to be anywhere else than looking through a scope at an enemy. At Payne blasting away with her heavy blaster; she had developed an attachment to her after their experiences on the forest moon.

Thoughts of that moon made Brandt look up and search the clear skies for it without success. Her eyes lowered to take in most of the hulking figure of Kekoa. She felt a stab of regret at having dragged him halfway across the galaxy on a whim. She realized that he would have volunteered for everything she had asked him to do. After all, he'd tackled a mech unarmed to save her. He wasn't going to walk away just because there were a hundred angry aliens the same size as him on their way up the hill to kill them all.

She looked at Specter. At Jake. And as his helmet turned to meet hers, she felt like he understood what she was feeling. He lifted his chin to her as though they had just bumped into one another unexpectedly but were too cool to make a big show of it. She chuckled in spite of the situation, returning the upward flick of her chin. The commander settled in ready to fire her rifle.

"Make 'em count," she echoed, vowing to do just that.

CHAPTER 29

Low Orbit Over Gaia Néos

The two frigates had become so accustomed to working in a pair that their crews were almost symbiotic. They had been in the worst position imaginable when they received their orders to provide orbital bombardment of the targets on the surface.

They were on the opposite side of the planet to the negotiation site, but three separate battles raged in space to block the most direct routes. This forced them to fly the longest route until they could drop down into low orbit. They went as low as their ships could maintain without heating up their bellies against the outer edge of the atmosphere and signaling their presence with glowing streaks of fire high in the skies.

Their haste led them to forgo accuracy. Instead, the frigates relied on sheer destructiveness to remove the Va'alen threat on the surface. Each fired three high-yield singularity warheads in sequence to blanket the site the aliens had adopted as their temporary home. They surged on, circumnavigating the planet in a bid to reach the ground team.

"Mayda–, –yday, may–" the speakers beside the captain's chairs crackled out in unison. "UN forces at … site in immediate danger of being overrun. … orbital forces … assist respond."

"That's Commander Brandt," Hayes's comm officer reported.

Hayes was already out of his chair and walking toward the tactical station where he gave his orders uncomfortably close behind the neck of the lieutenant manning the station.

"Cannons only," he ordered. "Prepare a full salvo on every enemy target you can see. Minimum safe distance is twenty meters, understood?"

"Aye, Captain," came the immediate and confident answer. "Get me the *Vengeance,*" he instructed the comm officer. He looked up to see Halstead's face already filling the viewscreen of his bridge. The two captains exchanged a nod, neither bothered with unnecessary politeness when there was work to be done.

"You get that?" Halstead asked.

"Yeah, ETA to their site is ninety seconds. I'm preparing an orbital strike with a minimum safe distance of twenty meters."

"Understood," Halstead replied. "We'll angle a different vector and do the same. Out."

The screen went black to remove some of the light bathing the somewhat gloomy bridge of the frigate. All they could do was wait for a minute and a half.

~

Ammo began to run out. To Brandt, this was always a clear indicator of two things.

One: they hadn't brought enough ammo. Or two: they were neck-deep in shit and sinking fast. She snatched the pistol off her leg and thrust it toward the nearest trooper who had emptied his rifle magazines and his own sidearm.

"Here," she shouted. She followed up the weapon with two spare magazines without taking her attention away from shooting aliens.

Payne's heavy weapon had gone quiet. She had burned through the charge packs with devastating effect on the enemy. The problem was that the enemy was now emboldened by the dearth of the heavy fire.

Every Va'alen they put down caused another Va'alen to roar in unimaginable fury before scratching themselves deeply with their claws and racing forward.

Zero was so tuned in to the battle that every time one of their enemies stopped to enter the enraged state he was lining up their temporarily still forms and drilling three or four shots into them. Most of them dropped. This might be the only reason their huddled little formation still survived. Just one of those things getting inside their position would spell game over quicker than an orbital bombardment to the face.

He called out more targets to the other snipers above him. Both cycled their railguns, as quickly as was humanly possible, drilling a slug through one, sometimes two, aliens if everything lined up right.

Specter, his rifle handed to the nearest trooper, had both arms extended fully with an oversized pistol in each hand. The weapons spat fat bolts of energy as he moved each hand and trigger finger independently of the other. His augmented brain and eyes lined up multiple targets.

Brandt tried not to think about the end, and how it would happen, but she knew that she would never stop fighting. Not until she was dead.

A bolt of pulse cannon fire hit her high on the left shoulder, spinning her slightly and forcing her to readjust her firing position. Red blood fountained ahead of her from her left and she turned to see the trooper who had taken her offered sidearm with a gaping hole in the chest of his armor. The shot had penetrated side-on, forcing its way inside the reinforced polymer plates. It took a moment for Brandt's shock to register that it had been the ricochet from her that had killed him.

She whipped her head forward again and fired repeatedly, wanting to take out every last one of the bastards for what they had done.

An enraged beast, three feet taller than Brandt was even in armor, sailed through the air as it was shot repeatedly. It landed on the body of the dead trooper beside her and roared as Specter plunged both blades repeatedly into its side. In a dying reflex, it lashed out savagely with one claw and knocked another trooper out of their ring of cover and into the open.

Brandt didn't think; she reacted.

She stepped outside the safety of the ring of mobile cover, what was left of it, and took three long strides closer to the advancing enemy. She fired unhesitatingly over the head of the soldier trying to get up.

"Commander," Kekoa said, surprising her. "Get your ass into cover or I'll have to come rescue you again."

She smiled, expecting the end to happen at any moment. "Hold your positions," she ordered. "No matter what."

She advanced, firing with each step. She expected a flurry of shots to batter her shield away to nothing and to cook her alive inside her armor as it melted and sparked. She reached down to grab the leg of the unmoving soldier and drag him back to cover, expecting the impacts to drill through her back at any second.

Instead, the ground a dozen paces in front of her screamed, shrieked and exploded to send her flying back riding the edge of a shockwave of dust, debris, and shattered parts of Va'alen exoskeleton.

"Wake up," a male voice said unsympathetically. Brandt's eyes fluttered but wouldn't open. A sharp dig to her left thigh, right in the sweet spot where she had been taught to kick and stab an opponent in a fight, made her flinch and contort her body away from the pressure.

Another sharp poke into the lower side of her ribcage made her twist to avoid the dig. She squirmed back the opposite way until laughter finally forced her to open her eyes.

She saw bright lights above her, unable to figure out why she would be sleeping with the lights on. She found it impossible to even relax in brightly lit rooms.

The pain in her side flared again and she inhaled a sharp hiss through her teeth. She turned toward the source of the annoyance to see the grinning face of Torres.

"Welcome back," he said.

"Good to have you back with us, Commander," Beale said, leaning over to smile at her.

"Thanks, Beaver," she said. That prompted snickering laughter among the others since she had finally figured out his callsign.

Beale blushed but said nothing.

"You going to get up or just let us keep doing the hard work?" Specter asked, jabbing a prosthetic finger into the nerve cluster in her thigh.

"Ow!" she complained. "Quit poking me!"

"Sorry," Turner said from the end of her bed. "I told them it was the best way to check you still had full control of your body."

"Asshole," she said. She shuffled up on her elbows to sit up.

"Turner, explain to me why I feel like I got sucked into an atmospheric compressor and shit out the other side?"

"Depends," he answered. "What's the last thing you remember?"

She thought about it, her eyes growing wide as the terrifying memories of the recent and doomed fight came flooding back to her. Alarms on the monitor began to beep as her heart rate went up dangerously.

"What?" she said, unable to prioritize which question she needed answered first.

"Relax," Torres told her. "We actually won."

"Wh... wha—" Brandt stuttered.

"The MEA screwed us," Torres said. "They did some kind of back channel deal with the Va'alen and transported a load of them out of the system. Only two of their ships got away and we trashed or captured the rest. The Va'alen are toast; their whole outfit on the surface got crushed."

"The kid..." Brandt said. She closed her eyes as the pain flooded her brain. Turner pressed a dermal injector to her neck after moving one of her messy braids out of the way.

"The kid you walked out into an orbital bombardment to save?" Torres asked. "He's doing okay. Got a concussion like yours and had to have a little surgery to alleviate some of the swelling. Probably wouldn't have made it if you hadn't pulled him back..."

"Dassiova?" she croaked, already feeling lightheaded from the painkillers.

"Pulled through," Turner said. "Courtesy of some new medical tech." He waved a dismissive hand at her confused look. "I'll explain it all when you're better."

"And... and..." She muttered in confusion as she tried to figure out what she needed to know.

"And you need to rest," a young female voice said. Ensign Curtis pushed her way politely to the side of her bed.

"I'm fine, Ensign," Brandt slurred.

"Oh, I'm sure you are, Commander," Curtis said sweetly. "But as you're deemed medically unfit for duty right now, you can just go ahead and assume there ain't no order you can give me that I'll obey."

"I surrender," Brandt said. She leaned back against the pillows with a stiff neck. She turned her head to one side and laid eyes on the patient in the bed beside her, prompting another attempt to sit up too fast. She almost passed out.

"Mister Rogers is just fine, Commander," Curtis assured her with an easy authority. "He spent a day too long in life raft, but I guess that's better than the alternative, given what happened to the rest of his crew."

Brandt looked at Torres who wore an expression of veiled anger.

"The MEA boarded the *Corvus* and took the Hive Lord," he explained through tight lips. "They blew her up, lost all hands except us and Rogers who just got to a dropship escape pod quick enough."

"We need to get after them," Brandt said, sounding as though she was drunk. "We need to get the... bastards..."

"We don't know where they've gone," Torres said flatly. "And even if we did, we've got too much to mop up in this system and back home without rushing off to war in another part of the galaxy... Brandt?"

"The meds have kicked in, Captain," Curtis explained. "She can't hear you. Best to let her rest now."

~

"So you're telling us that the negotiations were *intentionally* sabotaged by the Middle Eastern Alliance, and that *they* attacked UN assets in that system before fleeing to god-knows-where with the enemy?" the man asked. His small, angry eyes were rimmed red above a glorious moustache in the exact same steely gray color as his impressive shock of hair.

"Yes, Admiral," Torres said. "That's exactly what I'm saying." The man glanced aside, looking at another person's video feed displayed before him.

"And you can confirm this, Admiral Vernay?" he demanded.

"I can," the tough Frenchwoman declared. "Everything I cannot personally corroborate I can surmise from the sensor data. The MEA broke faith in our peace agreement and sided with the enemy. They murdered UN personnel in cold blood to steal vital... materials... and left the remainder of their fleet behind to face the consequences while they fled with the Va'alen they had rescued from the surface."

"You realize what this means? Both of you?" the admiral demanded.

"Like it or not, sir," Torres said, urged on by the full support of Dassiova, "we're already at war. We didn't pull that trigger, Admiral. The MEA did when they sided with the Va'alen and murdered our people. Other human beings, sir."

"I will have to consult with government," the admiral muttered. He was stalling as someone off camera was talking under their breath at him.

"That you, Mister Ettington?" Torres asked, taking a gamble.

The admiral's face went red then faded as a well-groomed and sharply dressed man sat in front of the comm and unbuttoned his suit jacket.

"Captain Torres," the head of the American UNID said in curt greeting.

"Sir," Torres replied.

"Looks like you've had a tough time of it out there," Ettington said in understatement.

"You could say that," Torres shot back. He had exchanged enough false niceties with a man he was fairly certain was soulless. "You read my report on what happened to Agent Crawford?"

Ettington nodded slowly with closed eyes, attempting to portray genuine emotion and failing.

"Are you in agreement with Admiral Vernay's and my recommendations?"

"That we declare open war on a recognized sovereign nation on Earth?"

"Yes," Torres said. "And that we unite Earth against a common threat because, believe me, sir, the MEA *will* give the Fold Drive technology to the Va'alen and they *will* come here for revenge."

"Perhaps you're right, Torres," Ettington conceded. "But these decisions go much further than merely you or I."

"That may be true for one of us, sir," Torres chuckled. He refused to believe the man's minimizing of his status or importance.

"In the meantime, the *Indomitable* is ordered to return to Earth for a thorough debrief. All MEA prisoners are to be aboard her."

"Understood, sir," Torres said.

"And a full security patrol is to be conducted around the clock in the Centauri system. That falls on you, Admiral Vernay, but we will be sending you more ships as soon as we can spare them. In the meantime we trust that you'll make it work."

Vernay accepted her orders with a somber nod.

"There will be contractors and civilian forces inbound your location within the week," Ettington went on. "We need to explore the possibilities of the system while we have clear skies, so to speak. If there's nothing else? Torres, I'll see you in New York. Vernay, good luck."

The screen showing the safe, comfortable office on Earth went black and Torres stretched his back before leaning forward to stand.

"Are you still there, Captain Torres?" Vernay said quietly.

"I'm here, Admiral," Torres said as he sat back down.

"How is Elias?" she asked. He was surprised by her use of Dassiova's first name.

"He was pretty badly banged up, but he's going to be fine."

"Physically, perhaps," Vernay said. "Don't underestimate what an injury that severe can do to the mind." Torres nodded. He didn't know how much he was supposed to say—the lines were blurring on who did and who didn't have access to secret information. The Nanomites had repaired the internal damage to Dassiova's organs and Curtis had done an outstanding job in sewing up the outside. In spite of the microscopic medical bots cleaning the wound, the admiral still raged a fever for three days that had threatened to finish him off. Curtis even commissioned a cruiser on UNID authority to jump back to Earth with a blood and tissue sample that showed a previously unknown pathogen. The sample was being tested to see if it originated with the Va'alen themselves or whether it was a hazard natural to the planet. While Dassiova'd been under, just to add to the host of physical problems he faced, the Nanomites had prioritized and diverted to begin breaking down the cancer cells forming in and around the admiral's stomach.

Torres was left in interim command of the carrier and was actually grateful for the orders to jump home.

"I'm sure Dassiova will be fine, Admiral," Torres said weakly. "He's a tough son of... he's a remarkably resilient man, ma'am."

"I'm sure he will," Vernay said, smiling. "And I'm sure he is. Safe journey, Captain. Send me something nice from home. Like twelve frigates captained by competent leaders and a few bottles of good Chablís. Vernay out."

EPILOGUE

The *Indomitable* jumped back into deep space beyond the moon and cruised at a steady speed toward orbital station number two. There it docked for a full overhaul and repairs. Torres felt for the crews left behind in the Centauri system. Many of them had been there for months with no sign of returning any time soon.

UN personnel were accustomed to deployments of up to eighteen months, but a year and a half spent millions of miles from home was rough.

Squads of armored troops boarded the carrier via dropship and took away the MEA prisoners to various black sites all over the globe. They would be subject to what was ominously called a debrief. Torres knew it would entail much more than that—mental and often physical torture if the drugs didn't work to get them talking. He found himself numb to caring about it in the slightest.

As ordered, Torres reported to the barracks nearest to the UN headquarters where he was assigned rooms more befitting an admiral than his actual rank. He had been officially relieved of command when the ship docked, reverting him to commander instead of the man in charge of a fleet flagship.

He reminded himself that command had been short lived and borne of an emergency measure.

Torres appeared from his quarters the following morning wearing a crisply pressed white dress uniform complete with his medals, prepared for him ahead of the meeting for which he had been summoned.

He stopped for a light breakfast, unsure if he would be invited to sit at the meeting, let alone offered a coffee. He found a familiar group of smiling faces eating their breakfast in PT gear.

"Working them hard, Leslie?" he asked as he sat.

"Always, Kyle," she said back. Their informality was a symptom of the relaxation of being safely back on Earth. "Is today your interview for that stripper job?"

"Hilarious," he said through a mouthful of croissant. "You had any orders yet?"

"Muster at fourteen hundred today," she said. "All of us. My guess is probably going back to Gaia Néos to guard the big corporation's mining plants."

"Probably," Torres said feeling a little sad that he had no idea where he would be going.

Specter's head whipping fast to one side grabbed their attention. His augmented senses picked up the arrival of a new person to the canteen before any of the others.

"Well this place has gone downhill," Rogers said as he ditched a large kit bag and walked over to them.

"What brings you here?" Torres asked, happy to see the pilot.

"Orders to muster at fourteen hundred today for reassignment," he said. "My last posting doesn't exist anymore so…" He shrugged.

"Well," Torres said as he stood and glanced at his comm device for the time. "I guess that's me. Look after yourselves."

They gave their individual goodbyes as they watched him stand tall and walk out of the room.

"Why does he look like he's taking himself to his own execution?" Turner asked.

"No idea," Brandt said. She stood to change the subject. "Get showered. The rest of the morning is yours. Lunch at twelve and full kit inspection at thirteen hundred."

~

Brandt let Zero play the part of the senior NCO, thoroughly enjoying himself as he tore through their kit with more humor than effective searching.

They stowed their kit and dressed in standard fatigues before mustering as instructed five minutes before fourteen hundred local time.

Nothing happened. Nobody arrived with their orders.

"Sooo…" Zero said. "This strike anyone else as a little weird?"

"It's kinda creepy," Kekoa agreed. "I'll give you that."

"Attention on deck!" barked a voice. They all snapped-to. "Stand easy," Torres said through a wide smile. "I'm screwing with you."

"What are you doing here?" Brandt asked.

"I'm here to give you your orders," Torres said happily, "as your Captain."

"Captain?" Brandt asked. "Where are we going?"

"Perhaps I can help with this," said a hissing voice muffled by a subtle breathing mask.

"Asha?" Brandt said.

She stepped forward to shake hands with the alien who wore dark goggles to protect his sensitive eyes. The tall, gangly alien wore a UN flight suit, custom made to fit him and shook her hand with enthusiasm as he enjoyed the human greeting.

"I will explain when we're aboard," Torres explained, gesturing to a nearby hangar and leading them there. He scanned his biometric chip to open the security door beside the massive blast doors.

"I'll give you the full mission packet when we're underway," he explained. The lighting came on automatically to display what was hidden inside. "In short, we're going to find the Va'alen home-world."

Sitting in the center of the hangar, shiny and looking better than new, was the *Böken Sha Ichi*.

"Hold up," Brandt said. "Didn't that asshat admiral say that the UN didn't justify this?"

"No, he initially said"—he simulated the appropriate voice of the particular asshat admiral—"we don't need a reconnaissance ship with that much of a substantial *credit* label attached running around in uncharted space doing god only knows what."

"What does he say now, Captain?" Rogers asked.

"Not much, I imagine," Torres said, "on account of his sudden retirement being announced."

He stepped forward and turned to his new crew.

"Who's ready to do some real exploring and try to prevent the war from spilling over to Earth?"

END OF BOOK FOUR

Remember to sign up for my emailing list at **www. devoncford.com**
Follow me on social media for cover reveals, release information and general shenanigans:

Facebook: @devoncfordofficial

Instagram: @dcf_actual

Also by Devon C Ford

The *After It Happened* series:

(Also on Audible)

1 – Survival (Performed by R.C Bray)

2 – Humanity (Performed by R.C Bray)

3 – Society (Performed by R.C Bray)

4 – Hope (Performed by R.C Bray)

5 – Sanctuary (Performed by R.C Bray)

6 – Rebellion (Performed by R.C Bray)

7 – Andorra (The Leah Chronicles, performed by Kate Reading)

8 – Piracy (The Leah Chronicles, performed by Kate Reading)

9 – Home (Performed by R.C Bray)

The *New Earth* series:

(Also on Audible Performed by Marc Vietor)

1 – ARC

2 -SWARM (with Chris Harris)

The *Burning Skies* Multi-Author series:

(Also on Audible read by Neil Hellegers)

1 – The Fall

2 – Fallout (by Jacqueline Druga)

3 – Uprising (by Chris Harris)